# JOHN MOSEDALE

# The Greatest of All

# The 1927 New York Yankees

THE DIAL PRESS

NEW YORK

Published by
The Dial Press
1 Dag Hammarskjold Plaza
New York, New York 10017

Library of Congress Cataloging in Publication Data

Mosedale, John.
    The greatest of all.

    1.   New York.    Baseball club (American League).
I.   Title.
GV875.N4M67      796.357'64'097471      74-3381
ISBN 0-385-27805-5

*This book is for*
*Betty*
*and for*
*Amy and Laura and Andrew and Michael*
*and for*
*Richard Marek, whose idea it was, and Margot*
*and to*
*the memory of my mother,*
*who took the kid out to the ball game*

# Introduction

O

As we plunge into the 1980s, the year 1927 becomes remote in ways that are measureless to man.

We now know that the world ends with a bang, not a whimper. Another poetic prophecy has become a cliché: *Things fall apart, the center cannot hold*—not in economics, in international affairs, in domestic relations, certainly; and as the All Star break approaches, not among the 1982 New York Yankees.

This is a book about a baseball team in its heyday. At that time baseball was the only major league professional sport. There is a single-mindedness about the spring and summer sports pages of 1927. The seeming simplicity of the 1920s compared to the present was clear enough when I wrote this book in 1973. But it has sharpened since. For 1973, although it did not seem so at the time, was a watershed year in the history of the New York Yankees.

It was the year George Steinbrenner took over, announcing as a twenty percent stockholder in the group that bought the team:

"We plan absentee ownership. We're not going to be something we aren't. I won't be active in the day-to-day operations of the club. I can't spread myself thin. I've got enough headaches with the shipping company."

Well, in 1982 *two* books were published about Steinbrenner's Yankees, which was the title of one of them. No one ever wrote a book called *Ruppert's Yankees* or *Topping and Webb's Yankees*. Here, in part, is what the dust jacket of *Steinbrenner's Yankees* says the book is about:

George M. Steinbrenner III, the self-anointed, undoubting Emperor of the Bronx—never have his antics and utterances, his cunning and bombast, been so nakedly revealed. Whether we see him storming the free-agent market with the quickest checkbook in the game, or manipulating the egos of his high-priced, temperamental players, or shuffling managers in a never-ending attempt to rule his ballfield and dugout as tightly as his front office, here is how George did or did not do it; exactly what happened, precisely what was said, expletives *un*deleted and no holds barred. Among scores of scenes from George Steinbrenner's Theater of the Absurd (and sometimes Theater of Cruelty) . . .

Does that recall another American industrialist of German descent, Colonel Jacob Ruppert? Where are the *players* in all that? Where is the game? Writing of Steinbrenner's trading, hiring, and firing between the 1981 and 1982 seasons, Roger Angell commented, "Each one of these parlous, impatient maneuvers, it will be noticed, focusses speculation and attention upon Mr. Steinbrenner, which is exactly as he wants it."

But in midseason 1982, there were indications that all that maneuvering had returned the Yankees to the condition from which Steinbrenner helped rescue them: During the eight years when CBS owned the team, you may remember, the Yankees were a bore.

The Steinbrenner stewardship quickly saw the Yankees restored to their customary position at the center of the baseball world, the hero-villains around which the sport revolves. It even resulted in two world championships. But at a price.

Roger Angell again, writing in *The New Yorker,* May 10, 1982:

I think that, without quite planning it, Mr. Steinbrenner is using sport in a new and singularly unpleasant way—to make us, the fans, feel rotten. Although his team is engaged in a game in which a sixty percent ratio of success is the very pinnacle of achievement, he invites us to be satisfied with nothing less than a victory every day. More particularly, his example urges us to scorn and despise the celebrity athletes on his enormous payroll whenever they fail to come through, and thus to release our bitter envy of them for their youth and their skill and their bloated salaries. When they falter on the mound or pop up with men on base—as they will again and again—we are licensed to curse them or throw things, for we and George have hired them only to win.

Now, baseball has always been a sport attractive to the fellow who suffers at the office and at home but is imperious in the grandstands. However, there seems to be a new ugliness in to-day's Stadium crowds. Thus, on April twenty-seventh, when Reggie Jackson of the California Angels hit a home run in his return to New York, thousands of entranced fans stood and chanted a school-yard obscenity at Steinbrenner, language which in more civil times might have gotten any one of them thrown out of the ball park. The sportswriters seemed to think the display was funny.

For all the graffiti, baseball retains a purity. Until the split season of 1981, no one had figured out a way to truly spoil the game. Baseball remains, as the blind old woman says in Anne Tyler's novel *Dinner at the Homesick Restaurant,* "clear as Parcheesi, clever as chess."

And the reason for this book, as I wrote back in 1973, is a simple one. Richard Marek, then editor-in-chief of the Dial Press, said, more or less, "You're always reading that the 1927 Yankees were the greatest baseball team of all time. Let's find out why."

Trying to find out why meant a cross-country flight, weeks

spent in the New York Public Library and its newspaper reference reading room, some 130 pages of single-spaced notes, more than a dozen cassettes of tape recordings.

Nineteen twenty-seven was forty-six years past in 1973, but there remained survivors of the team and its times, and their willingness to share memories is gratefully acknowledged. However, memory is a quirky thing, a trick mirror after nearly half a century. One survivor, for example, said it was important to remember that there was no particular significance attached to Babe Ruth's pursuit of his home-run record, when, in fact, the sports pages recorded little else along the baseball beat.

So the spine of the book had to be fact, untouched by memory, the day-by-day activity of the team called the greatest of all, to see how it won that accolade, what it did to set it apart from all the other teams in the game's history. Frank Graham wrote, "The defeat in the 1926 World Series was a dark interlude between the Yankees' unexpected triumph in the pennant race that year and their rise in 1927 to a peak which many believe they have never surpassed. This, they say, was the team. Greater than any that had gone before, greater than any that has followed."

How did the team win that superlative?

We are all familiar with good, even great, baseball teams. No one wrote about the 1970 Baltimore Orioles, "This is the greatest baseball team of all time," although it breezed to a pennant for a second successive year and beat the Reds in the World Series. What did the 1927 Yankees do that encouraged people, right then and there, to give them a title they haven't relinquished —certainly not in the past decade, although both Oakland and Cincinnati produced strong World Series champions?

The bare facts are not state secrets. The Yankees won the pennant by nineteen games in 1927, becoming the first American League club to sweep the opposition in the World Series. Babe Ruth hit sixty home runs in the regular season. Lou Gehrig drove in 175 runs. And so on. But whom did they beat and how? What were the events that earned them recognition as the great-

est of all? Hyperbole abounded in 1927, and the Yankees undoubtedly profited by the optimistic tenor of an age that believed
it was in on the greatest sideshow of all time. Underneath all the
varnish, what did the team do? That's what this book is about.

Since the Yankees took off like one of Ruth's home runs,
neither failing nor falling, there was a shortage of big, in the
sense of significant, games. The Yankees soared on opening day
and never looked back, never fell from first place. This can be
regarded as dull or seen as something marvelous to behold, like
a Roosevelt presidential campaign, or Joe Louis touching someone up, or a film by the Marx brothers. Following the Yankees
through 1927 is like watching an unconquerable army's greatest
triumph, except no one was killed, barely.

Watching them involved a felicitous expedition into the past.
Quite apart from baseball, 1927 was a compelling year, rich in
eye-popping events. It seemed obtuse to follow the Yankees
through the season without selective samplings from the larger
world—to treat the season as though it were played against no
backdrop at all. The year inspired two books of its very own—
Allen Churchill's *The Year the World Went Mad* and *1927:
The Picture Story of a Wonderful Year* by Carl H. Giles.

America seemed so confident then, so at peace with itself, so
bent on having a good time, so avid for the little pleasures, so
uncomplicated and direct in its pursuit of happiness. A certain
smugness attended, and Prohibition alone was enough to assure
the flowering of hypocrisy, but there was no agony remotely
approaching Viet Nam. There was plenty of domestic violence,
but there were no American assassinations in the Twenties.

Ever since the end of World War II, and to a lesser extent
before then, the Twenties have exerted a steady pull on the
American imagination. Partly this is because the decade seemed
for a good many people a good time to be alive. Twenty
years later the ink was hardly dry on the surrender documents
on the deck of the battleship *Missouri* before the literati, or just
interested readers, began waiting for the appearance of the new
Fitzgeralds, Hemingways, and Sinclair Lewises, not only for

literary reasons but to tell us we could go back again, even if we had never been there, and that soon all would be bathtub gin and incomparable parties and Mah-Jongg.

There have been plenty of good writers since then, although the new Hemingways never appeared, but it is expecting too much of history to furnish exact literary parallels—and, anyway, the 1927 Yankees didn't turn up again, either.

And it is easy to forget that, Era of Wonderful Nonsense or not, there was a strong minority sentiment in America, reflected in the careers of the writers mentioned, that the way to enjoy life in the 1920s was to get out of the United States and stay out, away from the narrowness and materialism and philistinism excoriated in so much of the best American literature of the period.

"By 1927 a wide-spread neurosis began to be evident, faintly signalled, like a nervous beating of the feet, by the popularity of cross-word puzzles," wrote F. Scott Fitzgerald.

"I remember a fellow expatriate opening a letter from a mutual friend of ours," he continued, "urging him to come home and be revitalized by the hardy, bracing qualities of the native soil. It was a strong letter and it affected us both deeply, until we noticed that it was headed from a nerve sanitarium in Pennsylvania."

But most Americans were not members of the Lost Generation or any other of the categories by which the Twenties are remembered. It was the golden age of the comic strip and, faithful to the period, they were frequently built around the family, whether as bizarre as *Moon Mullins,* created in 1923, or as homely as *Gasoline Alley*—the foundling Skeezix turned up on Walt Wallet's doorstep on Valentine's Day, 1921.

"There were 125,000,000 Americans in 1925," wrote Stephen Becker in *Comic Art in America,* "and probably 120,000,000 of them never saw a gangster, never wore a raccoon coat, never danced the Charleston. They were therefore not newsworthy at the time, and have since become a dull footnote to a lurid legend, stolid whipping boys to a generation of satirists. We find them in the comic strips of the Twenties—families and kids, normalcy in its purest form. . . ."

But this is a book about a baseball team in a kind of funny-paper world, and reminders of the great outside are chosen idiosyncratically, when it seemed appropriate to drop them in. Every effort was made to avoid the laundry list of the old documentary approach: "Silent Cal was in the White House, the nation whistled 'Mississippi Mud,' and Saks offered suits at fifty dollars. . . ."

Some few of the anecdotes in this book may be thrice-told tales—a condition that plagued Herodotus—but seem necessary to the story. Some turned up in yellowed clippings dusted by the decades. Some, as far as is known, appear here for the first time. There is a particular need, indigenous to sports, to avoid stories too good to be true, although, in the case of the 1927 Yankees, it is hard to say just what these may be. Where accounts of the same story differ, the most likely one was chosen. Babe Ruth's bellyache, for example, has more versions than the matter of Dr. Dogbody's leg.

The reader, if attentive, will notice the word *great* turning up from time to time in what follows. It is an overused adjective, but it fits the heroes of 1927. Not only on the Yankees but among the opposition, baseball was peopled with legends, and portions of some teams were hell-bent for the Hall of Fame.

We all stand on the shoulders of our predecessors, and never more so than in a book of this kind. "They were all keen, witty men," Paul Gallico wrote of his press-box colleagues of the Twenties, "and never a dull word fell from their lips." Reading their stuff, you almost believe him.

James R. Harrison, Richards Vidmer, and John Kieran—whose "Sports of the *Times*" column started in 1927—of the *Times;* Marshall Hunt, Will Murphy, and Gallico of the *Daily News;* Frederick G. Lieb of the *Post;* Rud Rennie and W. B. Hanna of the *Herald Tribune;* Frank Graham and Joe Vila of the *Sun;* and George Bailey, called "Monitor," and William Hennigan of the *World*—all were fascinating guides to the season of the greatest of all, informed, literate, and entertaining. The writers seemed to enjoy baseball then and to have fun writing about it.

There was, by the way, no particular pro-Yankee bias at the start of this project, no roots traceable to childhood. Growing up in Milwaukee in the Thirties gave one no hometown major league team to pull for. The Brewers of the American Association, playing out of a hatbox called "Borchert's Orchert," were the local heroes, and the favored big league teams played in the stadium of the imagination, pretty much on the basis of youth's attraction, to romance and glamour, so the first favorites were the St. Louis Cardinals. What boy would not be drawn to a team called "The Gashouse Gang," featuring names like Pepper Martin, "the Wild Hoss of the Osage"; Frankie Frisch, "the Fordham Flash"; Dulky Medwick; and, most memorably, Dizzy and Daffy Dean?

Then there were the National League champion Chicago Cubs—yes, *champions*—favored with a kid first baseman, Phil Cavaretta, not much older than the high school beaus of one's sisters, so that in imagination it was easy to believe that in a few short years . . .

It wasn't until 1946, on shore leave in Boston, that the author even saw his first major league game, the Boston Braves versus the Philadelphia Phillies, absolutely unmemorable, no hint at all that those same Braves, in seven years, would move to the old hometown, setting in motion a frantic series of franchise-jumping that led to expansion so inchoate that it became difficult to tell the teams, let alone the players, without a scorecard.

God may not have intended baseball to remain conveniently packaged in two eight-team leagues, and, sure, it made economic sense to follow the population west, but more than an unfair nostalgia insists that it used to be easier to keep the standings straight and the batting averages in mind—and hence easier to *care*—when there wasn't so much of everything.

More to the point, the 1927 Yankees, on close inspection, made it easy to become, retroactively, a fan. They were men of enormous skill and, off the field as well, enormous interest. It will soon be clear that, however it started out, this did indeed turn out a biased book.

Surprisingly, not much has been written about the most dominant team in baseball history. But credit for an assist is due Frank Graham's *The New York Yankees: An Informal History,* first published in 1943, and John Durant's *The Yankees: A Pictorial History of Baseball's Greatest Club.*

"If you had to limit yourself to one aspect of American life," according to Wilfrid Sheed, "the showdowns between pitcher and hitter, quarterback and defense, hustler and fish, would tell you more about politics, manners, style in this country, than any other one thing. Sports constitute a code, a language of the emotions, and a tourist who skips the stadiums will not recoup his losses at Lincoln Center and Grant's Tomb."

Sheed also warns that playing games can make one "incurably childish." Well, inside every adult male there is a small boy, struggling to stay there. This relic of childhood is one of the major differences between the sexes. A biologically mature woman who remains interested in cheerleading is silly. The most elevated gent, however, may turn to the sports page before finding out what he thinks today. The brain surgeon and the broker, each busy storing up the treasures of this earth, likely share deep interest in the pennant race.

And that classicist who dismisses sport and scoffs at his peers who retain an interest in games small boys can play, after making the point about the childishness of it all, turns himself over to ruminating among his stamp collection, which he started in fourth grade. Most men, no matter how far gone in debauchery, remain prisoners of the interests of their youth.

None of what follows would have been possible without the assistance of those earlier cited, the survivors, the writers, the librarians—particularly the employees of the newspaper reference reading room in the New York Public Library and, most particularly, the wise counsel of John F. Redding, librarian of the National Baseball Library in Cooperstown, New York.

Thanks, too, to Til Ferdenzi, former director of sports publicity for NBC, and Marty Appel, then of the Yankee publicity department.

And, finally, the book could not have been written at all without the aid and encouragement of my wife. That battered sentence, how many writers it has served down the corridors of time, how little it conveys. Only the writer and his wife know the meaning behind the words, even for a frolic like this book: the faithful guarding of privacy and fending off of interruption, the understanding of unaccountable moods and silences and peering out of windows, the assumption of duties belonging to both parents, the quieting of the telephone and the managing of bills and, most remarkably, the hours spent in that newspaper reference reading room, whispering into a tape recorder an entire season of New York Yankee baseball by a woman ineluctably uninterested in spectator sports.

But this could turn into a mash note, and it is not the time or the place.

*John Mosedale, 1982*

The Greatest of All

# One

O

On Thursday, September 22, 1927—the afternoon of the night Gene Tunney defeated Jack Dempsey in the Battle of the Long Count in Chicago—Babe Ruth hit a home run in the bottom of the ninth inning at Yankee Stadium.

It was his fifty-sixth home run of the year, more than any man except he himself had hit in a single season, and it was Ruthian, to use a popular adjective of the day, meaning timely, surrounded by emotion, and simply stupendous.

Timely because it also scored Mark Koenig from second base, thus defeating the Detroit Tigers, 8–7, after the Tigers had struggled from behind to take a lead. Ruth liked to uppercut the ball, lofting it so that it soared dramatically, like an artillery shell, or a rocket, and this one, according to a careful report in *The New York Times,* chipped a piece out of a seat six rows from the top of the bleachers.

One of the witnesses to the event was the doorman of the Yankee private offices in the Stadium. All season long he waited in darkness, the crowd noise his only reporter, locked away from adventure. Now he had been given a message to take to the dugout, and he stuck his head into Stadium sunlight during game action for the first time that season, just in time to see Ruth deliver his blow.

And then an affecting thing happened, symbolic of the love Ruth engendered and of the gulf which separates our times from 1927, which is more than just a matter of half a century. All afternoon long, a boy in knickerbockers sat in the grandstand, imploring Ruth to hit a home run.

When the Babe delivered, the boy did not wait to see the ball land in the bleachers, but leaped from his seat and, as Ruth rounded first, on to the field. He dashed across the diamond and intercepted Ruth at third base.

Ruth was still carrying his bat, and the idolatrous lad grabbed the handle with one hand, patting Ruth on the back with the other, and together the two trotted home. Together they touched home plate and swept together into the dugout, the boy hanging on like the tail of a comet, before they could be engulfed by the fans who streamed from the stands.

Altogether, not a tableau likely to be repeated these days. For one thing the fan in the newer stadium sits so far from the field of action that even a twelve-year-old's vital signs would flag before he reached the diamond, and he would collapse somewhere around Row BB. For another, a police officer would likely collar anyone headed for the field, fearing an assassination attempt on any popular figure. For another there would be an entirely proper concern that the lad was armed with pickax or Molotov cocktail. For yet another the player's lawyer or business affairs consultant surely would inform him that the incident—contact by a third person—constituted an interview, for which the player's fee was five hundred dollars, and would push on to the question of ancillary rights.

But this was 1927, when the gods seemed kinder to the United States of America, and so the incident passed with no more than the commotion customary when Ruth touched off an explosion. Rather typically, Lou Gehrig earlier in the day drove in two runs, bringing his season's total to 172, breaking Ruth's 1921 record of 170. Gehrig got the subheadlines, under the big news about Ruth, but then, Gehrig would always be remembered, in Franklin

P. Adams' rueful observation, as "the guy who hit all those homers the year Ruth set the record."

Not that many people at the beginning of the season expected either Ruth or the Yankees, who led the league by some sixteen games, to be in such exalted states that autumn afternoon. It was figured that Ruth would hit home runs, but when he shocked baseball by hitting fifty-nine in 1921, it was believed that the mark would last, in baseball time, forever.

The phrase is that he revolutionized the game. It has been said so many times that it slides easily on the tongue, and its truth is forgotten. Until Ruth came along, the home run was eschewed as almost vulgar. Although he worked as a pitcher, he first tied for the home run lead with 11 in 1918. The previous year, Wally Pipp, then Yankee first baseman, led the league with 9; Gavvy Cravath of the Phils led all hitters with 12, and there were just 339 major league home runs. By 1921, in only his third year as a full-time outfielder, Ruth set the record for home runs, lifetime, with 132, breaking a mark set in the nineteenth century by a man named Roger Connor, variously of New York, Philadelphia, and St. Louis. One hundred and thirty-seven home runs, lifetime, will not get you batting practice today.

Before the Babe the man perhaps most closely associated with the home run was J. Franklin Baker of the Philadelphia Athletics, who led the league from 1911–13, never collecting more than twelve in a single season. His nickname of "Home Run" came from the fact that he once hit two of them in a World Series—not World Series game, *World Series*—in successive games against the Giants in 1911.

By 1927 a lot of major leaguers were grabbing the bat at the bottom of the handle and swinging hard, conscious of the fact that the Babe's salary had jumped from ten thousand his first year in the outfield to seventy thousand. The club owners publicly, and perhaps in the heart of their hearts (for who knows what is in a club owner's heart?), deplored the financial element of Ruth's climb to fame—he and Charlie Chaplin were called the two best-known men in America, not excepting President Coolidge—but every ball park in the major leagues had been enlarged since Ruth's debut. And by the simple, flawless stroke of his bat he changed the pay scale for athletes for all time.

As to the club itself, it was figured to be a good team, one of the favorites for the pennant, but only one of them. Its 16½-game lead by September 22 did not seem likely back in the spring of the year. There were questions about its pitching, catching, and infield and about the ages of Ruth and pitchers Herb Pennock and Urban Shocker.

The myth of the Yankee pinstripe, which insisted that merely putting on the Yankee uniform made you part of a remorseless, invincible team, did not yet exist. The 1927 club carved out its beginnings.

True, the team had won the pennant in 1926. But it lost an historic World Series to the St. Louis Cardinals, and its league championship was regarded more as a collapse of the opposition than as any demonstration of lasting superiority. The 1925 club had finished seventh, and by winning the '26 pennant, the Yankees made the biggest jump to a flag in American League history up to that time, and there was feeling the pendulum might swing back.

So the Yankees that gathered in St. Petersburg, Florida, in March were respected but regarded as wearing no cloak of immortality. To begin with, there was Ruth. You always begin with Ruth. He was regarded as the game's Titan or, more aptly, its Gargantua, heroic from the cradle, but it was wondered how much longer he had to go; he was thirty-three, and there was some talk that his bat might be running out of home runs. He had hit forty-seven in 1926, but he had a way of following good years with bad.

In recent years there have been various attempts to strip away something called the legend of Babe Ruth, but there is no way to do this, for even after you strip away, you are left with the legend. Almost all the responsible things said about the man were true, the good and the bad, so the legend strippers usually settle by pointing out that the Babe liked women and drinking, which separates him from most healthy young men, and sometimes behaved badly, which sets him apart from humanity. And what is left is the swashbuckler who shaped the course of baseball and much else in modern sport, who set records that lasted for decades. In other words, a legend intact.

As early as 1921 there were attempts made to show just how singular and homeric a figure he was. Unlike the case with most giants, the stature was not stretched on the rack of nostalgia, retroactively. With Ruth people immediately knew what they had, something outsize and unique. *Baseball* magazine in 1921 argued that he could be compared to no other player, that Christy Mathewson in his prime had rivals, that Tris Speaker, then generally acknowledged as the greatest of center fielders, had competitors, that Ty Cobb even then was challenged by other base-stealers, but that Ruth stood alone, unchallenged.

Besides Ruth, the Yankees of 1927 had Lou Gehrig, in his third season as a regular, a .313 hitter the previous year, with 16 home runs and 107 runs batted in. Already his name was bracketed with Ruth's, although not in the way it would be after 1927, but he was not yet "the Iron Horse" who played in a record 2,130 consecutive games or Gary Cooper-Gehrig, whose farewell speech at Yankee Stadium is now part of a rite of passage for American youth, fixed in celluloid in one of Hollywood's few honorable approaches to the national game. He was called "Columbia Lou," because he had attended Columbia University, or "Biscuit Pants," for his running back's center of gravity, six inches off the ground, or, more often, "Buster," a name favored by Ruth, who never remembered anyone's name.

Tony Lazzeri was the second baseman, coming off a rookie year in which he played every game, batting .275, which would be well below his lifetime average. He was "Poosh 'Em Up," a name dating back to his first year in organized baseball, with Salt Lake City, when he was struggling, and a restaurant owner named Tony Roffetti took pity on him, feeding him spaghetti dinners three nights running, and urging him to "poosh 'em up," meaning hit. In 1925, when he was twenty-one, Tony Lazzeri set a couple of Pacific Coast League records with 60 homers and 222 runs batted in.

Mark Koenig was the shortstop, in his second full year, like Lazzeri and, like Lazzeri, a San Francisco native and a product of its sandlots. He was regarded, preseason, as a potential flaw in the formidable front the Yankees presented the world. He hit .271 the previous year, but he committed fifty-two errors, more than any other shortstop in the American League. It was asked if he ever would make a major league infielder. He had been the World Series goat, striking out seven times, sometimes at critical points, hitting into three double plays, and committing three errors, one of them crucial, in the seventh and deciding game.

Joe Dugan, who hit .288 in 1926, was called "Jumping Joe," and, in previous years, "the best third baseman in baseball." He could hit, field, run, and throw. He handled the bunt famously, dashing in to barehand it and whip it across the diamond in one of baseball's patterned graces, and the old Yankees and some newspaper accounts credit his nickname to this rare talent, but the name was first attached to him by a sportswriter named Tiny Maxwell with the Philadelphia *Ledger,* after one of Joe's frequent disappearances from the Athletics, his first major league club, which did not pay him enough, he thought, and which he did not believe was going any place. "Jumping Joe," according to one teammate, jumped the As thirty-six times, a modern record, going home to New Haven, or to Boston, or simply to check the ocean at Atlantic City a couple of days. In the spring of 1927 he was suspect because of an old knee injury.

With Ruth in the outfield there was Earle Combs, the best lead-off man in the major leagues, who hit .299 in 1926, more than 25 points below his lifetime average, but there was no doubt about him, a line-drive hitter who specialized in triples. Pitchers cried the couplet, "Hark! to the tombs/Here comes Earle Combs." He was a ghost on the bases, who, with Louisville in the minor leagues, was timed in ten flat for the hundred-yard dash in uniform and spikes by a clocker with Churchill Downs. Combs was a greatly respected southern gentleman, and, oddly, a cheerleader. He had only an average throwing arm, but no one was faster getting rid of the ball, and he covered a tremendous amount of outfield, having been advised to take all the space he wanted with no fear of running into Ruth or Bob Meusel.

Perhaps one of the reasons that Combs's throwing arm was so questioned was that he played next to Ruth, who had been a great pitcher, capable of making the Hall of Fame through that arduous calling alone, having once, as every schoolboy learns along with the pledge of allegiance, pitched 29⅔ scoreless World Series innings, a record that stood for forty-three years. He had become an outfielder only because his bat was too explosive to leave out of the daily lineup, but he retained his marvelous arm, so that base runners seldom challenged him, and it was said that he never made a mechanical error, never threw to the wrong base.

On the other side of Combs was Meusel, who had the best arm, by common consent, in baseball, a rifle, and who also hit for the average—.315 in 1926—and with power. The only year during the 1920s that Ruth did not lead the league in home runs—1925— Meusel was the leader, with thirty-three, and the runs-batted-in leader, too. He stood six feet, three inches, and was called "Long Bob," also "Languid Bob," because he was uncommunicative and because he tended to play the way he felt that day.

Fans remembered his performance in the 1921 World Series, when he lazed to first base and cost the Yankees a run that would have saved the game and, with Koenig, he was a 1926 Series goat, muffing a fly in the deciding game, but his manager once said, "I don't want to brag, but it looks to me as though Meusel is going to be the greatest batter-in of runs that baseball has seen in recent years." He traditionally led the league in assists for an outfielder.

There were three catchers with the 1927 Yankees. The nominal first-stringer was Benny Bengough, twenty-nine years old and in his fifth season with the club, a Merry Andrew who, at five feet seven and 145 pounds, looked more like the batboy than the catcher. He hit .381 in 1926 but played in only thirty-six games, having been hit on the right arm by George "The Bull" Uhle, a great Cleveland pitcher on his way to twenty-seven wins. Having unsuccessfully consulted medical specialists, X-ray artists, osteopaths, Bengough was visited by eccentrics and quacks claiming restorative powers for the damaged arm. One, a St. Louis dealer in hope, put Bengough in something like an electric chair, and the catcher leaped out at the current's first jolt and turned his ankle, thus becoming simultaneously sore of nonmatching limbs.

Tharon Patrick "Pat" Collins was a bigger man, solider, in the traditional catcher's mold, and he caught in 102 games in 1926, hitting .286 and, in the Series, .600, but he, too, had an injured throwing arm and doubted his own capacity to make the throw to second. He claimed, but gingerly, that he regained its strength through bowling—he was owner of a bowling alley in Kansas City—and he advised bowling in moderate amounts as a cure for ailing arms.

To back up this shaky duet, the Yankees dealt during the off-season for John Grabowski, inelegantly called "Nig," who hit .262 in forty-eight games with the Chicago White Sox in 1926, his third year in the major leagues. Grabowski handled pitchers well, it was felt, but there was concern about his dexterity, particularly in going after foul balls.

*Baseball* magazine observed unconvincingly, "The Yankee catchers are methodical, mere plodders, but, brother, these type are the salt of the earth, the backbone of the game."

The biggest question of all about the 1927 Yankees involved the pitching.

The ace was Herbert Jeffries Pennock, the Squire of Kennett Square, Pennsylvania, where he bred silver foxes. He won twenty-three games in 1926, losing only eleven, but this would be his fourteenth year in the big leagues. He had come up with the Athletics in 1912 and pitched for the Boston Red Sox before joining the Yankees in 1923 to win nineteen games en route to a World Series, and there was speculation as to how much longer he could be useful, particularly since he was a serious holdout at thirty-three.

But a Yankee coach said, "If you were to cut that bird's head open, the weakness of every batter in the league would fall out." One tremendous Detroit hitter, Bob "Fatty" Fothergill (lifetime batting average .326) said to an even more tremendous Detroit hitter named Harry Heilmann (lifetime batting average .342 and four times American League batting champion), that no left-hander could get him, Fothergill, out, and then went zero for four against Pennock. "What the hell happened?" said Fothergill. Heilmann explained, "You didn't face a left-hander, you faced Herb Pennock," a line that would be repeated, under other circumstances, before 1927 was over.

Right up with Pennock on the Yankee pitching staff was Waite Charles Hoyt, twenty-seven and in his tenth major-league season, but still called "Schoolboy," a name attached to him when he signed a baseball contract at sixteen out of Brooklyn's Erasmus High School. He won sixteen and lost twelve in 1926 and had not yet won twenty games in a season, but in 1921 he emerged from three complete World Series games with an earned run average of 0.000, a record he was to share with the legendary Christy Mathewson and one of those rare marks that will never be lowered.

Urban Shocker was back with the Yankees for his third year in 1927. He first joined the team in 1916, when he was twenty-six, but two years later he was traded to the St. Louis Browns, a move regretted later, for he became a Yankee nemesis, credited with knowing more about pitching to Ruth, in particular, than any other man in the game except for the great, tarnished Eddie Cicotte of the Black Sox. Shocker won 127 games and lost 79 for the Browns, a club even then studying for its role as the essence of big-league ineptness, before the Yankees finally got him back in 1925. The spitball was outlawed in 1920, but pitchers already using it were allowed to continue. Shocker was one of only seven legal practitioners in 1927, but he had such an assortment of curves and other dirty tricks that he said he sometimes got through a game without resorting to the spitter. He was thirty-seven now, clearly nearing the end of the baseball road, but with a reputation as "the greatest in the game at pitching to a batter's weakness or pitching to a dangerous batter," and only Shocker that spring had any intimation, which he kept to himself, that the drum banged slowly for him.

When Walter "Dutch" Ruether, a left-hander with ten major league years behind him after stops in Chicago, Cincinnati, and Brooklyn of the National League, and Washington of the American, came to the Yankees in 1926 for "cash well exceeding the waiver price," the deal elicited comment, since he was still regarded as one of the league's better pitchers, the Senators' staff was short of left-handers, and six clubs still in contention had to pass on him before he got to the Yankees. "One possible explanation is that Dutch's salary may have scared them away," wrote Rud Rennie in the New York *Herald Tribune*. "Another is that he may have been unruly. Dutch has been unruly."

This meant, in the code of a boozy era, that Ruether drank. He was accused of getting drunk before the first game of the 1919 World Series, when he beat Cicotte and the heavily favored White Sox, 9–1, in a game later accepted as being fixed.

"I beat them easily," Ruether later recalled. "What hurt me was the disclosure that they were merely fooling around. It's hard to believe. I thought I had worked a tight game."

He was nineteen and six with the Reds that season, and he may have pitched a winning game, at that. It was something a man could think about, over a drink.

Another veteran, Bob Shawkey, the oldest Yankee in terms of years with the team, was not counted on for much. After two and a half seasons with the Athletics, starting in 1913, he came to the Yankees, winning twenty-four games for them in 1916, thirteen the following season, before entering the Navy in World War I, picking up the lasting nickname of "Sailor Bob," resuming with six big seasons, twice winning twenty games but clearly wearing out and winning only eight in 1926.

Since the staff was in need of more dependable arms, it was time the cup not pass from the lips of George Pipgras, called "the Danish Viking," a Minnesota farm boy tagged by that fatal baseball cliché, "world of stuff, no control," coming out of the dugout only often enough to win one game, lose four over two seasons, before being farmed out to pitch 102 minor league games in two years, and this spring he was back for what could be a final look.

All the pressure was on him to prove he could be a major league pitcher.

"One of the most amazing characters ever to wear a Yankee uniform" and attracting instant notice was William Wilcy Moore, a big, yellow-haired Oklahoma dirt farmer who turned thirty that spring but was a rookie after a six-year career in the obscurity of places like Paris, Texas, and Ardmore and Okmulgee, Oklahoma. Two seasons earlier, his wrist was fractured by a batted ball, and, after he came back, he began throwing sidearm to relieve the strain and so developed a sinker, a low fast ball that breaks sharply as it reaches the plate. In 1926 he was thirty and four with Greenville, South Carolina, in the Sally League, walking only seventy men all season. A pitcher with a thirty and four record is worth looking at, it was said, even if he is pitching in the Scandinavian League, and so Wilcy Moore, who had thought the previous year of packing it in, going home, and settling down to the farm life, would be looked at closely that spring.

There were, of course, others in camp, rookies of great promise, utility men, veterans, a gaggle of substitutes like pitchers Myles Thomas, a Penn State man with a six-six record the previous year, and Joe Giard, thirteen-fifteen after two seasons; and backup outfielders like Ben Paschal, in his third season with the Yankees, who could field and who hit .360 in eighty-nine games in 1925 (but how do you, realistically, *how do you* break into an outfield of Ruth, Combs, and Meusel, unless you pray for a selective outbreak of the plague?); and infielders like Roy Morehart, out of Stephen Austin College in Texas, who hit .315 in seventy-three games with the 1926 White Sox, Julian Wera, and Mike Gazella, a weak hitter in his third year, who proved that a spear-carrier can mean more than his average the previous season, when the Yankees, having all but dissipated a huge July lead, lost a double-header to Cleveland, the second-place club, for their fourth defeat in a row. At dinner that night Gazella, a former baseball and football hero at Lafayette College, said approximately, "All right, you birds have been kidding me all season about the old college spirit. If you gutless bums had a little of that spirit, you would not have quit the way you did today." That little speech was credited with helping the team turn around and beat the Indians the next day and go on to the pennant.

Such were the men who gathered in St. Petersburg for training camp in the spring of 1927.

All happy ball clubs are alike, as Count Leo Tolstoy almost observed on another occasion, and each unhappy ball club is unhappy in its own fashion.

The '27 Yankees are remembered as a team of swashbucklers who trampled their way through the seven other American League cities, sacking the opposition. But there is a perilously thin line between high spirits and behavior that is out of control and so reflected on the ball field. The failure to understand and act on this difference sends managers to join poor Anna under the familiar locomotive wheels of history.

Two seasons earlier, the Yankees were a divided and bitter club that finished seventh, in the second division for the first and what proved to be the only time under Manager Miller Huggins. The chief source of the discontent was Ruth. You always begin with Ruth.

He opened their relationship by scorning Huggins, an attitude that became widespread in the dugout. "The Yankees," one sportswriter cruelly observed, "think their manager is a girl."

The reasons, as with any tangled relationship, were complex. Huggins, a manager of no great statistical distinction, came to a ball club with a record that was ditto in 1918. It is difficult to think of the Yankees, even after the indifferent clubs of the 1960s, as just another ball club, but that is what they were when Huggins first came to New York.

There were times, in fact, when the club appeared to exist, as in the early days of a later team called the New York Mets, only because it is a law of American commerce that to consider yourself major league if you operate a string of businesses, even if they are pussy farms, it is necessary to have a New York franchise.

The chief distinctions of those first New York entries in the

American League, itself called the junior circuit, coming into existence with the dawn of the new century after a quarter of a century of National League history, were as a graveyard of managers (seven in the twelve years following the team's birth in 1903) and as a property of fractious owners.

The franchise had an almost unbroken string of losing years, artistically and financially, when it was bought on January 11, 1915, for $460,000 by a couple of millionaires named Colonel Jacob Ruppert, inheritor and head of a brewery bearing his name, and a sport rejoicing in the name of Tillinghast L'Hommedieu Huston, a civil engineer who stayed on in Cuba after fighting there in the Spanish-American war and made his fortune.

As marriage counselors report every day, responsibility is hard to share. Ruppert, as president of the Yankees, overruled Huston, as vice-president, by bringing in Wild Bill Donovan as manager, a baseball veteran who in 1914 won the International League pennant for Providence, aided by a young pitcher, who also hit well, named Ruth. Huston, who wanted his friend, Uncle Wilbert Robinson, manager of the Brooklyn Robins, to lead the Yankees, never forgave Ruppert.

There were temperamental differences. Ruppert was a former four-time congressman, well-connected, a Teutonic dandy who, although born and raised in New York of American parentage, spoke with a pronounced German accent that became all but impenetrable when he grew excited.

Fresh out of high school, he went to work in his father's brewery, washing beer kegs, twelve hours a day for ten dollars a week—learning the business from the ground up is the explanation. By the time he was twenty-three he was general manager, and he headed the business before he was thirty, a particular branch of the American success story of the sort that leads to widespread cynicism in the Republic. With a fortune estimated at seventy million dollars he lived in a fifteen-room upper Fifth Avenue apartment and a twenty-five-room Tudor mansion at Garrison, New York, where he kept monkeys, peacocks, and a kennel of prize-winning St. Bernards.

He was a resolute bachelor, claiming that he enjoyed the company of women but that men married only because they were lonely or needed a housekeeper. Although his view was expressed in the public prints, there appeared no flood of angry comment. Psychology was in its first American vogue in the twenties, and Freud was alive and well in Vienna, but no one seems to have asked what this rich old bachelor was displacing, suppressing, or replacing with all those monkeys, peacocks, and dogs.

Huston went off to World War I, still upset over the choice of Donovan, who in three years did no better than fourth place. At the suggestion of Byron Bancroft "Ban" Johnson, founder of the American League, Ruppert brought in Huggins, manager of the St. Louis Cardinals, to take over the ball club, informing Huston by telegram. Huston, already edgy, never forgot that the management change was made without consulting him. He disliked Huggins sight unseen and still wanted Robinson.

Huggins, who was five foot seven, and had played at under 150 pounds as a scrappy and aggressive second baseman called "Little Mr. Everywhere" (and, later, "the Mite Manager"), grew up on the sandlots of Cincinnati's rugged Fourth Ward, the son of an English-born grocer who disapproved of Sunday ball, so the boy played under the name of Proctor. Once, when his older brother, a more promising ball player, forgot he was in new trousers and essayed a slide, young Miller cried, "The pants, Clarence! The pants!" but the trousers ripped, and, so the story goes, Clarence received a hiding that permanently discouraged his interest in baseball. Miller knew that his father wanted him to be a lawyer and he took a law degree at the University of Cincinnati, although he never practiced.

He played baseball with semiprofessional teams, surely with his father's knowledge, while acquiring an education. He was one of those admirable few determined to live up to his image of himself. Small and by nature puny, he spent four winters working with weights and pulleys to build up his left arm and foreleg. With St. Paul in the American Association on Sept. 17, 1902, he flawlessly handled nineteen chances—eleven outputs, eight assists—more than any major leaguer had ever done, and so made the newspaper wire services.

He broke in with Cincinnati in 1905, going to St. Louis as a combative, intelligent player, batting .265, and telling a sportswriter, "I'll tell you when I'll quit. When the fans tell me I'm no longer filling the bill," the most frequently broken promise in sports. When the day came that he was booed after failing to handle a couple of grounders, he took the same writer to dinner and said, "Well, my public gave you the answer this afternoon. You've seen the last of Miller Huggins as this club's second baseman."

He had become Cardinal manager in 1913, never bringing the club in higher than third, but as a sportswriter put it, "In the first two decades of this century, third place for a St. Louis ball club was a sensation."

Huggins was, like Ruppert, a bachelor, and baseball was his life, his monkeys, peacocks, and St. Bernards. His only other interest was the stock market, at which he was canny and successful, sometimes investing wisely on the behalf of his players, a job he apparently regarded as part of his managerial duties.

The idea that it is easy to manage is largely a new one, an aphorism of the seventies putting it that the only requirements are "to be white and a drunk." But this is said by people who have never tried managing; done well, it is like any task at which few succeed, and it eventually cost Huggins his life.

With St. Louis, he came upon a weak, skinny nineteen-year-old from Texas with a bad batting average and no ability to play his position, passed over by other baseball people. Huggins worked with him, and Rogers Hornsby became the man generally regarded as the hardest-hitting right-hander of all time, a record six-time National League batting champion who hit more than .400 over a stretch of five years. This talent for development of young players should be part of any manager's portfolio; just about any of the better ones can point to his Galatea. Huggins could point to Hornsby, Gehrig, and Lazzeri before drawing a breath.

It took him only three seasons before the Yankees won their first flag, but the cost was dreadful. Huston's animosity was open. Huggins inherited a club of players that did not respect him; he would have to earn it. Because he was small, and because his tendency was to hold the reins loosely, believing on the face of no solid, supporting evidence that he was dealing with grown men, some of his players regarded him as weak.

"I know of no one who could have taken over a bunch of artificial prima donnas," wrote Joe Williams later in the New York *World Telegram,* "such as was handed to Huggins when he first came to New York and turned them ultimately into a perfect, machine-like organism."

Huggins himself, recalling the attitude of his players, the feuding owners, and Huston's willingness to side with malcontents, said, "I would not go through those years again for all the money in the world."

His health was never robust. He could not eat, frequently did not sleep. His teeth were bad. He was an easy victim to infections. Not in an obituary, but while he was in no need of canonization, a writer observed, "Never in more than a dozen years of friendship with Huggins have we heard him utter a single, derogatory word in reference to any human being."

Huggins' first Yankee ball club finished fourth in 1918 and rose to third a year later. In 1920 he suggested to Rupert that Ruth could be purchased from the Red Sox. It turned out to be the biggest deal of its time, and one that would not be approved today. The Yankees, in addition to the purchase price of $125,000, made a $350,000 loan to Harry Frazee, the perennially hard-pressed Red Sox owner, a theater buff who needed ready cash for the purpose, it is said, of backing a new Broadway musical called, *No, No, Nanette.* Frazee mortgaged his ball park as security.

Ruppert, although he was no tightwad, had recently turned down an offer to buy Eddie Collins for $50,000. Collins left baseball after a record twenty-five years in the majors, hitting .340 over a ten-year span, once stealing eighty-one bases in a season, but Ruppert didn't want to be gouged. Now he asked, "Is any ball player worth that much money?'' Assured that Ruth was, he made the purchase.

So we come back to Ruth. In much that is written about him, and in conversation with anyone who knew him, the basic characterization is that he had more than the ordinary man's share of small boy in him. This can be charming, but it also can present discipline problems. Ruth went from a loveless, poverty-ridden childhood to riches and adulation about as quickly as it can be legally done. He had no talent for curbing his impulses—''Obey that impulse!'' a cant exhortation of the twenties, might have been written by him, although it wasn't—and he resented outside assistance.

He divided the world into good guys and bad guys. Bill Carrigan, his first manager, was a good guy, chiefly because he pretty well let the young ball player alone. Ruth announced publicly and repeatedly that Carrigan was the best manager he ever had.

The year after Ruth arrived with the Yankees, as they moved to their first pennant in history, Ed Barrow came from the Red Sox as general manager, probably as part of the Ruth deal, and one way of measuring his accomplishment is to say that he meant almost as much to the club as Ruth did. He had been Ruth's field manager in Boston, winning the pennant in 1918, and knew enough about Ruth to side with Huggins. This made further opportunity for combustion.

Barrow was a tough cookie. He is remembered as chief architect of what became the Yankee dynasty, organizing the best scouting staff in baseball, headed by Paul Krichell.

''Barrow's three favorite words,'' Krichell once recalled, ''were 'Proceed at once.' The way I used to get out of town, you'd think the cops were after me.''

Barrow, who quit as a sandlot schoolboy pitcher after tearing a muscle on a rainy day in 1883, managed the Tigers as far back as 1903. In more than half a century as the most successful major league executive of all time, he was sometime club owner, boxing promoter, minor-league official and manager, but his monument, of course, is the Yankees, and it is ironic that baseball's most tremendous force acquired a reputation for bloodless efficiency when it was built by a knockabout of the old school, who just missed being born in a covered wagon and grew up fighting floods, fires, and Indians on an Iowa prairie, and who would come to you over the desk, not with a platoon of lawyers and cost-efficiency men, but with two big fists. In his later years he cheerfully estimated that he had some fifty bare-knuckle fights, encouraging the other fellow to see things in a different light; once he flattened a man named Sandy Ferguson, who had a fair reputation as a heavyweight, and once, facing it out with Ruth, he ordered the other Red Sox to clear the clubhouse, just he and Ruth would settle the matter. Ruth demurred, his wife supposing in retrospect that the young Ruth thought the better of fighting a fifty-year-old man, but there are fifty-year-old men and fifty-year-old men, and no one argued that Barrow was anything but one of the tougher ones.

His arrival in New York, shortly after Ruth, came at a time when Mark Roth, the traveling secretary of the Yankees, said, "If the crowds get any smaller, they'll have to put fractions on the turnstiles." Barrow told Ruppert, "If you ran your brewery and real estate business along the lines of this ball club, you'd go broke in no time."

In 1918 the Yankees drew 282,000 customers to the Polo Grounds, which they shared with, and rented from, the Giants, long the indisputable first team of New York. In 1920, Ruth's first year, the Yankees drew 1,289,422. That same year, their landlords drew 929,609, and after it became clear that more New Yorkers wanted to see Babe Ruth hit home runs than watch the Giants win pennants, the landlords suggested that it was time for the Yankees to move.

Ruppert obliged by building, just across the Harlem River from the Polo Grounds, Yankee Stadium, the first three-tiered concrete and steel baseball park. "Colonel Ruppert's concrete cashbox," it was quickly called, but not as quickly or as frequently as the House

That Ruth Built, a name given it by the sportswriter Frederick G. Lieb.

Still, prosperity did not ease the friction between Ruppert and Huston—or, at first, between the team and its manager. A player faction, led by Ruth, continued deriding the pickle-faced, pipe-smoking little man who came over from the other league to manage them.

Once a group of Yankees gathered at 3 A.M. under Huggins' hotel window when the team was on the road. "Oh, Hug," they crooned, "your ball club is cockeyed drunk again! Miller, come get your drunken ball club."

Twice, at least once with Ruth involved, drunken Yankees held the little manager off the observation car of a speeding train, letting him twist slowly, slowly over the track. Ruth said, "It was a nutty thing to do, but Hug forgave me. I'll never figure out why." One who knew all the parties said, "Huggins probably figured Ruth would be Ruth, Meusel would be Meusel."

Huggins was, after all, older, wiser, and educated.

The bickering was not confined to either the dugout or the locker room. In the eighth inning of the deciding game of a World Series against the Giants Huggins ordered his pitcher, Bullet Joe Bush, to walk a man intentionally with a man on third. Bush yelled back from the pitcher's mound, "What for, you stupid oaf?" He walked the batter, but the next man singled, the game was lost, and the Yankees were outraged.

Some of the players immediately went to Huston. Huggins ordered the clubhouse doors shut. He lectured Bush, an uncharacteristic thing; the old Yankees revere Huggins' memory because, among other things, he customarily called an offending player into his office, alone, the day after a game, to discuss sin. But now he spoke sharply to Bush, whom he would not forgive, sending him out of the league to St. Louis in 1924. The clubhouse was in a turmoil. Someone whispered to Ruth, and he growled, "Shut up, before I stick my fist in your trap," and kicked a trunk.

Huston rode away with a couple of newspapermen, staring in

silent, purple-faced fury at the taxi floor. When they reached a midtown hotel, he strode to the bar, still silent. Then he let loose a war whoop, sweeping his arm so that it cleared bottles and glasses from the bar and sent them crashing to the floor.

"He's through," Huston shouted. "Huggins has managed his last Yankee team. He's through! through! through!"

Huston was wrong about that, but a bad situation worsened. The manager could not control his imperious star, the most commanding figure in baseball history. Apart from general matters of discipline and responsibility—the statistics aren't helpful, since Ruth kept hitting home runs and the Yankees won—there was damaged morale and a questioning of the chain of command. Huggins got rid of some troublemakers, like Bush and another pitcher, Carl Mays, but there remained the matter of Ruth.

The thing would not have worked at all without Ruppert. He sided with his manager, even though this put him in conflict with his partner. Ruppert loved the Yankees and wanted to win. His idea of a good ball game, he said, was 10–0, Yankees. "Close games make me nervous."

With his other business interests, he was in some ways a dilettante about baseball. Early on, he expressed concern that the team wasn't hitting in spring training. Huggins reassured him that the pitchers always were ahead of the batters at that stage.

A couple of weeks later Ruppert was overheard informing some visiting tycoons, "The pitchers are ahead of the batters. But don't worry. Next month it will be the other way around, and then everything will be all right."

But he was no dummy; he had the money and he believed in Huggins. In the World Series of 1921, the Giants defeated the Yankees so badly that it was widely viewed as a disgrace for the American League. In 1922 the Giants won again. Finally in 1923, the Yankees beat the Giants for their first world championship. The victory was followed by a second-place finish the next year and a plunge to seventh in 1925.

Part of this was due to the normal attrition that hits a ball club while the search for replacements goes on, but there was more to it than that.

On the way north from spring training Ruth got off the train in some southern pesthole and consumed, quickly, a large quantity of hot dogs, washed down with what was identified, probably properly, as poisonous soda pop. The ensuing bellyache was heard round the world. A London newspaper reported Ruth's death. He was rushed to New York and underwent surgery. History is tangled as to what really happened. The bellyache story is the most widely supported. There are the customary innuendoes that something more serious, even "sinister," was involved. On the other hand, Mrs. Ruth, in a book called *The Babe and I,* says the ailment was a groin injury the Babe suffered sliding on a rocky Atlanta diamond during an exhibition game and that the club, faced with having to say "groin" in public, preferred having its star identified as a glutton. This seems hard to believe, but baseball traditionally lingers behind the times and, for all the talk of the roaring twenties, the period wrestled with vestigial Victorianism.

Ruth played in only ninety-eight games, hitting below .300 for the first time since he joined the Yankees and getting only twenty-five home runs. "As Ruth goes, so go the Yankees" already was accepted baseball wisdom, and the Yankees went nearly to the bottom of the standings. Huggins understood what his difficult star meant to the team. He called Ruth "the most destructive force in baseball. I don't mean the force of Ruth's homers alone. The mere presence of the Babe creates a disastrous psychological problem for the other team. We won the 1922 pennant because of that factor. The last month of 1922, Ruth didn't hit at all. But the opposing pitchers kept walking Ruth to get at Wally Pipp, and Pipp was hitting .400 at the time."

Still, no cease-fire marked the hostilities between Ruth and Huggins. There were periods when they did not speak to each other. There were periods when they spoke to each other, but sharply. Frequently, they spoke to each other through invisible third parties, a man on the shoulder, like the French. Huggins would talk grouchily of ball players who stayed up all night, showing no consideration for the team. Ruth would speak about a manager who knew nothing about managing, whose strategy lapsed, and who could not handle pitchers. A sample set piece, widely reported:

Ruth: "I wish you were fifty pounds heavier."

Huggins: "It's a good thing for you I'm not."

All very childish, but as history frequently informs us, particularly recent history—thanks to the miracle of electronic surveillance—no more so than behavior and dialogue in other corridors of power.

In 1923, encouraged by Barrow who one day simply exploded over the continued quarreling between the partners, Ruppert bought out Huston. He then made one of his infrequent clubhouse appearances and made the most of it dramatically, uttering one of those two-sentence communiqués which sometimes alter the course of events more sharply than tendentious documents, the point being clearer. "I am now sole owner of the Yankees," he said. "Miller Huggins is my manager."

Results are not always immediate. Ruth's behavior roller-coastered. His youthful first marriage began to dissolve, and he undertook a more than five-year courtship marked, in the second Mrs. Ruth's recollections, "by frustrations, not a little humiliation and an uncommon amount of terror." There were a lot of ladies, at home and on the road, a lot of drinking, a lot of partying, defiance.

It blew up in St. Louis, in August of the bellyache year, 1925, when the club was foundering next to last with a 49–71 record. Ruth, who had appeared in only sixty-eight games, batting .266 at a time when fifty-four American League batters were above .300, and with only fifteen home runs, arrived late at the ball park, told Huggins breezily that he had been detained on business, and was told, in turn, not to put on his uniform, he was suspended indefinitely and fined five thousand dollars.

That was the largest fine ever imposed by a club on a player. The explosion rocked baseball. Ruth protested. Bootleggers, he said, were not fined that much. He went to Chicago to see Baseball Commissioner Kenesaw Mountain Landis, to New York to see Ruppert. In the end, after tumultuous press conferences at every stop, he apologized, like a man, publicly.

"You can call it the turning point in the history of the New York Yankees," Barrow later said. "Thereafter, the so-called bad boys realized that we meant business."

Huggins crowed. A little. "The fine stands," he told a press conference. "I reiterate that it will not be lifted. Please note the word 'reiterate.' I like it. Up to now, I have just repeated and reasserted, but now I reiterate."

Toward the end of the season Christy Walsh, Ruth's business agent, arranged a small party for Ruth, some baseball writers, and State Senator James J. Walker, soon to become mayor of New York City.

It is not a Hollywood fiction but a matter of record that Walker, an eloquent after-dinner speaker with an impressive blarney quotient, and fueled by whatever potables of the evening, made a speech in which he told the Babe what the Babe meant to America, particularly to "the dirty-faced kid in the streets," and how he was failing his duty.

"The Babe arose with tears streaming down his face. He apologized to the writers. He apologized to the dirty-faced kids," wrote one witness. "He promised to be good. He was the most contrite man I yet have seen at a public function."

Good intentions aside, the element of resolve is not the dominant strain in childish natures. Ruth previously had promised to reform: in 1922, when he announced that he had gone through an estimated half a million dollars on frivolities, including high-priced cars; in 1924, when he published a magazine article about his new, good intentions. It would be too much to expect reformation; a smattering of maturity was probably all Huggins hoped for.

But there is evidence that whether it was the fine, or the Walker speech, or simply that march of time which slows us all, Ruth toned down the extravagance. Ruth-watchers, who constituted a nation, detected some seriousness in his approach. Given his nature, it was always a quirky business; adult behavior stuck to him tentatively, like adhesive tape after a shower or California to the continent.

He turned himself over to Arthur A. McGovern, who ran a gymnasium near Grand Central Station, and who wrote an article about it, titled, starkly, "Salvaging the Wreck of Babe Ruth." McGovern put him under a tough dietary and weight-control program which appeared to pay off in 1926, when Ruth hit .372, with forty-seven home runs, as the Yankees won the pennant, and, as spring training approached in 1927, McGovern was at Ruth's side in Hollywood, where he was making his first major motion picture.

So what you had was a team whose big man was just a season away from the only season in which it can be clearly established that his off-the-field behavior caught up with his performance; in which there was a still-developing first baseman, and second-year men, one of them unquestionably questionable, at second and short; in which there was age at third and on the pitching staff, mercurial genius in the outfield and journeymen behind the plate, but which, most importantly, appeared at last to be under the control of, and responsive to, the manager.

All of this was being played out against a baseball season which did not look promising, over which the dark cloud of scandal lowered as the year broke. What was called baseball's darkest hour had tolled when eight men were charged with fixing the 1919 World Series; that story broke the following year, just as Ruth, putting the game forever in his debt for that reason alone, helped distract the fans by hitting fifty-four home runs.

As what became known as the Watergate affair reminded us, scandal, once revealed, does not go quietly; it subdivides, producing its own progeny, like protozoa. In the fall of 1926 disquieting rumors floated around Detroit about Manager Ty Cobb of the Tigers. Similar stories drifted around Detroit's sister city of the spirit, Cleveland, about Manager Tris Speaker of the Indians. The passage of time has not dimmed the glory of these two men; they are not only in the Hall of Fame but ornaments on just about every all-time team chosen, gods, worthy, almost, of mention in the same breath as Ruth.

Each capped the rumors by suddenly announcing that he was quitting his team, Cobb after five years as manager, Speaker after seven and a second-place finish, just three games out, in 1926. The news leaped to the front pages; it was development of historic proportions, almost as though a President and a Vice-President of the United States should be simultaneously accused of crimes as serious as conducting a secret war and as shabby as accepting bribe money.

The Cobb-Speaker affair seemed bad enough. Commissioner Landis made public two letters turned over to him by Ban Johnson. The letters were from "Smokey Joe" Wood, baseball coach at Yale University but formerly a great pitcher for the Red Sox (and, in 1919, with Speaker in Cleveland), and from Cobb, both written to Hubert "Dutch" Leonard, a former pitcher with Boston and Detroit. The letters seemed to support Leonard's contention that Cobb, Speaker, Wood, and Leonard met under the stands between the games of September 24 and 25, 1919, and agreed that Cleveland, which had clinched second place, would lose the following day to Detroit, which was battling the Yankees for third. There was no money for a fourth-place finish in those days.

Enter now Charles August "Swede" Risberg, one of the more culpable of the Black Sox, who said from the farm of his enforced, premature, and deserved retirement near Rochester, Minnesota, that he could divulge information about a matter "not quite as silly as the thing Cobb and Speaker were accused of participating in."

Said Landis, a theatrical former federal judge whose passion for the headlines rivaled that of Bernard M. Baruch, "Won't these goddamned things that happened before I became baseball commissioner"—which was January 12, 1921—"ever stop coming up?"

Risberg's charges involved the alleged "sloughing off" of a Tiger-White Sox game in 1917, with repayment by another dump in 1919. It also involved the common practice of the day of players contributing to a kitty for members of a rival team who had been particularly tough on a pennant rival in late-season games, one of those *quid pro quos* of commercial enterprise which do not seem questionable, because no one questions them, until exposed to light of day, when they are clearly the source of great potential mischief.

Supporting Risberg's contention was Chick Gandil, another Black Sox of low repute. All the charges were full of holes. Arrayed against Risberg and Gandil were players whose probity nearly rivaled their skills—Cobb, Collins, Schalk, Heilmann, and Howard Ehmke among them. Leonard, it developed, had threatened revenge on Cobb for dropping him from the Tiger team and on Speaker, a former Red Sox teammate, for not claiming him on waivers after the Tigers let him go.

Landis quickly exonerated Cobb and Speaker, saying he made public the letters only because the man had asked about their status. Speaker, after a trip to New York in the late winter, when it was rumored that he might replace Meusel or Combs in the outfield, signed with the Senators; Cobb joined Collins and Zach Wheat, for eighteen years a Brooklyn monument, in Philadelphia, where the trio, in some opinions, just about clinched a pennant for the As. The Risberg-Gandil charges also were dismissed as the work of vengeful and dishonest men.

But the total effect clouded the baseball horizon. It was believed by some that the shaken faith of many fans would be torpedoed by the charges. A winter of headlines threatened the future of what was then, without rival, the national game.

Compounding the problem for the Yankees was Ruth's movie acting. His absence from New York cleared the news pages for the Giants. And his contract was up. He had signed for $60,000 the previous year. From the coast came demands for $100,000 and a three-year contract.

In addition to his fitness consultant, Ruth had acquired Walsh as a business manager. The practice was unusual then. The comparative simplicity of the age is nowhere more clearly demonstrated than in the views of a St. Louis Cardinal executive, Sam Breadon, who gave even the tight-fisted Branch Rickey lessons in penuriousness, speaking for the baseball establishment in negotiations with Tommy Thevenow, a small shortstop who starred in the World Series. Breadon said Thevenow immediately became a holdout on "acquiring a manager in salary negotiations.

"I am sick and tired of this third party business when it comes to dealing with ball players. It's not a question of salary now but of 'third party' advice that is holding Tommy back."

A similar tack was taken more than thirty years later by a professional football coach named Vince Lombardi, but his attitude was regarded as isolated and reactionary. Breadon spoke the conventional wisdom of his day. In the thinking of the magnates the idea of frequently uneducated, even unlettered, naïve men who would play a game for the sheer love of it, asking sharp operators schooled in economics for assistance in financial dealings posed as grave a threat to baseball as the fix. The fact that the wretched Black Sox acted as they did at least partly because of the fifteenth-century slave conditions under which they labored was not discussed.

The irritation of the establishment was expressed in *The Sporting News*, the *Osservatore Romana* of baseball, on the matter of Ruth's negotiations.

"I see the newspapers have filled their columns with nauseating slush," it quoted Ruppert, in a style he never approached, "concerning Ruth and his motion picture stunts in Hollywood. It appears that the Bambino has a salaried corps of press agents, a manager and a trainer who think the world is hungry for news of the great man. But getting down to brass tacks, the public cares nothing for his literary mush. What they really want to know," he added, his finger on the pulse, "is Ruth's physical condition and desire to play baseball as soon as possible."

John B. Sheridan, a "veteran scribe," weighed in with the opinion that "the fantastic salaries paid Ruth and Cobb derive from other members of the team, who make them contenders," a view clearly designed to promote harmony. "They would be worth far less with the Phillies or the Red Sox," he argued, without checking the Red Sox to see what, besides the Boston Commons, they would give to get Ruth back.

Trial balloons, floated from the Coast about the possibility that Ruth might devote full time to the screen, or what time he could find after he and McGovern established a nationwide chain of gymnasiums, dissolved in pools of literary mush from Ruppert and other sources arguing that Ruth without baseball would be a man of practically no interest at all.

In addition to his salary, it was estimated that Ruth picked up $20,000 from the World Series and exhibitions, $65,000 from vaudeville, $75,000 for the movie, and $10,000 for syndicated newspaper articles. "Some figures are open to suspicion," said one newspaper, "but the overall total can be toned down and still arouse the envy of the wage slave."

The Yankees, it was written "are not likely to be persuaded for a long-term contract. No member of the team has a contract for more than one year. . . . Some see Ruth seeking protection against the decline in skill and fleetness of foot rapidly taking place."

Contrary to Ruppert's statement, there was an almost creepy fascination with everything Ruth did, on or off the field. There was no television for him to dominate, but he commanded newsprint the way the Kennedy family did in the early 1960s, and he would be eclipsed in 1927, and then briefly, only by Charles A. Lindbergh, the greatest overnight wonder in the history of the world.

The Yankees already were arriving in camp when Ruth departed Hollywood. His every train stop was the scene of a press conference. Far from not caring about his salary demands, the wage slaves cried, "Get the hundred thousand, Babe!" "Make Ruppert pay!" In Chicago, the conference included twenty-five news cameramen, as Ruth insisted he wouldn't play unless his demands were met. Ruppert and Barrow were reported hiding out in New York.

In the seventies the media affectionately report the loyalty of fans clustered in airline depots to greet teams returning from playoffs or World Series. In 1927 more than a hundred persons sneaked past guards at Grand Central Station to welcome, not a ball club, but one man, returning from no great triumph but on his way to see about a contract before spring training even got under way. And two thousand more milled about in the streets.

The result, rare for Ruth, who customarily rose to the occasion as routinely as other men put on their trousers in the morning, was anticlimactic. He proceeded to the McGovern gymnasium to show what fine shape he was in, posing an hour for photographs, then to St. Vincent's hospital for a brief visit with his estranged wife, suffering from an undisclosed ailment, then to the Yankee offices, where he was told Ruppert was at the brewery. There, the door-keeper said pointedly, "Colonel Ruppert wants to see you. The other gentlemen will wait outside."

The third parties joined the fourth estate in watchful waiting. After less than an hour, Ruth, Ruppert, and Barrow appeared, "It's all settled," said Ruth. The terms were $70,000 for each of three years, the $210,000 total the largest yet in baseball history, Ruth giving in on the matter of money, management on a contract covering more than one year.

"Putting the shoes on the other foot," editorialized *The Sporting News,* a sore loser, "it is up to Ruth to earn the money. He can do it by attending to the business of playing baseball as he knows how to play it. He can become a $70,000 liability if he doesn't."

"So endeth all the ballyhoo," wrote a man named L. C. Davis, in imitation of the great cartoonist Milt Gross, "About Bambino's wages./He goes to join the Yankee crew/To train by easy stages./ The Colonel threw him for a loss/Of $30,000 maybe,/He et up all the applesauce—/He did, ooo-ooo, nize baby!"

The sights and sounds of spring training have not changed much since Adrian C. "Pop" Anson first took his Chicago Nationals to Hot Springs, Arkansas, in the mid-1880s to sweat the winter's beer from them. Television is there now, and computers and pitching machines and organization charts, but newsfilm in a time machine would produce goings-on so familiar as to make *déjà vu* an inadequate phrase.

HOLDOUTS, CONT.—"It was gathered," said *The New York Times* about Ruppert on the subject of Pennock, who sat in Kennett Square, demanding $20,000 and a long-term contract, "that he considered Pennock's demands all right, except that they were ridiculous, excessive and impossible.

" 'Pennock wants a salary greater than was ever paid to any pitcher in the American League, and, I am certain, in the National League,' said Ruppert. 'This goes for Walter Johnson, Uhle, (Dazzy) Vance and others. Now Pennock is a great pitcher and pitched wonderful ball last year, but I don't think he deserves to be paid the highest salary paid to any pitcher in baseball. He is covering a lot of ground there.' "

Pennock, it was pointed out, "struggled along on a paltry $15,000 last year. Now he's asking $20,000 in the interests of the increase for Grade A milk, shoes, neckties and other necessities of life." The Yankees were reported willing to give him $18,000 "an increase of $10,000 in four years."

THE OWNER AS DUTCH UNCLE—"Another thing to remember is that Pennock"—who had eight winning seasons left—"is getting older and may have passed his peak," confided Ruppert. "He ought to be down here, getting in shape."

GETTING TOUGH—"No contract, no repast," said Huggins, affirming that unsigned Yankees would not be welcome in the hotel dining room. "If a player can sign his name at the bottom of a dinner check, he can also sign at the bottom of a contract."

Combs reported late, looking lean after a tonsillectomy, then signed. Meusel's brother, called "Irish," an outfielder with the Giants, came to Florida with a contingent of other Californians, including Lazzeri, but Bob was not with them, leading to speculation that he was holding out. It developed that he was only being languid.

"Are you a holdout?" he was asked, after he turned up.

"No," he replied.

"Do you expect to have any trouble reaching an agreement with the club?"

"No."

"After this long speech," a correspondent reported, "Bob paused to draw a breath and then went out to the golf links." He signed with no delay. This left Pennock.

ULTIMATUM—"If Pennock hasn't signed by early next week," said Ruppert, "we intend to send him formal notice to sign the contract or return it. If he fails to sign, he will be put on the ineligible list, and then he will have to make his peace with Landis before returning to the game."

This actually was a preliminary to an ultimatum. "This might be called the sub-ultimatum. Ruppert is just winding up in the bullpen. He is winding up, but he hasn't delivered. He has plenty on the ultimatum when he lets it go. The papers will be full of it next week. In the meantime, the experts will write analytical stories, looking at both contenders. The betting commissioners were reporting odds of 2–1 on Ruppert tonight, with the odds likely to go to 11–5 tomorrow."

That was from the typewriter of the gifted James A. Harrison of the *Times*. Such stories are as much a part of spring training as the first peeps of the robin and the appearance of the croci. Pennock came around, but late, and had to remain behind when the rest of the club moved north, warming the winter's kinks out of his system in the Florida sunshine. He got $18,500 and a three-year contract.

WEATHER—Some days the sun shined. Some days it rained. Other days it was cold, paining Huggins who invested in Florida real estate.

INTERESTING ROOKIE—When Moore signed, there was no big story. The retort might have been, "Who's Wilcy Moore?" But the day might come, it was noted, when Moore would sign amidst the popping of flash bulbs. He showed a sinker, a good fast ball, a good curve, a good "slow ball," and excellent control.

"You would like him if you met him," a reporter wrote. "He is big, broad-shouldered, modest and unaffected. He is an Oklahoma dirt farmer in the off-season, and he looks the part."

He proved something of a sensation in camp, working twenty-five innings in exhibition games, allowing eleven hits. "I figure it is more sensible to take a pessimistic view because of his age," Huggins said. "He is one of those old youngsters. He is breaking into the majors at thirty—old for a pitcher."

His concern seemed legitimate. Shawkey was thirty-seven; Shocker, thirty-four, Pennock and Ruether, thirty-three. And "it is believed some of the boys are giving themselves the best of it."

"If any of the young pitchers shows me anything," Huggins said, "they will get a chance. I admit that in the past I've been cautious about using rookies, but that was in the past. Sometimes, a young arm is better than an old head."

SPRING PHENOM—Elias Funk, "a pint-sized outfielder from Oklahoma City," drew Huggins' praise.

"He stands well at the plate, fields beautifully and is as fast as a ray of light." He stole fifty-one bases in the Western League in 1926, batting .339, scoring 129 runs and "did other commendable things."

Big league scouts fought for him. " 'Sure to make good,' said the ivory hunters, and there was unhappiness when the Yankees outbid the competitors."

His career with the Yankees, it developed, consisted of one appearance, in 1929. He left them with a batting average of .000. He spent three years with the Tigers.

CASEY STENGEL—In 1927 Stengel was two years retired as a player in a major-league career that started with Brooklyn in 1912, all the glory years as manager of an unbeatable Yankee machine three decades in the future and his ultimate triumph—making a bad ball club lovable—even beyond that. But he already was as much a part of spring training as the robins, the croci, and the spring phenom, and he had become quotable. "The rookies have had their weeks of glory," commented a correspondent. "Some of them are like the rookie in Casey Stengel's story, who wrote, 'I'm coming home, mother. They're beginning to curve them.' "

INFATUATION WITH THE GREAT MAN—Introducing him as a movie star, vaudeville headliner, journalist, and head of a gymnasium trust, the writers found fun in the persistent concern about Ruth's physical condition. As he did with other elements of sport, he revolutionized coverage of spring training. A record thirteen newspaper writers went south with him when he joined the club in 1920, giants like Grantland Rice and W. O. McGeehan among them, and the word got around about lazy days on the warm peninsula—a writer didn't die of overwork down there, either, out from under snow and slush and the editor—and spring training became almost as big a lure for nascent journalists as the thought of a byline.

Now it was reported that Ruth was in the best shape of his life, only six or eight pounds overweight when he got to camp— depending on which exclusive story you read—his best playing weight being 210 or 213. He was not then a fat man, not the roly-poly deity of later years, but more than solid, with a thirty-eight-inch waist and a normal chest of forty inches, forty-seven inches expanded, the remarkable seven-inch expansion seen as the source of great power, three or four inches being the norm for big prize-fighters, so this appeared as the fount of his tremendous swing.

" 'Hit me as hard as you can,' Ruth said, thrusting his famous stomach in the direction of a newspaperman. The fist nearly sank from sight, but the Babe merely smiled."

He showed a surprising aptitude for the game, it was reported. He explained he had been a baseball player in his younger days, before the cinema and journalism and gymnasium finance intruded.

"Rival players will stop and put their ears to the ground" when Ruth came to town, John Keiran wrote. "He is responsible for the full dinner pail. Whatever he does is as interesting to the players as it is to the fans.''

His first home run of the spring disappeared ''in the general direction of Tampa. It landed at the feet of a truck farmer who said to his son, without looking up, 'Well, I see Babe Ruth is in camp again.' ''

VISITING FIREMAN—Statesmen, entertainers, politicians in need of office, anyone who can use a mention, traditionally visit training camps. Now that all sports seasons overlap, eating up newspaper space, it is not the surefire bet to make a two-column cut that it used to be, but it is still worth a try. In 1927 the visitors to St. Petersburg included Billy Sunday, a former major leaguer and reformed drunk who was the most famous revivalist of his day, a Billy Graham with liniment. ''The evangelist can still hit the old onion, as Babe Ruth would say,'' a newspaper reported. ''He smacked one over second that was smoking.''

LEGS—''Legs will play an important part in tabulating certain important results of 1927,'' wrote Rice, citing Collins and Cobb and, particularly, Ruth. ''Those rather slender props have been carrying a rather large body around for 14 years,'' or since Ruth was 18, an age Rice apparently divined as the beginning of leg stress.

Tris Speaker subscribed to the general belief that no player as unevenly constructed as Ruth with a huge body and pipestem legs could stand up under baseball's day-by-day ordeal for any great length of time.

'' 'Ruth made a grave mistake when he gave up pitching,' Speaker said. 'Working once a week, he might have lasted a long time and become a great star.' ''

That was in the spring of 1921, the year Ruth hit fifty-nine home runs.

TACTICS—Whatever the sometime view of Ruth and other ball players, Huggins was regarded by the press as a shrewd and knowledgeable manager, whose dugout commentary offered the true gen.

"One thing Gehrig can't do right is come in on bunts," he said one day. "He never knows when to come in and when to stay out and let the pitcher handle the bunts. We're working on that every day. You've seen the long bunting drills we've been holding.

"I'm going to start working on Koenig next week. Any shortstop who can't go to the left with one hand is not a great shortstop. Many a game has been saved by a one-hand stop near second base, and Koenig will have to learn to do it."

MANAGING THE MANAGER—As the Yankees moved north in 1927, the fan-newspaperman managers knew what Huggins did not know: Koenig must go.

He committed seven errors in sixteen exhibition games, batting .046. He was "a good ball player and a nice boy" but he represented insecurity. The answer, the newspapers reported, was simplicity itself. Morehart, leading the team with a .360 average through the spring, handling fifty-two chances without error, showing speed and acumen on the bases, would take over at second, Lazzeri moving to short.

Koenig played 123 games at shortstop for the Yankees in 1927, sitting down only because of injury.

INSIGHT—The Yankees, it was heard that spring, were "a one-year ball club" and so would not repeat.

THE ENEMY CAMPS—And what about the opposition?

After the Yankees set a record for games won in 1927, forests were felled for newsprint to carry the freight of the argument that they didn't beat anybody. Whenever anything athletic is done surpassingly well, the question is, But who did they beat? It is part of the cussedness of man. When Dempsey was heavyweight champion, followers of John L. Sullivan (c. 1890) argued that all Dempsey's victims were hospital cases, even before the fight. John

Lardner feared for the health of Joe Louis, because, on the type-writer, he suffered such horrible beatings at the hands of Dempsey and Sullivan and anyone born before 1920.

But if the critics didn't love the Yankee foes in December as they did in May, there was plenty of argument for other clubs going into the season.

A poll of "hundreds of players" taken before the season established the Athletics as the favorites. Frederick G. Lieb, who "picked 10 of the last 12 pennant winners" and who, with Ruth, was the only one to predict in print that the Yankees would win in 1926, also chose the Athletics.

YANKEES' ABILITY TO BLUDGEON WAY TO ANOTHER PENNANT SEEN DOUBTFUL was one headline. Billy Evans, "the umpire-scribe," wrote, "Of all the ball clubs I have looked at this spring, the Athletics are by far the most impressive. The club doesn't appear to have a single weakness."

There also was support for Washington and Detroit, hard-hitting clubs like the Yankees, and, like the Yankees, possessed of suspect pitching. Cleveland, with the best pitching staff in baseball, was a dark horse. Ban Johnson saw a five-team race, including the Red Sox because Bill Carrigan had come back from ten years outside baseball, to take over as manager, a demonstration of belief in the supreme importance of managing not paralleled until Stengel, three decades later, affirmed that he could not have won the pennant without his players.

Gambling, or "Broadway" money—there was no Las Vegas in 1927, not in the present-day sense, and the Minneapolis line had not been established—was variously reported on the Yankees or the Athletics.

The young Yankee pitching was not impressive in the exhibition games. But "the boys are batting," the New York *Post* reported. "There is something pulsing in the Yankee club that has not been there since Bob Meusel broke his leg in midsummer and made the entire squad so lame it was fortunate to limp home to the pennant.

"Ruth continues to lead the way. The big slugger is on a streak. He is hitting two or more balls every day which would be home runs in most American League parks. His ebullient spirits are being transmitted to the ball club. . . . With all due respect to all concerned, Babe Ruth is the dynamo and barometer of this team.''

Record crowds turned out. ''They go to see the Babe. The Yankees are under no illusions about it, and neither are the Cardinals.'' The team played eighteen games in Georgia, Alabama, and Tennessee, with ten victories, seven losses and one tie against the Reds, the Braves and their World Series conquerors, the Cardinals. The games drew a record total of $600,000 in gate receipts, ''which nearly paid all training camp expenses.''

And so spring training ended, one of baseball's timeless joys, the recovery from winter's fat and sloth, the telling of old stories in Florida twilights, the tricky business of judging new talents, the puzzling over the game's eternal mysteries, the team as team and other arcanae; all accomplished for the spring of 1927. The rites had been affirmed for another year, and ahead with all its delights, like a surprising and complaisant woman, stretched the season.

# Two

○

Mark Anthony Koenig was seventy in the spring of 1973, a somewhat stocky, somewhat rumpled man, pleasant-looking, with a square, ruddy face, iron gray hair combed straight back, dramatic black eyebrows, and an open gaze. He is one of those for whom the setbacks of life remain evergreen; the triumphs wither, but the grubby undergrowths of loss flourish; defeat is yesterday.

"I should have had it," Koenig says. "I couldn't get the damned ball out of my mitt." He is talking about 1926.

He does not whine but gets on himself for getting on himself.

"I was never the player I should have been," he insists. "I was too hard on myself."

He remembers Ruth as, sure, a good guy, but he does not remember him with the reverence the other old Yankees display. He disparages Ruth's apartness, his drawing room on the train where others slept in Pullman berths, the suite instead of the hotel room, the cutting through baseball society like a monarch. All this seems to Koenig—recalling it not with jealousy, for he is not a jealous man—as putting on airs.

And there was that day of an exhibition game in Baltimore, when Koenig made no attempt to field a ball that was far over his

head, beyond any conceivable reach, and Ruth called in obscenities from the outfield, loud enough so the stands could hear, and
Koenig says when they returned to the dugout, he told Ruth, loud
enough for the stands to hear, Don't you ever call me anything like
that again, the whole world knows that you are yellow, you thus
and such. Koenig says he then turned to watch the game and Ruth
grabbed him from behind—''but he wasn't very tough; I don't
think he could have licked his sister''—and Koenig turned and the
two grappled briefly and, as Koenig tells it, he had wrestled Ruth
to the ground and was on top when the others came in and broke
the two apart. Their lockers, and their sleeping accommodations
on the train had been near each other, Koenig recalls, but Huggins
separated them as distantly as he could, and the two men did not
speak to each other until the last day of that season when they were
prevailed upon to shake hands.

As the star, Ruth could have made trouble for Koenig after that.
But there is no evidence that he did, it was not in that childish and
essentially generous nature. Oh, Ruth was a good guy, Koenig acknowledges, there is no question of that. Still. ''You never saw
him,'' he says. ''He was always up in the room with his girls.''

But Koenig, fed upon by some worm of what-was-not, is
toughest on himself. He wears glasses only for reading today, but
there was a time, when he was a ball player and after he left the
Yankees, when he wore them on the field, and that was uncommon
in the twenties and thirties. ''I thought I needed them,'' he says,
''but it was all in my head.''

Koenig lives in Glen Ellen, a widening in the road in Jack London country, Sonoma County, some forty-five miles north of San
Francisco, having moved there from the suburbs to get away from
pollution and other discontents, but now the low-slung California
hills are attracting hippies—''twenty-five of them in one house last
year, and one septic tank. You can imagine.''

He traveled the old ball player's route, quitting school—he
would not use a soggy euphemism like ''dropping out''—at sixteen, in his sophomore year, to play ball. He never made more than
twelve thousand dollars a season, but, heeding his working-class

parents' admonishment to watch his money, he put some aside and invested prudently, and, after baseball, operated a filling station, and then another, and, as a result, he says, sitting on the patio, dark against the brilliant California sunshine, he is comfortable.

His speech can be dotted with the meaningless obscenities and casual slurs of the locker room, but it also can be formal when he chooses. "You are welcome," he wrote in the winter of 1973, "to come and reminisce about the halcyon days of the golden Yankees." Asked about the rhetorical flourishes in a man whose formal education ended in his mid-teens, he said, "I always read everything I could get my hands on. Homer. I liked to read about old Penelope and the little men sprouting from the ground like dragon's teeth. Kenneth Roberts, I guess he's dead now, but he wrote a wonderful book, *Arundel*. And Stone, who wrote about Michelangelo."

The educated ball player is a recent development, we are told, but it is an overrated one. Self-educated or not, the old Yankees, for all the low-life reputation, were mostly all high school graduates and some touched on the American equivalent of higher education. The really dumb and illiterate ball players Ring Lardner wrote about were pre-World War I products, although he wrote in the twenties. Some were around in 1927, of course, as some are around today, but Morehart was an engineering graduate of Stephen Austin College in Texas, Combs was a schoolteacher and graduate of what is now Eastern Kentucky University, Gehrig, although he made one of his infrequent stabs at humor by saying his only BA was "batting average," attended Columbia University, with its Ivy League taint, and there was Gazella of Lafayette, Dugan briefly attended Holy Cross, and Hoyt, Middlebury. And, of course, none of them could addle their senses by getting into the television habit, sex and violence were at least first hand, and the old Yankees are sharp as tacks.

Koenig respects education. He is not without the old-timers' traditional wariness of the young, but this is partly an impatience with shortcutting and the slipshod. He still hears from autograph seekers and the merely curious, and in the winter of 1973, he received a fan letter from a boy in Brooklyn. "The grammar was atrocious," Koenig said. "The spelling was worse. I wrote back and answered his questions, and I told him if he wanted to give his parents unexpected pleasure, he should spend some time in the library and show half as much enthusiasm for books as he does for baseball."

Showing enthusiasm for both, Koenig grew up in the early days of the century in San Francisco. "Oh, it was a wonderful city then, beautiful. Now I wouldn't go into that jungle if you paid me."

His father worked with his hands, taking care with the product. Koenig takes pride, sixty years later, in a photograph of a crib built by his father that converted into a pot, a table, and a chair. The family had the essentials, food, clothing, and love, and Koenig started team play young with a squad called the Sunset Midgets that played in Golden Gate Park. " 'Big Rec,' we called it, and we had some damn fine clubs. Anson Orr, a window dresser, staked us. He was kind of an effeminate guy, but he was crazy about baseball. He put out all the money for uniforms, bats, and balls."

When Koenig quit school, it was to join a club in the lowest minors in Saskatchewan. The manager also caught, with a glove that had the stuffing coming out of it. It was not much of a club, even for a teen-ager. It dropped fourteen or fifteen games in a row, so when a man from another club came to scout it, looking for pitching help, the manager lined up his staff and said, "Take any of them sons of bitches you want," adding plaintively, "I get so damned sick and tired of seeing those guys run across home plate."

It was all very different then, all very informal, so often there was no kind of line on a player at all, and a tryout was just that. The manager, in need of pitching help, decided to look at a left-hander of unknown quality, saying, "I'll see what this guy's got," and the first pitch hit him right in the back of the head, stretching him. The left-hander disappeared into obscurity.

Understandably, the manager spent as much time in his hotel

room as he could. Koenig recalls the place as being so littered with beer and whiskey bottles that you could only move about through a carefully engineered pathway.

The league folded after two months, but Koenig was called to the hotel, and there Bob Conrey, a prominent Yankee scout, said he would give Koenig five hundred dollars to sign a Yankee contract, but to wait there a couple of days. Meanwhile, Koenig got two wires, offering him contracts with Oklahoma City and St. Paul, the latter a Triple A team that promised four hundred dollars, which was good money in those days, and the Yankees, who could have had him for that five hundred, wound up paying St. Paul fifty thousand for him.

St. Paul farmed him out to Jamestown, South Dakota. "I think I had more fun when I started playing ball," he says, "then I ever did afterwards." It was rugged enough. Traveling from Jamestown to Aberdeen, he rode a little Toonerville trolley, pulled by an automobile. He joined Jamestown in the last month of the season, going up to Des Moines the following year and then to St. Paul during a pennant drive.

After warming up a pitcher in the bullpen, Koenig sat down and fell asleep, dreaming perhaps of Penelope, and had to be wakened to pinch-hit. He smacked one into the right-field corner, but the base runner, a pitcher, was caught at the plate, although Koenig feels he could have scored himself. He did come in with the winning run a moment later, and St. Paul won the pennant in 1924.

He was a regular with St. Paul the following year, and then was brought up by the big team toward the end of its dismal season, the Yankees' worst finish since before World War I, appearing in twenty-eight games and hitting .208, but Huggins must have seen something, for when Tony Lazzeri joined the club in spring training the following year, Huggins predicted the Yankees could win the pennant if the young shortstop and second baseman held up, and before the season was over, they were being called "the greatest keystone combination in baseball."

Neither the Cardinals nor the Yankees were expected to be in the World Series that year. The Yankees, rallying from the seventh-place finish of 1925, won the pennant with a .591 percentage, at the time the lowest ever for a New York club; the Cardinals, after a struggle with Cincinnati, finished at .578, one of the lowest figures for a National League champion. Still, it was the first baseball title for a St. Louis team since Chris Von Der Ahe's Browns in the old American Association of 1888, when it was considered a major league, and so in 1926 prohibition was waived as the city went on an all-night celebration unrivaled since the Armistice.

Rogers Hornsby was the Cardinal manager, and he took baseball seriously. The pressures of his office caused him to surrender his batting championship after six years; he hit only .317. His mother died between the end of the season and the start of the Series. He did not attend the funeral, choosing to remain with his team, "a move some considered heartless . . . but he could no more have left his players than a commander about to lead his troops on a beach could walk out on his command."

The Series came down to the seventh game, lofted by heroics on the field that were reflected in the prints. The St. Louis *Globe-Democrat* gave over its entire front page to one Cardinal victory. GREATEST DEMONSTRATION IN CITY'S HISTORY STAGED AS FRENZIED MULTITUDES LIONIZE BASEBALL HEROES AMID BEDLAM OF NOISE AND JOYOUS ENTHUSIASM.

Few episodes in baseball history inspired the kind of a branch of mythology growing up around that seventh game. Thirty-nine-year-old Grover Cleveland Alexander, with St. Louis only because the Cubs could no longer handle his drinking, already had beaten the Yankees twice in his first World Series in eleven years. He came strolling in from the bullpen to relieve starter Jess Haines with the bases loaded in the seventh inning, the Cardinals leading, 3–2, and Tony Lazzeri, the rookie who had played in every game that year, at bat.

Before calling on Alexander, Hornsby had asked Haines, "Can you make it, Jesse? " and was shown a hand dripping blood, so tightly had the pitcher been gripping the ball for his knuckler. Hornsby waved in Alexander, whose 10–2 victory over the Yankees only the previous day, came on a Saturday, as the fates would have it, giving him two reasons to celebrate that night, and Alexander was a celebrator of major-league caliber.

Part of the legend is that he weaved in from the bullpen, drunk. Another version has it that Hornsby, knowing his man, looked at him closely, saw his eyes were clear, and said simply, "You can do it."

Lazzeri had hit only .275 for the season, but he was second to Ruth in runs batted in with 114, and he was murder in the clutch. Alexander fed him a strike. Lazzeri then lined a vicious foul down the left-field line, putting it in the stands—"less than a foot made the difference between a hero and a bum," Alexander said later— and then Alexander threw another strike. It is all there on Alexander's plaque in the Hall of Fame.

Alexander did not give a hit the rest of the way. He walked Ruth in the ninth on a 3–2 pitch, coming in to ask the umpire what was wrong with it, and, told "It was just that far outside," retorted, "If it was that close, I'd think you'd give an old geezer like me the break," and trudged back to the mound. Ruth, who then walked, took it into his head to steal and was thrown out at second, ending the Series on a minor note, but he had hit four home runs, three of them in one game, and the receipts set a record that lasted for ten years.

That, seen from one perspective, is the story of the 1926 World Series, one of baseball's enduring moments, myth made real. It is almost as though Koenig played in a different ball game, remembering chiefly his error on a double-play ball, "It came right into my glove. I came out with a brand new glove like a damned fool, and I booted it.

"Then there was a fly into short right field. It was Combs's, but Meusel ran over to take it, he had the big arm, and he dropped the ball."

And again, Meusel and Koenig couldn't decide on a fly and let the ball drop for a single. The winning hit was a single by shortstop Thevenow, a .256 hitter who had one of those series, leading both clubs with .417 and so acquired an agent. "A little popping fly that fell behind Lazzeri at second base, and they beat us. Jesus, they never should have beat us. We had a better club.''

None of that is on a plaque in the Hall of Fame, but it is engraved on Koenig's mind.

Part of the story of the 1927 Yankees always has been that the memories of that Series defeat goaded the club to greater efforts. Koenig doesn't remember it that way. There was strong feeling that the team should not have lost, but it was no rallying cry.

No added incentive was needed to draw attention to opening day, Tuesday, April 13. The stories of the spring set forth a scenario that could be acted out immediately: the opposition was the Athletic team many figured as the best in the league.

All the conventions of the time conspired for epics of competition. The twenties are recalled as the golden age of sport—Dempsey, Tilden, Bobby Jones, Man o' War, Red Grange, and all that. Every subsequent decade, as the old records fall and gates are exceeded, is pumped up to supplant the third decade of the century, but somehow the honey doesn't pour, and ''golden age'' was certainly apt for boxing and horse racing, baseball's chief rivals of the period, and baseball was the only professional team sport of any consequence.

E. B. White wrote that with New York's many and self-contained attractions, ''the inhabitant is in the happy position of being able to choose his spectacle and so conserve his soul.'' Considering what lay down the road for the United States of America, there were not a lot of things to worry about:

U.S. JOINS SHARP DEMAND

FOR NANKING REPARATION

AND CANTONESE APOLOGY

Contending Chinese forces, including those of a young commander named Chiang Kai-shek, struggled for control of China, but even with seven foreigners dead, including one American, at the hands of Chiang's troops in what was called ''the Nanking outrage,'' China was very far away.

The curiously reassuring presence in the White House entertained Senator Frank B. Willis, Republican of Ohio, who foresaw a Coolidge-Dawes ticket defeating Alfred E. Smith, 2–1, in 1928, getting everything right except the name of his candidate. One hundred and thirty-five thousand readers, at five dollars a copy, of Will Durant's *The Story of Philosophy* could find in *Cosmopolitan* magazine his views on "the wave of suicide among the young," who were also up to other matters; Doris Blake in the *News* worried about "Too Much Tolerance . . . there is a pagan spirit abroad in our land."

Hardly the stuff to furrow the brow of later generations of Americans. But if spectacle was needed to wash these trifles away, there were 264 new and revived attractions on Broadway, including Helen Hayes in *Coquette,* Vivienne Segal in *The Desert Song,* Ethel Barrymore in *The Constant Wife,* Jeanne Eagels in *Her Cardboard Lover,* and Jane Cowl in *The Road to Rome.*

If the spectator desired a little more leg, there were Earl Carroll's *Vanities* and George White's *Scandals.* Obsessed as ever by sex, reform groups pressured Mayor Walker to crack down on "dirt shows," including *The Virgin Man,* "the story of an unkissed youth from Yale beset with the temptations of New York," and an adaptation of Theodore Dreiser's *An American Tragedy.* Mae West, as star, author, and producer of *Sex,* dealing with "a prostitute's revenge on the society matron who sent her to jail," was fined five hundred dollars and remanded to the public workhouse for ten days, amidst loving attention from the penny press.

The concertgoer that week saw the American debut of Ballet Mécanique," by the New Jersey-born George Antheil at Carnegie Hall, months of publicity producing a crowd jammed "chic by jowl." New York's reaction placed it somewhere between Paris, where there was quiet enthusiasm, and Budapest, where the police were called out. New York contented itself with simple booing, but the event made the front pages.

Film spectacles included Cecil B. DeMille's *King of Kings,* Janet Gaynor and Charles Farrell in *Seventh Heaven,* Clara Bow's *Child of Divorce,* which asked "Can You Blame Us for Going the

Limit and Leading the Life We Do?'' The world's largest theater, the Roxy, seating 6,200, opened with ''the world's largest pipe organ, played simultaneously by three organists on three separate consoles, and the largest symphony orchestra in existence, a permanent choral group of 1,000 and a permanent ballet company of 50 dancers,'' all to warm up the spectator for Gloria Swanson in *The Love of Sunya*.

The night before the opener there was another Broadway hit, S. N. Behrman's *The Second Man,* featuring Alfred Lunt as a sophisticated New York man of letters, attracted by a post-flapperette, Margalo Gilmore, but disposed to marry an older woman, Lynn Fontanne, with whom his name was not yet hyphenated. His sophistication was established by lines like ''he talked like a commuter.''

Mrs. Walker, Grover Whalen, chairman of the Mayor's reception committee, and others hustled to the Battery to welcome the Hamburg-American liner *New York* on its first appearance in the city for which she was named, and demand exceeded supply for tickets to the trial of Ruth Snyder and Henry Judd Gray, beginning that week, for the murder of her husband. Damon Runyon called it ''The Dumbbell Murder. It was that dumb.'' It was a wow of a spectacle because personalities as disparate as Dr. Frank Crane, a syndicated thinker, and Alexander Woollcott, a critic and wit, agreed that ''Ruth Snyder was so like the woman across the street that many an American husband was soon haunted by an unconfessed realization that she also bore an embarrassing resemblance to the woman across the breakfast table.''

But the spectator with an eye for the biggest spectacle that sunny but cool April afternoon went to the Stadium. There were doubters like Paul Gallico, sports editor of the *Daily News,* who wondered why Cobb and Speaker were not back with their old clubs ''although judged guiltless'' and growled:

''These weird scramblings and unexplained pieces of businesses do more to shake my own faith in the integrity of the game than a hundred petty scandals. . . . Baseball has always chosen the longest way around [and] never been administered with real intelligence. Landis does the best he can, but he has the stupidity and cupidity of the magnates tying his hands. The game is not at its best right now.''

But W. O. McGeehan, the legendary sports editor of the *Herald Tribune,* coiner of the phrase ''the manly art of modified murder'' for boxing, predicted;

''The New York Yankees have the center of the stage for their New York debut, and the indications are that it will be the biggest baseball opening in the history of the business. . . .

''For years, one baseball prophet has been sounding the slogan, 'Watch out for Connie Mack!' meaning that Mr. McGillicuddy was once more on his way to a pennant. It looks as though a stadiumful will watch Mr. McGillicuddy, also Mr. Cobb, Mrs. Collins and Mr. Wheat for at least one time.''

A stadiumful was right, the mood being caught by Marshall Hunt in the *News*—verse popped out like hits off the Yankee bats in 1927, the atmosphere clearly was more carefree and people kidded around—''Again that joyous, thrilling shout,/The happiest cry of all./The hardened umpire's gruff command,/'Come on, you gents, PLAY BALL!' '' A record crowd of more than seventy-two thousand jammed the gates. The attendance broke the previous record of sixty-six thousand for the second game of the '26 World Series.

''The baseball magnates still are sitting uncomfortably on the top rail of the radio fence [wrote Stuart Hawkins (''Pioneer'') in the *Herald Tribune*] looking enviously with one eye at the proven publicity value of [Graham] McNamee's description and blinking dubiously with the other eye at the supposedly bad effect of a widely press-agented broadcast on today's box office score.

''That, as in former years, is why we of the public prints have had to keep silent until this morning about the important news that WEAF and WJZ will broadcast Mr. McNamee's play-by-play account. . . .''

Mayor Walker tossed out the first ball, Sir Thomas Lipton, the tea and boats man also being on hand, the ''famous Seventh Regiment Band dispensed gay and blithesome airs'' from the opening of the gates to Umpire Billy Evans' gruff command.

It was widely pointed out that Mack was so rich in talent he could field two teams—the addition of Cobb, Collins, and Wheat meaning either the pennant, according to Grantland Rice, or nothing at all (Frederick Lieb)—but Mack could field only one team at a time, of course, and although his starter was Robert Moses "Lefty" Grove, the record bonus $100,000 Mack paid for him after he won 109 games helping Baltimore to five consecutive International League pennants did not this day seem a particularly prudent investment.

Grove, generally considered the greatest left-hander in the history of the American League and on his way to the first of seven consecutive twenty-game seasons, possessed a blazing fastball. He and Hoyt pitched scoreless ball for three innings before he began to soften. Koenig beat out a tap in front of the plate and went all the way to third when Grove threw a fireball to the left-field fence. Ruth, who had been presented with a silver loving cup before the game, came to the plate in this modestly dramatic circumstance but only popped up, and Koenig was run down after Meusel hit back to the box.

But the long sad season for the opposition was hinted at in the next inning, when Dugan singled after Grabowski walked, and Hoyt bunted to Dudley Branom, the first baseman, who dropped the ball. Combs doubled, scoring two runs and putting Hoyt on third. Koenig rolled out and Ruth, who was suffering from a head cold and slight fever—"he said he felt dizzy and looked that way," was one comment—struck out. Grabowski's bad-hop grounder eluded Collins, scoring Hoyt and Combs.

Cobb, whose legs were suspect at age forty, beat out a bunt to open the sixth inning, went to third on Sam Hale's single when Combs threw short, pulling Dugan from the bag, and scored on Branom's out.

Lazzeri, who was playing under full strength after a winter of battling boils, opened the Yankees' half with a double over the head of Cobb and Al Simmons. Dugan bunted, and Grabowski scored Lazzeri with a single to left. Hoyt sacrificed the runners along, and they scored on an error by Joe Boley, the shortstop. Koenig tripled, scoring Combs and came in himself when Ben Paschal, batting for Ruth, singled to right. The As picked up another run in the eighth, but Hoyt's eight-hitter was sufficient, and the Yankees won the opener, 8–3.

The team thus applied its trademark—Combs, Gehrig, and Lazzeri doubled, in addition to Koenig's triple—but it bunted and ran, too. So much for the image of Murderer's Row, a tag honestly earned by the group, as strong, solid types, rooted to the ground.

Typically, Ruth drew attention although he did nothing. A boxed account of his hitless day ended: "It is 4:55. It is the sixth inning. Three runs have scored. There is a man on base. Seventy thousand stand. It is the mighty Babe's turn. Another run! Seventy thousand shudder! That isn't the mighty Babe Ruth! No—Ben Paschal, who singles and scores that run. The mighty Babe is a flop—he had three chances and failed."

Demigods draw that kind of lower criticism for one bad day at bat, but victory and the size of the crowd made the rebuke seem irrelevant. "Gone was the aroma of the baseball scandal last winter," wrote Hunt, "when captious critics made significant gestures and dolefully predicted that baseball has been shaken to the very roots and would collapse immediately. Seventy thousand!"

By the following night, however, the question was whether the Athletics knew that the season had started. Led by Koenig with a perfect day in five at-bats, the Yankees assaulted three Philadelphia pitchers for sixteen hits and won, 10–4. Dutch Ruether gave up hits in every inning but the third and sixth, fourteen of them, but there was no need for more than adequacy on the mound.

Since the previous day had reestablished that the Yankees still hit the fastball, Mack started Samuel Gray, a southpaw called "Dolly," who had won sixteen games in 1925 and who would win twenty the following season, and who threw a curve. The Yankees drummed him out with six hits and five runs in the fourth inning before he was relieved.

"Koenig," noted the *Times,* "for whom the experts had been feeling more pity than scorn, turned the laugh on them by hitting five singles in a row." All the long years later, he attributes much of this to the pinstripe myth:

"Just putting on a Yankee uniform gave me a little confidence, I think. That club could carry you," he says. "You were better than you actually were. If I'd been with a tail-end club the year I went up, I don't think I'd have been around for 1927."

After only two games against the club they had to beat, the Yankees were "at the head of the parade and all is well on the banks of the Harlem," Harrison wrote in the *Times.* "The apathetic Athletics have displayed nothing that should cause a Yankee fan to walk the floor at night. . . . Connie Mack at first blush appears to have an interesting but not highly valuable collection of antiques."

Gallico was more cautious. "The Yankees looked very good, but I am not misled. I know my Yankees. Yesterday, they looked like a team playing in the World Series. Tomorrow they may look like the Phillies on a sultry Thursday afternoon in August. When the Yankees are hitting, they are the greatest club in the world. When some lefthander has them swinging away, they resemble DeWitt Clinton's second team. . . . I am not going into laudatory hysterics so early in the season. Still, the crisp work of Mark Koenig . . . was something to make me a little less apprehensive of the future."

But the As snapped back the following day, warming the chill afternoon by jumping on Bob Shawkey for three runs in the first inning, on singles by Cobb and Simmons, a walk, and Hale's triple. New York retaliated when Combs led off with a single, Ruth walked, Meusel singled, and Lazzeri tripled.

The Athletics kept plowing ahead—Lamar and Cobb scoring on Hale's second triple and Mickey Cochrane's single scoring Hale—and the Yankees kept coming back. Koenig and Gehrig walked in the sixth, and a single by Ruth loaded the bases. Meusel cleared them with a triple and scored on a wild throw by Poole.

The As wiped out Wilcy Moore, who had relieved Shawkey in

the first, with two runs in the eighth, but the Yankees seldom lost just because their pitching was bad. They came right back on singles by Gazella—who replaced Dugan, spiked by Hale in the first inning—and Grabowski. Paschal pinch-hit for Urban Shocker (who reportedly found the cold weather congealing his spitter) and singled, scoring Gazella and sending Morehart, running for Grabowski, to third.

Combs's sacrifice scored Morehart, and Ruth walked after Koenig popped up. With the score tied and darkness falling, Gehrig came to the plate. The ball he hit was described as throwing off sparks, but Hale made one of those catches in which the fielder can't believe he has the ball. "Check your glove," suggested Boley. All it went for was an out, and the game was called on grounds of chill and darkness. The beginning of baseball wisdom is never to judge teams on the basis of one game: the co-favorites for the pennant had eached scored nine runs off four pitchers and failed to win.

The Yankees closed out the series with a 6–3 victory, highlighted by Ruth's first home run of the season, his throw to the plate from deep right field which nailed Simmons, and Herb Pennock's first start of the season.

He had pitched only three innings that spring, as a result of his holdout, and there was some surprise when Huggins named him for the game, but he gave up only seven hits, four of them scratch, and the newspaperman-fan managers were silent. A series doesn't make a season, but three wins and a tie was an impressive opening against the most feared contender, and even more gratifying to the bleak eyes of the business office was the near-record attendance of 125,000 for four games.

The *Daily News,* however, didn't get around to revealing the score until the twenty-second paragraph of its story, after playing off a verse in honor of the day's big event: "Let cymbals crash their eerie din/Let trumpets burst the ear/The mighty Babe, egad! has smacked/His first homer of the year."

"We used to slay Boston," Koenig recalls. "We used to start off the season, win four or five games to get a big head start, and

Boston always seemed to be a part of it.'' Indeed, through the years, the Hub, as it calls itself, as in Hub of the universe, has been good to New York baseball. Perhaps it never really recovered from the sale of Ruth when ''it was shocked out of a year's growth and half a century of dignity,'' according to one commentator. ''Overnight, crudely lettered signs reading 'For Sale' appeared on the Public Library and Boston Common. Fenway Park was cartooned as lying in barren gloom, a mass of undeveloped real estate available to the first bidder.''

The Red Sox, who also gave the Yankees Hoyt, Pennock, and Dugan, came to town in 1927 with a record of two last-place finishes behind them, scoring three hundred fewer runs than the Yankee champions of the previous year, and they couldn't field, either. The appointment of Carrigan, loser of only two World Series games with his Red Sox champions of 1915 and '16, and the new ownership of Bill Quinn, replacing the theater-sunk Frazee, generated some optimism, but realists noted that this time around, Carrigan lacked pitchers like Ruth and Ernie Shore, to say nothing of the immortal old outfield of Duffy Lewis, Speaker, and Harry Hooper.

The team was built around rejects, outfielders like Ira Flagstead, a former Tiger, and Johnny Tobin, a former Brown whose arm was gone, and, at short, Paul ''Pee Wee'' Wanninger was trying to replace Emory Rigney, another former Tiger, Wanninger having been hauled up from Class C too soon by the Yankees to take over for Everett Scott with the bad lot of '25.

Boston opened with a young man then called Charley Ruffing, who in more than five years in the Hub of the Universe, would lead the league in defeats, putting together a 43–103 record. Out of its boundless generosity, Boston then traded him to the Yankees, to become Red Ruffing of the Hall of Fame, four 20-game seasons in a row and a reputation as the hardest-hitting pitcher of his day. But although he was staked to a first-inning run and his teammates outhit New York, ten to six, the Yankees won, 5–2, behind Shocker, Koenig again starring on the field and at bat. ''The Frisco boy gets a big cheer every time he wriggles his little finger,'' the

*Times* observed. "He is rivaling Ruth for April popularity." But he remembers, "I never got along too well with the fans. They said I didn't smile enough. I had a black tooth up front, and I was embarrassed about it."

"The Yankees had the dandiest time yesterday, collecting their Easter eggs in the Bronx," Hunt started his account of the next game, played as COLD WEATHER CHILLS SOCIETY'S EASTER PARADE.

"It is true the eggs were not concealed in obscure places, which made it easier to spot them than it might have been, but the Yankees ran and skipped hither and thither, clasping their hands in childish glee and yelling with the joy of youth, 'See, see, see what the nice bunnies have brought you!' "

The fine, ironic tone covered a 14–2 Yankee victory, powered by two tremendous Gehrig home runs. He also singled, to drive in a total of six runs, more than Hoyt needed in picking up his second win. Every Yankee scored, their eighteen hits being good for eighteen bases. And again, Koenig starred in the field, going deep to his right to throw out Wanninger in the fourth inning.

After six games the team was batting around .400, had earned no worse than a tie, had to change pitchers only once and had put together three games without an error. And the following day, Slim Harriss, after giving up two runs in the first inning, pitched well for Boston, but Ruether pitched even better, a three-hitter on what was called "a sweeping curve, a steaming fastball and a canny change of pace," and so New York won, 3–0. In the first inning Ruth stole home.

"The lowly, derided worm turned" the following day, ending the Yankee streak at six. "It was," Harrison noted, "the Red Sox' first victory, but probably not their last of the season." More ominously, if the word is not inflated, Collins threw to first when he should have thrown to second, which led to one run, then dropped the ball at the plate, allowing another, and Ruth suffered his worst batting exhibition of the year, hitting into two double plays and striking out once, while Koenig's boot of a third-inning grounder ended the team's errorless streak at forty-five innings.

On this off-key note the Yankees took off for their first road trip. For many of them, Koenig recalls, the end of the ball game meant the start of a search for beer, or maybe even something stronger. At home it was not hard to find. Prohibition, it was conservatively estimated, more than doubled the number of places where a person could buy a drink in New York. The safe estimate was 32,000 speakeasies. One official put the total at more than 100,000.

Liquor was available in "dancing academies, drug stores, delicatessens, cigar stores, confectioneries, soda fountains, behind partitions of shoe shine parlors, back rooms of barber shops, from hotel bellhops, from hotel headwaiters, from hotel day clerks, night clerks, in express offices, in motorcycle delivery agencies, paint stores, malt shops, cider *stubes,* fruit stands, vegetable markets, groceries, smoke shops, athletic clubs, grill rooms, taverns, chop houses, importing firms, tea rooms, moving van companies, spaghetti houses, boarding houses, Republican clubs, Democratic clubs, laundries, social clubs, newspapermens' associations," according to a team of reporters for the New York *Telegram,* cited by John Kober in *Ardent Spirits: The Rise and Fall of Prohibition.*

And so some of the Yankees, demonstrating the stubbornness of genius, crossed the river to a place called Jimmy Donahue's in Passaic, New Jersey, Koenig remembers. Koenig, Dugan, Meusel, and Bengough would be a likely party. There was nothing particularly festive about the place, he recalls, you just went upstairs for pitchers of beer and fat sandwiches, although there was a memorable night when Ruth decided to swim the Hudson and his teammates only just convinced him that it was not a good idea, the darkness and the hour making it unlikely searchers could find him.

"When I think of all the wasted hours, my God," Koenig says. "What somebody with brains could have done with them, you know? I mean, the hours you kept. You could go to bed at three o'clock in the morning, because you wouldn't have to be out until one o'clock. You could sleep until eleven." He shakes his head. "All those wasted hours."

Of course, there were a lot of laughs, a lot of partying. But not, as implicit in the folk wisdom of a thousand jokes, in Philadelphia. "We used to eat in a place where the waiters were ninety years old, and the hotel elevator was a wire cage."

As for the matter of official business, there was no reason to suppose that the Athletics were going to continue to furnish batting practice for the Yankees. "There is no other team in either league which has been more patiently strengthened than the As, or which rates as strong in reserve material," wrote "Monitor" in the *World*.

Al Simmons, the Duke of Milwaukee, who hit .308 his rookie season, already was established as the batting star of the club, in the third of eleven consecutive .300 seasons, with more than a hundred runs batted in annually. He was joined in the outfield by Cobb and Bill LaMar, called "Good Time," who hit .356 in 1925 and was playing with the greatest enthusiasm of his career. Wheat and a promising young player named Alex Metzler were reserves.

Mack had two complete infields, Jim Poole, Max Bishop, Chick Galloway, and Jimmy Dykes in one; Dudley Branom, a rookie who led the American Association the previous year with 222 hits, Collins, Joe Boley, and Hale in the other. Boley, held back by injuries for a half dozen years in the minors, already was regarded as being on a par with the league's best shortstops, Joe Sewell of the Indians and Detroit's Jack Tavener.

Grove, Howard Ehmke, and Eddie Rommell were the big three of the As' pitching staff, with Sam Gray and Rube Walberg added starters and Joe Pate and twenty-one-year-old Charley Willis in relief. "There was nothing wrong with my pitching last year," said Mack, already at sixty-four regarded as an elder statesman but only a kid by the geriatric standards he would set. "If the rest of the league had been as good, we would have finished ahead of the Yankees."

Clearly, the catching was in good hands. Mickey Cochrane, a former Boston University halfback, was just rounding into the form that would put him into the Hall of Fame, a combustible leader with a lifetime batting average of .340. He was supported by a nineteen year old named Jimmy Foxx, who would become one of history's great right-handed sluggers, missing Ruth's record in 1932 when rain erased two of his home runs and hitting thirty or more in a record twelve consecutive seasons. The As, in fact, were only two years away from becoming one of history's great ball clubs.

And they beat the Yankees in their home opener, 8–5, before the largest crowd in their existence. For the Yankees it was one of those infrequent days when things never right themselves. Pennock hurt his foot in batting practice, and so Shocker, who had put away a big lunch, anticipating the day off, was called on to pitch in spite of what was described as "the burden of his noontime fodder"; at that, he did all right until the fourth inning, when Gazella dropped a foul off the bat of Simmons, who then tripled and scored on Hale's fly. The teams traded off runs until the seventh, when Simmons singled with the bases loaded to put Philadelphia ahead to stay.

The Yankees came back the next day with their second batting orgy of the young season, Gehrig and Lazzeri each hitting three-run homers in a 13–6 victory. Lazzeri also tripled and bunted safely, to drive in five runs, the same number as Gehrig. Hoyt was lifted in the fifth after Combs, the reliable, dropped a fly and Koenig mishandled a grounder, leading to three Philadelphia runs.

Large numbers of fans, in the manner of the uncompromising Philadelphia clientele, left by the eighth inning. "Oh, Otis," crowed the *News,* "these Athletics ain't so tough—not so tough when they don't get the pitching and the Yankees feel like hitting."

Philadelphia won the series after a day's delay on account of rain, welcomed by a Yankee pitching staff suddenly short-handed because of Pennock's injury. With the score tied, men on first and second with one out in the ninth, Cochrane batted for Dykes and grounded to Lazzeri. He tossed to Koenig, who threw high to Gehrig in a try for the double play. Gehrig should have caught it, but stood on his dignity and first base, the throw went to the fence, and Boley scored the winning run, 4–3. It was an unhappy turn for Koenig because earlier in the inning, he grabbed a Zach Wheat drive behind his back and threw him out, "one of the finest plays seen this side of Alaska."

Ruth had hit his second home run of the year in the first, with one on. Gehrig hit his third in the following inning, "an even more powerful clout that landed on the roof of a house in 20th Street and bounced on and on."

"The fans applauded Ruth's home run," the *Herald Tribune* noted. "That's his business. Not so Gehrig's. He's just a first baseman."

If you excepted the pitchers, Fred Lieb wrote, "Washington has, in my opinion, the finest team in baseball." The outfield was composed of Speaker, Goslin, and Rice, who didn't reach the majors until he was twenty-five, but lasted for twenty seasons, hitting .300 in all but five of them, and the outfield, intact, is in the Hall of Fame. The infield didn't insult it by comparison—Joe Judge, midway of a career as a .298 power hitter, Bucky Harris, the boy-manager second baseman, Buddy Myers, and Ossie Bluege.

"I've got $140,000 tied up in pitchers," lamented Griffith, the woe understandable since he didn't have much to show for the money. Walter Johnson was sidelined with a broken bone in his wrist, but it was the first time in two decades when this would not be a blow; he clearly was nearing the end of a fabulous career. Hollis Thurston came from Chicago, where he won twenty games for a last-place club. Garland Braxton, who was acquired from the Yankees in the mysterious Ruether deal, joined a promising young rookie from Memphis named Horace Lisenbee, called "Liz" because "Horace seems too classical for baseball."

The Senators battled the Yankees even in home-and-home single games. Ruth's third home run of the season and second in two games, traveling four hundred feet before disappearing over a forty-five-foot high fence; Meusel's second home run and a pinch-hit triple by Cedric Durst with the bases loaded accounted for five of six Yankee runs before 20,000 fans. That was more than Shocker needed in a 6–2 victory.

But back in New York, the Senators won, 5–4, when Bluege

scored the tie-breaker in the eighth inning on an infield hit by a rising young outfielder named Sam West, whose speed beat Lazzeri's
throw to first. "Some of the grandstand managers were heard to
remark that Huggins should have walked West to get at the
pitcher," the *Times* noted. "Well, Huggins is only a young fellow
and will learn some of these tricks when he has been around as
long as some of the fellows in the $1.10 seats."

The fan-managers were silent now, except in praise, about
Koenig, who was hitting .429. His turnaround from his sorry
spring showing and the World Series justified Huggins' faith in
him. Morehart, the sensation of the exhibition season, still warmed
the bench. "Koenig played good ball for me last year, and I'm
confident he will come around for me," Huggins had insisted all
along.

"He made you feel like a giant," is the way Koenig recalls the
little manager. "If you made a mistake, he took you aside the next
day, called you into his office. Barrow could make you feel like a
midget, but Huggins made you feel like a giant."

After the World Series the previous year, Huggins had called his
rookie second baseman aside, not to criticize him, in spite of the
ample cause, but "to warn me against buying an expensive car or
some such frippery. He advised me to invest in some good, sound
securities. 'What do you think you will buy?'

" 'Mr. Huggins,' I said, 'I have been watching this ball club of
ours all season. I believe that I will be making a fine investment if I
bought stocks in a company that manufactures gingerale and club
soda.' "

The two men understood each other. Although Huggins was not
a professional pessimist, he had not expected the Yankees to
approach their running start of 1926, when they tore off sixteen
games in a row. As the team worked its way north from spring
training, it did not look like a club that would get off so well, more
probably one that would make trouble as the season progressed,
and Koenig's form reversal somehow complemented the Yankees'
early foot.

Alexander Cartright, current holder of the title "the man who invented baseball," probably had not finished laying out the first diamond before an onlooker, one of those lanky, grass-chewing types, an acid fellow pointing out the obvious, suggested that a game won in the spring counted just as much as a game won in the autumnal blaze of a pennant fight. This is only a mathematical truth, as demonstrated by the annual need as the long season draws to a close for the dogfight of the crucial series, the crucial game so often that it is one of sport's continuing wonders that after 150, now 160-plus games, the outcome often is decided by just one game, but the mathematical, ledger-book side of it remains true: the game won in the spring counts just as much as the Big One of September.

And Ruether, apparently revived after an operation for "tonsils, adenoids or whatever" over the winter, added to the joys of the time by pitching his second shutout, beating the Red Sox, 9–0, the score of a forfeited game, it was pointed out, so the Yankees could have saved themselves the trouble of the trip to the Hub. Ruth hit a home run, a double hit as hard as the homer and stopped only by the fence, and a single; Koenig, Meusel, and Collins tripled.

After going scoreless for seventeen innings, the Sox rose up in the ninth inning the next day, when Wilcy Moore walked Fred Haney with the bases loaded, to win, 3–2. Shocker pitched well earlier, and even drove in New York's second run before seventeen thousand, the season's largest crowd at Fenway, including the visiting Mayor Walker, warming up for a European tour.

The winning pitcher was Harold Wiltse, who had handed the Yankees their first defeat April 19 and was perceived by the *World* as "one of the best young southpaws in the league . . . the new Yankee pitching jinx." The *Times* reported, "Brilliant play by Koenig was the treasure of the game. He handled 12 chances without a slip, miscued on one that was understandable."

Seventy thousand, more than sixty-five thousand paid and so creating a new record in receipts, turned out the next day to see the Athletics, suddenly tied with New York at the top of the league, in "the first crucial game of the season." Pennock opposed old John

P. Quinn, program age thirty-two, but you could add three or four
years to that, according to insiders.

Ruth hit a first-inning home run with Koenig on base, the ball
sailing almost on a line to the bleachers, and Cobb didn't even turn
to look at it. In the second inning Hale beat out a bunt down the
first-base line and kept going when Dugan, who returned to the
lineup two days earlier, threw the ball to the grandstand. Cy
Perkins scored him with a single, and when Boley also singled,
Pennock was in trouble. But he stopped Quinn's drive with his leg
and threw him out to end the inning.

The As opened the third with two more singles, but Pennock
pulled himself together and prevented any scoring. But in the
fourth, Meusel lost Quinn's easy fly in the sun, and two more runs
scored. The As had collected nine hits in four innings but, thanks
to two double plays, only three runs.

In the sixth inning Koenig walked and Gehrig homered and the
Yankees, although only three men had reached base between the
two homers, were ahead to stay, 4–3. Quinn walked Meusel and
was walked himself, after giving up only two hits and four walks
in six innings, a victim of opportunism.

Rube Walberg, pitching in the eighth, was the victim of something else. Ruth hit another homer, "the biggest and best of the
day," with no one on. Gehrig singled, scoring when Meusel
doubled down the right-field line. Meusel moved to third on the
play and scored on Lazzeri's sacrifice fly.

The 7–3 victory left the Yankees in first with a 10–5 record,
Philadelphia second, 9–6, and Chicago third, 10–7.

They were still in first by a game when they opened their first
western road trip with an exhibition in Fort Wayne, Indiana. As
always, it was an occasion for Ruth. He played first base against a
semipro team, the Lincoln Lifes, Gehrig taking over right field.
With this relaxed arrangement the score was tied in the tenth inning, 3–3. Ruth held a reception for several hundred small boys
who couldn't wait for the game to end, then stepped to the plate,
signaled to the crowd that it was all over—a gesture he did, or did

not, repeat under more theatrical circumstances in the 1932 World Series—hit a tremendous drive over the right-field fence, and disappeared in boys as he scored.

Almost as surprising as the Yankees' fast start was the performance of the White Sox team they next faced, which had been labeled likely to battle with Boston for seventh place. The pitching was anchored by young Ted Lyons, who joined Chicago right out of Baylor University and was destined for the Hall of Fame as winning more games, more consistently, for a losing team than any pitcher except Walter Johnson. Urban Faber and Ted Blankenship were also reliable starters, but the team's hitting was suspect, and morale was a problem after a suicide attempt that winter by the promising Johnny Mostil, a center fielder jammed up over imaginary illness and romance.

Destiny and the crowd. Surely, monographs wait to be written on the subject. On Saturday, May 7, 1927, Captain Charles Nungesser, a French war ace, lifted off for America, seeking *la gloire* and twenty-five thousand dollars put up by M. Raymond Orteig, owner of the Lafayette Hotel in Greenwich Village for the first person to fly, solo, nonstop, across the Atlantic Ocean. Nungesser was cheered on by a large crowd in evening dress.

And in Chicago, a crowd of thirty-five thousand, the city's largest of the season, Vice-President Dawes among them, watched Lyons step smartly along, giving up only six hits in the first seven innings, three of them leading to a run in the third.

Meanwhile, Pennock kept looking up to find men on base, but "the skill of the master worker was then evidenced as he gave hitters just what they didn't want," escaping twice with two on and no one out. The Yankees picked up another run in the eighth on singles by Ruth, Meusel, and Lazzeri.

The team demonstrated its infinite potential at bat in the ninth. Grabowski singled to left. Pennock bunted, and Grabowski was safe at second when Bill Hunnefield, a shortstop of questionable skill, dropped the ball. Combs bunted and was safe when he was hit by the throw to first. With the bases loaded, Koenig singled, scoring one run. Earl Sheely, regarded by some as the best defensive first baseman in the league, threw low to the plate on Ruth's grounder, allowing Pennock to score.

Gehrig then hit a home run, his seventh of the year, putting him one up on Ruth. The bases-loaded drive was the first ever to reach the new right-field pavilion in Comiskey Park. What had been a pitchers' duel ended with the undignified score of 8–0.

While there was no word from Captain Nungesser, New York went ahead with plans for a dramatic welcome, and in Chicago, what was estimated as the largest crowd ever to see a ball game in the Midwest, some fifty-two thousand, including Commissioner Landis, turned out the next day to watch another lopsided game, Hoyt winning, 9–0, behind Collins' home run and the customary Yankee mixture of artifice and luck, the day being further brightened by a scoreboard showing Cleveland beating the runner-up As for the second day in a row.

As so often happens, the two wild-scoring games were followed by a pitching duel, Comiskey Park's finest of the season. Faber and Ruether matched up for seven stride-by-stride innings. Gehrig tripled in the fifth and scored on Meusel's sacrifice fly, but Chicago tied it in the eighth. Ruether ran out of gas in the ninth and was replaced by Moore, now called "one of Huggins' promising young hurlers," and Metzler greeted him with a single to center, moving to second in a cloud of dust when Combs was slow fielding the ball.

Kamm bunted to Moore, who threw the ball, and the ball game, over Gehrig's head. An error by Lazzeri in the first inning was his first in twenty-one games, during which he had handled 122 chances.

The Yankees moved on to St. Louis. Traveling men, ball players, and drummers develop for certain cities affections which generally are based on superficialities—food, drink, entertainment, this hotel or that. They learn nothing of how the people live, housing, education, that sort of thing.

It is superficial, but at least the standards of judgment for the traveler remain the same for all cities, and St. Louis was a favorite stopping-off place, although it is unconscionably hot in the summer. For one thing, there was a notorious cathouse, the House of the Good Shepherd, for those who were interested, and there were gustatory attractions and, for another, St. Louis was excellent for professional reasons: The Browns had George Sisler and little else.

In spite of a first-inning home run by Ruth, which gave the club a three-run lead, the Yankees came to the ninth inning of the first game trailing, 7–6. Durst opened the ninth batting for Dugan and walked. Grabowski singled and gave way to Gazella as a pinch runner. A walk to Combs filled the bases, and Koenig drove in one run with a long fly to center. A mistake then was made which was not often repeated. Ruth was intentionally walked to get at Gehrig. His single won the game, 8–7.

In the 1926 World Series, Ruth became the first man to hit a home run into the center-field bleachers of Sportsman's Park, and now, in the second game with the Browns, he did it again, with Ernie Nevers pitching. The ball sailed higher, though not as far, as his World Series homer. Shocker, his spitter in fine shape, gave eight widely scattered hits, and the Yankees won, 4–2.

A double by Ruth won the next game, 4–3. Jones, called "Sad Sam" because he was so genial, and Pennock pitched well against each other, scattering the hits, and Pennock was aided by a couple of masterly Koenig-Lazzeri double plays.

"Koenig," said the New York *Sun,* "has improved amazingly in one phase of the defensive game . . . the handling of pop flies just beyond the border of the infield. Last year he was very weak in this department and, on numerous occasions, scared off Babe Ruth or Earle Combs or both as he pursued balls that he either muffed or failed to get his hands on. His sole virtue where pop flies are concerned was that he always tried for them, and in the end his persistence paid off. Now he not only goes after them but gets them."

The Yankees swept the four-game series and made it six of seven in the West the following day, Hoyt squeezing by with a ten-hitter, 3–1. Hoyt was in danger so often that Moore pitched almost nine innings in the bullpen, waiting for the call, but Hoyt toughened when he had to. Koenig and Meusel each tripled to position runs, but the winning run was set up on a double by Hoyt after he missed a bunt attempt. The fielding standout was a deft Gehrig-Koenig double play, the two uncertain fielders exchanging throws that nailed runners. Although it was only May 14, it was noted, "they have practically conceded the pennant to the Yankees already in St. Louis."

By this time, in the greater world beyond the diamond, hope faded for Captain Nungesser, the fog-shrouded Atlantic balking searches, even as crews for three American planes, rivals, prepared to take off for the prize that brought about the captain's death and, although there were fears the French might regard the flights as untimely, Paris prepared a welcome on the order of that bon voyage party only days earlier.

Before leaving town, the Yankees always made a couple of stops, Koenig remembers. "We'd always go to a brewery like Anhueser-Busch, and they'd give us a tour and beer, and there was a restaurant that'd give us big racks of barbecued ribs. Geez, I remember those ribs, the best I ever tasted."

And Koenig remembers that he and his teammates would bring the beer and ribs back to the train. Sometimes, they would take the food and drink into the boxcar as the train pulled out of the station, and sit, eating and drinking, this team many call the greatest of all, and, like schoolboys as the train bucketed through the gathering heat of the night for Chicago or Detroit, metaphorically for destiny, these players of a summer game would whoop and shy the bottles and stripped ribs at the telegraph poles.

# Three

○

One of the raps raised against baseball is that it is old-fashioned, and, in a country that takes the new so seriously, this is a grave charge.

The sunshine game, it is argued, comes from another century, and is too slow, too ordered a process to compete with the hard hitting or speed or scoring of football, hockey, and basketball, which are thus more attuned to the spirit of the violent and frenetic seventies. Looking around at the unglued society of the sixties and seventies, with its atmosphere of breakdown and failures of both nerve and taste, it can be argued that a game out of touch with the spirit of the times is intrinsically admirable, but, of course, which sport is preferred is a question of choice, and such arguments are fundamentally pointless.

At the same time baseball's age is part of its allure, its nineteenth-century origin and memories charming, like certain foreign accents. No other sport, it has been said, relies so much on memory. In a society in which Thoreau's cursed busyness is difficult to escape, baseball reminds us of picture-postcard villages and a day when conscience didn't nag over the thought of dawdling for a couple of hours over a beer and a ball game.

A ball player named Terry Turner, a shortstop with the Indians admired by his father, served as Roger Angell's *madeleine* when he wrote in *The Summer Game:*

Within the ballpark, time moves differently, marked by no clock except the events of the game. This is the unique, unchangeable feature of baseball, and perhaps explains why this sport, for all the enormous changes it has undergone in the past decade or two, remains somehow rustic, unviolent and introspective.

Baseball's time is seamless and invisible, a bubble within which players move at exactly the same pace and rhythms as all their predecessors. This is the way the game was played in our youth and in our father's youth, and, even back then—back in the country days—there must have been the same feeling that time could be stopped. Since baseball time is measured only in outs, all you have to do is succeed utterly, keep hitting, keep the rally alive, and you have defeated time. You remain forever young. Sitting in the stands, we sense this, if only dimly. The players below us—Mays, DiMaggio, Ruth, Snodgrass—swim and blur in the memory, the ball floats over to Terry Turner, and the end of this game may never come.

Since nothing in America is very old, except some trees and rock formations, baseball, which was invented or evolved into something like its present form around the time of the Civil War, and so was played, or watched, by men with memories of men who fought in the American Revolution, the game has links, however tenuous, with the very origins of the nation. And to talk with a baseball old-timer is to talk with someone who was, figuratively speaking, present, if not at the Creation, at an age comparable to the Cro-Magnon, with someone who can say he has seen it all more truthfully than the historian in almost any other line.

There is a shock of recognition, then, in meeting with Dan Daniel, who is eighty-three and who saw the first game played by a New York American League team in 1903, "the Highlanders or Invaders or whatever the hell you want to call them. I was a boy in knickerbockers and I went with my cousin, a semipro pitcher of some consequence, and, that first day, we sat in the bleachers. It rained, and due to goddamned inexperience, the front office hadn't provided for rain checks and made an announcement that anyone present could get in free the next day.

"Well, the next day my cousin and I, elevated by the rainout from the bleachers to the grandstand, sat in a box on the third-base side of the old ball park, which was at Broadway and 162nd Street. Of course, hearing about the previous day's announcement, everyone in New York turned up, claiming they'd been there when it rained, and there was a riot." He shakes his white-haired old head. "Inexperience in the front office."

That first front office was presided over by partners as temperamentally unsuited to each other as their successors, Ruppert and Huston, proved to be. They were a fat, walrus-mustached man of the sort familiar in turn-of-the-century political club or Elks picnic gravures, named Bill Devery, who called himself "the best police chief New York ever had," and a flashily dressed racetrack plunger named Frank T. Farrell.

At first they appeared the answer to Ban Johnson's problem. The founder of the American League, comprehending the remorseless law of American commerce cited earlier—the one about even pussy farms needing a New York outlet to be considered major league—anxiously wanted a team in the Apple, but found himself frustrated by the owner of the not only established but already storied New York Giants, John T. Brush, who disliked Johnson and had friends in Tammany Hall, which was all you needed to succeed in any commercial aspect of New York life at the time.

Devery and Farrell, the one a former top cop and the other a big sport, both bragged of even more important Tammany connections than Brush's, as can be imagined, and when Farrell dropped into Johnson's office with a check for twenty-five thousand dollars, Johnson was impressed, although not as much as he was a little later when it was explained to him that Farrell frequently bet more than that on a single horse race, and so the two men were granted the franchise.

They installed as president an inoffensive businessman named Joseph W. Gordon and, in honor of his name and the club's loca-

tion on a north Manhattan hillside, called the club the Highlanders.

Its first manager was Clark Griffith, a pitcher of substance since
1891, who is recalled today as "the Old Fox" because, for what
seemed forever—including the twenties—he and a former catcher
born Cornelius McGillicuddy but known as Connie Mack, stared
out from the sports pages as examples of geriatrics active in American life, thin, white-haired, ascetic-looking men, owners of ball
clubs, Griffith in Washington and Mack in Philadelphia, each
guided to world championships and then to lifetimes in the second
division.

But in 1903 Griffith was still pitching, and, after the Yankees
defeated the Senators, 6–2, in their first game ever, young Dan
Daniel as witness, the club did no better than one second-place
finish for him, although it was not without some good players. Its
first resident of the position Ruth held was his antithetical opposite, a five-feet, four-inch Brooklyn Irishman, a legend from the
legendary Baltimore Orioles of the 1890s, Wee Willie Keeler, who
immortalized his batting philosophy with a phrase, "Hit 'em
where they ain't."

Griffith left after five years, succeeded by Kid Elberfeld, who
piloted the club to last place, and so was succeeded in turn by
George Stallings, who, in 1914, would lead the Boston Braves
from fifteen games out in last place on July 4, the date established
by tradition for teams to have found their level, to a first-place
finish ten games in front. They were called "the miracle Braves,"
and even more miraculously they defeated one of Mack's truly
great Athletic teams in history's first sweep of a World Series,
what is called "the most sensational of all Series victories." The
defeat of his three-times championship As was so galling to Mack
that, not for the last time, he broke up a great team by selling off its
stars. Stallings had set the Highlanders seemingly on their way to a
first pennant when he quarreled violently with the owners and was
dismissed four days before the season ended.

He was succeeded by Hal Chase, sometimes called "the greatest
first baseman of all time," and, sometimes, by those anxious to

make points, or perhaps demonstrate retentive memories and encyclopedic knowledge, or perhaps out of simple conviction, he is placed ahead of Lou Gehrig as the best of all the Yankee first basemen. It is difficult to accept this judgment, since among other lapses of character, Chase associated with gamblers.

One of his skills was, with a man on third, charging across the diamond from first to field a bunt dragged down the third baseline, tagging the runner heading for home and firing to first for the putout, a piece of pretty business not seen often these days. But as a manager he was unmanageable, and a man named "Fighting Harry" Wolverton moved in to succeed him, unmemorably, to be replaced by Frank Chance of the Chicago Nationals. Chance was "the peerless leader" of Cub teams that won four championships in five years, the last in 1910, and also was the subject of baseball's most famous verse:

These are the saddest of possible words,
Tinker-to-Evers-to-Chance,
Trio of bear Cubs fleeter than birds,
Tinker-to-Evers-to-Chance.
Ruthlessly pricking our gonfalon bubble,
Making a Giant hit into a double,
Words that are freighted with nothing but trouble,
Tinker-to-Evers-to-Chance.

Franklin P. Adams wrote those words for the New York *Globe* in 1908, but glory is not always transferable. After Chance fired the enormously popular Chase, who had remained at first after being let go as manager, he was himself cashiered and shortstop Roger Peckinpaugh took over.

One reason for this parade of leaders was the fact that Devery and Farrell habitually managed from the grandstand, shouting advice and imprecations and frequently invading the dressing room to replay lost games, a practice frowned upon by managers, in general a proud lot, often touchy. The owners also detested each other.

Matching the team's generally nondescript record, it was very much a poor relation to the enormously popular Giants, sometime champions (1904–05, 1911–13), almost always in contention and managed since 1903 by the choleric McGraw, called "Little Napoleon," a term not without pejorative possibilities, but loved by the fans and a leading figure not only in sport but on Broadway.

With a touch of *lèse majesté,* and perhaps avarice, the Giants allowed the American League club to share the Polo Grounds, beginning in 1913, by which time they were called the Yankees, a name given them by Jim Price, sports editor of the New York *Press,* because it fit more easily into headlines.

On January 11, 1915, Devery and Farrell, who had seen only one profitable season, sold the club to Ruppert and Huston, walked out of the office and never spoke to each other again. Farrell, the plunger, left an estate of $1,072, a cautionary figure cited in Yankee histories for young readers.

All of this was seen or read about by Dan Daniel, still around to tell about it in the fall of 1973 in his crowded and relic-strewn office at *The Ring* magazine, for which he has written for fifty-two years. Heavy-set, with close-cropped white hair, a large, friendly nose and bright brown eyes behind heavy-rimmed glasses, he embodies much of New York's sporting and journalistic life of this century. As a cub reporter, he received the break dreamed of in all those B movies about the newspaper game when, in 1909, he was working for the New York *Herald,* and a telegrapher named Al Curtair, crazed by who knows what dreams of avarice, demanded a raise to five dollars a day from his three-dollar wage. Al Steimer, the sports editor, was so outraged that he fired Curtair and sent young Daniel south with the Brooklyn Robins to spring training in Macon, Georgia.

Daniel didn't finish the assignment because his parents wanted him to come home and continue his education at CCNY. He returned but stayed with newspaper work, covering basketball, billiards, and intercollegiate chess championships, then on the sports pages, before moving over to the New York *Press.* There destiny waited in the person of Nat Fleischer, "Mr. Boxing" for five decades, his magazine, *The Ring,* becoming "boxing's bible," and Daniel's name was on the masthead from the beginning.

Daniel's career, however, was with the crazy quilt of New York newspapering, and you could pretty well write the history of one by following the other. The *Press* was absorbed by the *Sun.* Frank Munsey, who called himself a publisher but is more often remembered as a kind of butcher, or packager, acquired the New York *Telegram* and merged it with the *Sun,* and Daniel "went along with those crazy combinations, as Munsey murdered newspapers left and right."

Daniel sighs, smiles, removes his glasses, and wipes a hand across his tired eyes. "Of course," he says, "Munsey was right." This is sacrilege for an old-line newspaperman. "Those papers were losing money."

By the 1930s, the mergers formed the New York *World Telegram,* by the 1950s, the New York *World Telegram and Sun,* and by 1966, briefly, the push-me-pull-you of American journalism, the New York *World Tribune Journal,* which sank, not so much under the load of three staffs for everything, three columnists for every scandal, but under the burden of three publishers with their own scant but stubborn and mutually exclusive philosophies—"that was murdered by incompetence"—and through it all, "Dan Daniel" was a by-line familiar to generations of baseball news readers.

When Colonel Leland Stanford MacPhail owned the Yankees in the 1940s, he chartered a plane to be used by writers covering the team. "I didn't want to fly," recalls Daniel, "and I went to Mac-Phail and told him so. The clubs at that time paid the writers' traveling expenses, and, no, I never felt that influenced the way I covered the team. If the newspaper had had to pay for the writers, the way the thinking ran then, nobody would have gone on the road.

"Well, MacPhail told me he wasn't going to pay for anyone riding the train when he had this plane, so I went to Lee Wood, who ran the *Telegram,* and said, "The time has come." He thought about it a while and said, 'We'll pay your way,' and the next thing you know, all the writers were traveling at the newspapers' expense, rather than the ball clubs'," a condition widely hailed at seminars conducted in the name of John Peter Zenger.

Daniel, then, witnessed or was around, for just about all of the century's baseball in New York, not only covering teams but conducting one of those columns answering hard questions from Gus Fan, questions sometimes so hideously obscure or complicated as to raise doubts about their origin—could R.L.J. of Ozone Park really want Daniel to name his all-time, all-Polish team? He served an unprecedented five consecutive terms as president of the New York chapter of the Baseball Writers Association of America and, perhaps the emotional highlight, acted as master of ceremonies that impassioned day the Iron Horse was honored.

Far from being the one-dimensional, uncomplicated plodder of legend, Gehrig was, in Daniel's estimate, "a strange young man." Part of the strangeness is the contrast with Ruth. Both, as youths, shared the common denominator of a bottom-level poverty so galling as to surely leave scars, but that was all they shared.

For Ruth, streetwise at age seven, already a sampler of liquor and tobacco, rejected out of hand by his saloon-keeper father and shipped off to little better than a reform school after a gun was fired in his father's tavern, not just a poor kid, but a poor, unloved kid, grew into a free-spending extrovert, friend to all the world, lover, companion, full of fun and forever seeking it out, womanizer, *bon vivant,* idol of a nation, glutton of life's pleasures, in Gehrig's own assessment, "a man who knew how to live."

And Gehrig, for whom the poverty was no less marked, grew up the only surviving child—three others died in infancy—of German immigrant parents who adored him, counseled him, coddled him. He was so stuffed with simple fare that his early nickname was "Fats." His was the kind of home often recalled in middle-aged oversimplification as being "poor but there was so much love we didn't know we were poor." Gehrig grew into a secretive, isolated, frequently depressed, clumsy loner who found it hard to believe he was liked, let alone loved.

Beyond the comfort of wool-gathering, the fact is that Gehrig followed every precept of Puritan ethic and Horatio Alger almost

from the moment of his birth, June 19, 1903, in New York City.
His father was an ironworker, frequently unemployed because of
chronic illness, and his mother was a domestic. The parents, as
Gehrig grew up, were janitors in various low buildings, longest on
the northernmost, unfashionable west side, the father ultimately
becoming so ill that it was the mother who was the chief source of
income.

Gehrig, as he did all his life, worked hard, did the right thing.

His father took him to the *turnverein,* that German sporting society centered on pulleys, weights, and bars, and young Henry Louis
sweated his fat into muscle. He earned his first pair of long trousers
by working for them. At age fifteen he achieved his first taste of
fame when, playing for the High School of Commerce against
Chicago's Lane Tech at Wrigley Field, he dazzled the spectators
by hitting the ball over the fence.

The feat made the newspapers, which wrote of "a schoolboy
Babe Ruth," so that comparison was established early, and attracted college and professional scouts. In truth, Gehrig was not
yet much of a ball player, hitting around .200 and being an uncertain fielder. Sometimes he pitched, throwing hard enough to get
away with it.

His parents became employed at a fraternity house at Columbia
University, and Lou started waiting on tables, the brothers calling
him "the little Dutch boy" or "the little kraut," as he "writhed at
the caste system by which some brothers who couldn't carry his
morals or ethics made him feel as poor as he was."

Working, working all the time, he became good enough at both
football and baseball so that some twenty colleges expressed interest in him. He chose Columbia, typically, because it meant that he
could study engineering while living at home.

He played tackle and running back on the football team. Accounts vary concerning his ability. He was naïve enough that when
a scout told him he could earn some money playing minor-league
baseball under an assumed name in the summer—"a lot of college
boys do it, son, or I guess there wouldn't be any minor
leagues"—he went off to Hartford and played, the money desper-

ately needed at home, and when this was discovered, it nearly ended his college career.

So far are we removed in time that the solution seems fanciful. Columbia's graduate manager of athletics, a frat brother when young Lou waited tables, simply told the truth, doctored no transcript. He wrote letters to all of Columbia's football and baseball rivals, explained that Gehrig acted in innocence and suggested that he be withheld from competition his sophomore year and then allowed to compete, and, since the greater institutions of learning had not yet discovered that winning is the only thing, the solution was regarded as just.

Paul Krichell discovered Gehrig. It was an accident. None of the New York college teams being at home one spring day, Krichell went to New Brunswick, New Jersey, to see Columbia play Rutgers. Krichell was friendly with Andy Coakley, the Columbia coach, and asked him what kinds of players he had, and Coakley told him he had a pretty good pitcher but didn't plan to use him that day.

Gehrig teetered around under some flies in the outfield but hit with enough power, shredding the leaves off a tree beyond the fence, to impress Krichell. Krichell asked Coakley about him and was told slyly, "That's the pitcher I was telling you about." Krichell wondered—a kid who hit with that power. The next time he saw him, Gehrig hit the ball over Columbia's South Field fence, sent it bounding up the library steps across the street, just the way it happened in the movie, and Krichell called Ed Barrow and said he had found the new Babe Ruth.

Gehrig signed for a fifteen-hundred-dollar bonus, quitting college because the money was needed to pay for an operation on his mother; she survived her son, but she seemed always going to the hospital for an operation. College ended then, because of a hospital bill, one of those moments in the annals of American medicine not celebrated in the institutional advertisements of the pharmaceutical houses.

Work, work. And save. What with medical and other expenses at home, Gehrig joined the Yankees for the first time at their training site in New Orleans with twelve dollars in his pocket to see him through six weeks. The club paid food and lodging, but some money was needed for incidentals, which is how baseball players got the reputation as ten-cent tippers, and, even in the twenties, twelve dollars did not go far in terms of six weeks.

Daniel recalls sitting in the lobby of the Bienville Hotel one evening when Gehrig entered, "tired, bedraggled and worried. I asked him what was wrong, and he said, 'I'm broke. I've walked all over this city looking for a job as a soda jerk, but there aren't any openings.'

"My God. I went to Huggins and said, 'You've got this very promising kid here who's going around after workouts looking for work as a busboy.' So he called Mark Roth and said, 'Why do you let this guy go around broke?' and Roth said, 'He never said anything to me,' and the club settled it with an advance."

Huggins was suspicious of college ball players, although reminding himself of Eddie Collins, also a Columbia man, but the six-foot, two-inch Gehrig pleased him; Huggins liked his players big. Gehrig was thunderstruck in the presence of Combs and Meusel and, most of all, Ruth, of course, and they liked the quiet young man with the shy smile, but, for a while, he was just around.

In Gehrig's first major league at bat he struck out against Washington. In his second appearance he pinch-hit a double against St. Louis. This was in 1923, and he appeared in thirteen games for the Yankees before Huggins sent him down to Hartford, a minor-league club with which the Yankees had a player agreement, for seasoning.

Harry Hesse, Gehrig's roommate at Hartford, remembered a young man always broke because he sent his money home for the continual medical expenses. "I realized the guy didn't have a dime. Not a dime. He didn't have money for clothes. He looked like a tramp."

Gehrig went into a terrible slump. He was batting .062 when his manager called New York and begged Barrow to take the boy off his hands. Krichell was dispatched from South Carolina, where he was scouting, to see what was wrong. He found a homesick, emotionally convoluted young man, sure he would never hit. Krichell took him to a steak dinner. Over dessert he said, "Ty Cobb told me what he does when he is in a slump. He just works at hitting the ball back to the pitcher. That's all. Just nice and easy, and in a few days, he is back in the groove."

The story seems too pat, and since Cobb hit .367 in twenty-three seasons, radar is needed to detect a slump, but Gehrig broke out of whatever he was in, hitting everything in sight, winding up the season, after flirting with .500, at .304 with twenty-four home runs.

Huggins first put him in the lineup for a full game against the Senators the next season, over the objections of the short-fused Bush, who was working toward a twenty-game year. In the first inning, Gehrig held a bunt while the runner scored from third. Bush loudly denigrated the values of a college education.

But in the seventh inning, with two men on, Washington walked Ruth to get at the rookie. Huggins simply told the terrified young man to get in there and hit the ball. Gehrig doubled the first pitch off the fence, driving home the tying run and scoring the winning run himself, the inadvisability of walking the Bambino to get at Buster thus being demonstrated early.

After Gehrig appeared in ten games for the Yankees in 1924, Huggins sent him down again, promising him that this would be his last trip to the minors.

He remained lonely. "He took everything to heart," Hesse said. "He was a guy who needed friends, but he didn't know how to go about getting them. He'd get low and sit hunched over and miserable, and it was pretty tough to pull him out of it."

Hesse set Gehrig up with what he thinks was his first date. Gehrig didn't say a word. When the girl spoke to him, he blushed.

There was one thing in his life, however, that worked right. On June 1, 1925, Gehrig pinch-hit for Pee Wee Wanninger against the Senators, to the accompaniment of no drum rolls. The day marked the start of his consecutive game streak, 2,130, which three decades later remains, apparently, the safest record in baseball.

The next day Wally Pipp, the first baseman, complained that he had a headache. Huggins replaced Pipp with Gehrig. Pipp, a graceful major-league veteran who had been helpful in coaching Gehrig, shortly wound up in Cincinnati. "I took the two most expensive aspirins in history," he later said.

By 1927 Gehrig was established at first base because of his bat. His fielding was improved, but it was as uncertain as his social confidence. "He used to come up to the apartment Benny Bengough and I shared," Mark Koenig recalled, "and sit around, waiting for us to introduce him to girls." He had enough money now to dress decently, but he sat, wordlessly, neat in a new suit, waiting for a girl.

Still, at the plate, he was the complete man. "If there's anyone in the league now who will break my record," Ruth's ghosted column began one May afternoon in 1927, "I have a hunch it will be Lou Gehrig, and I certainly wish him luck."

Gehrig gave signs of having the same thing in mind as the Yankees opened in Detroit. Rain and then snow—on May 16— delayed the start of the series, disappointing thousands of fans who, by circumstance of birth, were denied the variety of spectacle taken for granted by New Yorkers, and showed up at the park in spite of the weather. The weather irritated Detroit club comptrollers, who figured on good crowds when Murderer's Row showed up, and gave Huggins occasion to worry publicly if his "smoothly running machine was likely to develop knocks." An additional concern was whether to risk starting his younger pitchers or go with proven quality on the game-won-in-the-spring-counts-the-same-as-a-victory-in-the-fall theory.

Vexing as the weather pattern may have been since it snarled up the schedule with make-up games and extra doubleheaders, it was a minor note to floods sweeping the Mississippi River valley. "There never was such a calamity in our history," said Secretary of Commerce Herbert Hoover, on the scene in Louisiana, where he predicted the homeless there would number half a million, most of them Arcadians who refused to move until the stove was floating, "a romantic, clannish folk as like the peasant farmers of France as two dots.'' They were removed to what the press called ''concentration camps.''

Not until 1973 would there be a greater spring runoff in the Mississippi valley, but in 1927 there were fewer levees to control it, 313 died, seventeen million acres flooded, and the loss was put at three hundred million in Coolidge dollars.

Detroit's rainouts, although modest in comparison, gave New York writers time to assess the Tigers. They were a club, said Monitor, which could finish first or sixth, ''depending on the pitching they get.''

The outfield of Heilmann, Manush, and Fothergill, who had finished first, third, and fourth in league batting in 1926, was ''as good as the best, possibly stronger at bat than Washington's but not quite as good on defense.''

Five decades later, the mention of Ruth, Combs, and Meusel means the ultimate; in 1927 there were two other outfields considered just about as good, even better. The Tiger trio was so gifted that Al Wingo, who hit .370 in 1925, was a reserve; in 1926 he was joined by Cobb, the manager, who benched himself in favor of his starters. Fothergill, when the Yankees came to town, was leading the league. His batting hint wasn't much of a help to beginners: ''I just walk up to the plate and slam it.''

George Moriarity, a former Highlander third baseman and, later, an umpire, had succeeded Cobb as manager. There was ''no man in the game with a better analytical mind or keener understanding of a ballplayer's temperament,'' said Monitor.

Lou Blue, a .300 hitter and ''one of the game's better first basemen,'' anchored the infield; at second was Charley Gehringer, ''one of the game's infield finds last year,'' whose lifetime batting average of .321, a batting swing regarded as the smoothest in the sport, and an effortless fielding talent reflected in the phrase ''the mechanical man'' put him in the Hall of Fame. Tavener was the shortstop, and third was shared by Jack Warner and Marty McManus, who was acquired from St. Louis, where he had trouble with the management. The pitching staff, topped by Earl Whitehill, Liz Stoner, Sam Gibson, and Ken Holloway, did not encourage hope for Detroit's first pennant since Hughie Jennings' great clubs of 1907–09.

Detroit jumped off to a two-run lead in the first inning of the season's opener between the two teams. Gehrig homered in the third with one on to tie with Ruth at eight homers each. Meusel then singled and stole second. Lazzeri, after singling, was trapped off first. Meusel took third and, as the Tigers tried to run down Lazzeri, dashed for home, beating the throw with a slide.

Combs, who might have written the book for leadoff men, opened the seventh with a walk. He went to third on Koenig's single and scored on Ruth's fly. Gehrig doubled to right center, scoring Koenig when the throw went past the catcher. Gehrig tried for home but was tagged in the stomach so briskly that "he rolled over and played dead."

Collins, Combs, and Koenig were walked in the ninth by George Smith, who had replaced Holloway, the starter. Ruth singled home two runs. When Ruether walked the first man to face him in the ninth, Huggins called on Moore. After walking a man he got rid of Warner and Heilmann and struck out Fothergill, preserving a 6–2 win.

Gehrig's "wretched day at bat" included a homer and two doubles, and the *Times* observed "he ought to begin hitting any day now."

Fifteen Yankee hits, including Ruth's ninth home run of the season, accounted for a 9–2 Yankee victory in the getaway game of the truncated series the following day. The box score makes it look like a laugher, in the baseball phrase, but Detroit left two men on base in the second, third, fifth, and sixth innings and three in the fourth, against Pennock.

"The spectacle of the slight lefthander holding his hard-hitting foeman off," the *Sun* was moved to observe, "was not unmindful of a slender boxer skillfully outpointing a burly opponent who seems on the verge of landing a heavy punch, and still is on the verge when the bell rings."

Pennock said, "I haven't been so tired in a long time. In the first place, I didn't have anything on the ball, and in the second place, I didn't have any control. It was the hardest game I ever pitched, I think." A team gets you nine runs, he might have added, you can afford to struggle a little.

With Detroit threatening constantly, only the fact that Pennock was Pennock prevented Huggins from taking him out. And the pitcher was aided by a heart-stopping catch by Combs in the fifth, when he dashed to deep center, his back to the plate, and stuck a glove over his shoulder to grab a drive by Fothergill. It was the Yankees' ninth win in ten games of the western swing.

Cleveland, noted John Kieran "would be a good ball club if they could borrow the Detroit outfield, or Detroit would be good if they could borrow the Cleveland pitching staff." George Uhle, Emil Levsen, and Joe Schaute won fifty-seven games in 1926, when the Indians whittled a ten-game early September Yankee lead to a game and a half before finishing three games out, but the Big Three had accounted for a meager four in the spring of 1927. The replacement of Speaker in center by Fred Eichrodt, .234 lifetime, was hardly a plus, but George Burns was back at first, the league's most valuable player the previous year when he hit .358, "one of those rarities who didn't bloom until he was past 30."

Crowds gathered, hundreds of cars lining the highways outside New York City, as the word spread that a persistent fog was beginning to lift off the Atlantic and Lindbergh announced that he would take off in the morning, weather permitting.

But all remained the same in baseball as the Yankees won their seventh straight, beating Cleveland, 4–3, Gehrig providing two runs on his ninth homer of the season. People were paying increased attention to Moore, too, who relieved Shocker in the second with two on, two out, and the score tied. One pitch retired the Indians, and, in the next seven innings, only two Indians got as far as second and fifteen of them were retired in a row. Like Fothergill, Moore demonstrated that genius is inarticulate about the gift.

"My sinker is my natural fast ball," he explained. "I just wind up and turn her loose, and she sinks. It's hard to hit squarely," he added unnecessarily. "They land on top of it, mostly, and it goes into the dirt."

He won the game for himself in the ninth. Dugan singled with one out, went to third on Collins' single, and Moore came to the plate, designated bunter. He was ludicrous with the bat, but this time he bunted perfectly down the first baseline, and Jumping Joe scored, standing up.

The winning streak ended the following day when George Uhle beat the Yankees, 2–1, but not even Yankee fans much cared.

LINDBERGH SPEEDS ACROSS NORTH ATLANTIC, KEEPING
TO SCHEDULE OF 100 MILES AN HOUR; SIGHTED PASSING
ST. JOHN'S, NEWFOUNDLAND, AT 7:15 P.M.: ALL OF THE
BREAKS ARE IN HIS FAVOR, FOLLOWING WINDS HELP TO
SPEED HIM ALONG ON HIS HAZARDOUS VENTURE

LINDBERGH DOES IT! TO PARIS IN 33½ HOURS, FLIES
1,000 MILES THROUGH SNOW AND SLEET, CHEERING FRENCH
CARRY HIM OFF FIELD: CROWD ROARS THUNDEROUS WELCOME

Banner lines across *The New York Times* front page and stories that pushed everything else into the land of the want ad signaled a journalistic jag and public orgy of affection without parallel. Sixty trans-Atlantic flights by plane and dirigible preceded Lindbergh's, but he was the first person to do it alone, and, as John Lardner wrote, "probably excitement never grew with more horrible momentum, from a puff of curiosity to an earth-shaking tension than it did through the night of May 20 and the morning of May 21. . . . From that moment, which seemed to be the beginning of the end of the most glorious story of the era of glorious stunts, two forces—circumstances and Lindbergh's character—set to work to prevent such an ending."

Cleveland honored its own hero, presenting George Burns with a silver bat filled with fifteen hundred one-dollar bills, and then won its second straight over the Yankees. Jumping Joe Dugan, the bunt maven, fielded a roller in the style that won him his nickname, but his throw drew Gehrig off the bag, and Cleveland won, 3–2. "If there hadn't been so many people looking at him," it was observed, "Miller Huggins would have broken down and cried."

"We was going good until the Yankees hit town," the *Sun* heard the western clubs lament, as Ruth hit his tenth homer the next day, and New York beat the Indians, 7–2, making it an even split in Cleveland, and ten of thirteen in the West.

Twenty-three thousand overflowed the park, filling the stands and so were allowed to sit along the foul line and in left field, leaving no dollar uncollected no matter the threat to the conduct of the game, in the finest tradition of *laissez-faire* Coolidge economics.

Rain postponed doubleheaders on successive days in Philadelphia, while the larger canvas showed Lindbergh's reception in Paris, where he received the Cross of the Legion of Honor, as the Chamber of Deputies hailed him as "the audacious hero of the century" and crowds burst windows, jamming for a look, as he attempted to dine at a private club. All of this moved the flood stories from the front pages. HOMES OF ONE HUNDRED THOUSAND IMPERILLED AS DIKE BREAKS, washed to secondary status, along with the information that a congressional majority was opposed to any extra session on flood relief. The big lesson of the Thirties, i.e., sometimes government must act, was not yet learned, and the feeling was the Red Cross was handling the situation well.

"The New York Yankees are repeating their early season dash and have not yet met the expected opposition," is the way Monitor saw it. "Looking back to the second week of April, when it all started, it will be recalled that Philadelphia, Cleveland, Detroit, Washington, and Chicago were all viewed with alarm as very much in the contending class and likely to push the Yankee league champions into the second division. The league looked like it would offer a tremendous struggle between six clubs. . . .

"From a six-team race, the American League may develop into a two or three club affair, unless the west can come here in June and stop the Yankee rush. The Yankees will be home almost all of that month."

An exhibition game at West Point offered Ruth the opportunity for a couple of *beaux gestes*. He didn't fail. The rest of the team arrived at noon for an ear-splitting reception by the cadets. Ruth drove up in a car the size of a tank, presented baseballs to the top players of twelve companies and, before a cloudburst halted the game with the Yankees leading, 2–0, went down swinging. Cadet Tim Timberlake, the pitcher said, "He just wanted to make us feel good. He was so anxious to hit a home run for us, he went after bad balls." Another Ruth fan was born.

There is an exhibition game recollection about Gehrig, too. Koenig remembers the team on some ratty field, perhaps in Texas, in the preseason. Only a wire fence separated the benches from the stands. "The fans," observed a Yankee, "can hurl epithets at us."

"Gee," said Columbia Lou, "do you think they'll fit through the screen? " He was, as usual, dead serious.

It was another talent he shares, in Koenig's memory, with Ruth. "They're coming out in groves," Ruth might say as the stands filled. Or, "There's a vacancy in the sky," oddly poetic, as the sun broke through.

Twenty-five thousand Washingtonians saw two of the finest pitching exhibitions of the year on May 28, but only one of them was by a Yankee. In the opening game of a doubleheader the astute Pennock not only offered a rare demonstration of shameful throwing but looked positively dumb, or raw, when with men on first and third, the Senators brought off a double steal. He whirled to try for Judge, going to second; Speaker delayed, then broke for home. Alerted by his teammates' shouts, Pennock spun around, but it was too late, and he stood, ball in hand, like the new man in town.

His opposite number, Lisenbee, winning, 7–2, and beating the Yankees for the third time, looked so good the critic could not imagine anyone looking better, until he saw Hoyt in the second game. Scattering three hits, Hoyt threw the Senators their first shutout of the season, allowed only one man to get as far as second, only five to first, retired the side in order in seven of the nine innings, and allowed only six balls, apart from the three hits, to reach the outfield. The score was 5–0.

Gehrig hit a home run in that game, tying Ruth at eleven. The news was buried in appreciation of the pitching. The 'fan who caught the ball brought it to Ruth to be autographed. ''The Babe obliged. He is glad to see Lou get them.'' Gehrig's reaction was not recorded.

There was another split the following day. Again the Yankees were profligate with hits in one game and with good pitching in the other; the team had no sense of waste. A couple of runs from the 12–2 first-game victory would have bailed out Moore, making his first start and losing, 3–2, in the second, when Lazzeri threw over Grabowski's head and allowed the winning run to score on another Senator double steal.

Ruth's twelfth home run before forty-five thousand fans put him one up on Gehrig. It was not overlooked that he also tripled and singled in four at-bats, and dashed back to the wire screen, gloved right hand over his left shoulder, to grab a fly off Harris' bat, getting almost as big a hand for the catch as for his home run. He attracted attention, by himself, as easily as the gaudy, one hundred-member band of the Black Watch, the famed Canadian World War I regiment, which marched before the game as guests of the management.

It is generally accepted that the Twenties created heroes out of a sense of war weariness, a fatigued people turning gratefully towards any escape from responsibility. But this was 1927, nearly a decade since the Armistice, and America hardly qualified as a nation which had suffered terribly. There was a lot of drinking going on, of course, and perhaps the generally festive mood contributed to an easy sense of celebration. But Prohibition inflicted itself only on the United States. Europe, which was genuinely recovering from battle fatigue, searched just as desperately for heroes.

Lindbergh was now conquering London, as the word was used, the police saving him from a crowd of 150,000, after he conquered Paris—the final flourish was his visit to Nungesser's mother, wearing his "now famous borrowed suit," just the right touch, the French thought—and conquered Brussels, where he met his first king and reported, "Albert knows a lot about flying."

In Detroit his schoolteacher mother rejected a $100,000 movie offer "to depict the American mother"; she tried to hold her chemistry class as usual, but the students rebelled, giving her an ovation, difficult though it was to turn away from their studies.

If it was heroes the fans wanted, the Yankees could oblige, overcoming a five-run deficit, sending eleven men to bat in the eighth inning, scoring seven runs and beating the Red Sox, 15–7, "about what you expect when the front-runners and tail-enders meet." Ruth drove in three runs with a single and his thirteenth homer; Koenig's bases-loaded single was the day's most timely hit, and Myles Thomas pretty well controlled the Red Sox after they clobbered Ruether for their early lead.

Ruth smacked a heroic, not to say timely, home run in the eleventh inning of the second game that beat Philadelphia, 6–5, and saved the Yankees from losing both morning and afternoon games on Memorial Day. Before the fell hand of socialism gripped baseball, admissions often were charged for two games in one day, the total being given as the attendance figure; in this case, thousands more stormed the gates and were turned away.

The As unsuccessfully protested the game, which was saved by another heroic act. With Collins on second and Cobb on first and one out, Grabowski chased a foul by Al Simmons over near the Philadelphia bench. He made a diving catch, falling over an iron railing, hitting the dugout floor and half-diving down a flight of stairs, his feet waving energetically in the air. The As pulled him out, still clutching the ball.

Both Collins and Cobb had scored by then, but Huggins complained to the umpires that the runners should have been given only two bases. Collins' run was granted, but Cobb was returned to third, where he died, and this was the decision Mack took to the League of Nations.

The Yankees should have won the first game, hammering Grove for fifteen hits and eight runs, but the Athletics separated Pipgras and Shawkey from nine. Simmons, almost automatically the star, scored the winning run when he doubled, went to third when Dugan dropped a throw, and crossed home on a fly.

By now there were occasional references to what Ruth and Gehrig were doing as "the great American home run derby," or handicap. The sense of strain that later marred relations between the men did not exist at this point in their careers. Ruth was outwardly, and apparently inwardly, cheerful over the prospect that Gehrig might break his records.

He knew, although it would be forgotten by 1962, when Roger Maris hit sixty-one home runs in an extended season, and by 1973, when Henry Aaron closed in on Ruth's lifetime home-run total, that whatever happened to the records, no damage would be done to the legend.

You cannot compete with a ghost, as the lovesick swain protests to the pretty war widow in bad movies. In this sense, the Englishman was right, if kinky, when he said that statistics are like the bathing suit, revealing everything except what is important. You don't become Babe Ruth, the Babe knew, just by hitting home runs.

Gehrig knew that, too, in a sadder way. In 1927 he still very much idolized Ruth. For a time during the season, he told an interviewer, he tried to alter his swing, to make it more like the Babe's. "But now, I'm going back to just try to meet the ball." On the evidence of the record, it is difficult to see when he experimented. He seems to have smashed the thing straight through the season. But he also had acquired a rueful wisdom.

"I'm not a headline guy, and we might as well face it," he said. "I'm just a guy who's in there every day. The fellow who follows the Babe in the batting order. When Babe's turn at bat is over, whether he strikes out or belts a home run, the fans are still talking about him when I come up. If I stood on my head at the plate, nobody'd pay any attention."

A strange young man. In some ways, he was haunted. Old Dan Daniel, sitting in the cluttered offices of *The Ring* magazine, amid the bounce and clatter of garment-center traffic, his memory swimming with seven decades of Yankee baseball—Keeler and Keller and Mantle and Mays (Carl) and Baker and Berra and McCarthy and Lopat and, who knows, Terry Turner—remembers him that way. A strange young man.

"All his career," says Dan Daniel, as wise as Maria Ouspenskaya, "Gehrig feared that his ability to hit a ball would leave him over night."

# Four

○

He was bred in old Kentucky,
Where the feudists' bullets whirl.
There's the die-hard of old Breathitt
In every raven curl.
He was bred in old Kentucky,
Gee, but Hug, you're mighty lucky,
When you grabbed off a man like Earle.

He once estimated that there are ten or fifteen thousand people named Combs in Kentucky, recalling a day when he played with a semiprofessional team for Pleasant Grove in which there were only two surnames in the lineup, three Snowdens and six Combses, only one of them, brother Matt at first base, a direct relative.

The father was a cold-comfort farmer who scratched out a living in the blue grass for a wife and seven children and swore that there would not be another farmer in the family, or a ball player, for that matter.

The important thing to understand about the meanness of the family finances is that a career as a one-room-school teacher was seen as a step up on the economic ladder. And so Earle went to college, Eastern Kentucky State Teachers, it was then called, now

Eastern Kentucky University, where there is an Earle Combs Hall, an athletic dormitory—honoring not only a Hall of Fame ball player, but a businessman, former member of the State Banking Commission, and former chairman of the State Board of Regents, all of them the same man.

After he graduated from college, where another distinguished alumnus was Cassius Clay, a nineteenth-century ambassador to Russia and namesake, although any other relationship is unclear, of a celebrated twentieth-century pugilist, Combs taught the three Rs, hiking eight miles to and from the little red schoolhouse in the Lincoln tradition for thirty-seven dollars a month, before giving it up for a forty dollar-a-month job as ball player and carpenter with the High Splint Coal Company.

He had learned baseball as a kid in pickup games, recalling, "I was always assured of a position on the team, not because of my athletic ability, but because I always furnished the ball. My dad made them for me. He'd wind yarn or twine around a small rubber ball and cover it with leather from old kid shoes."

The recollection is unnecessarily modest. It seems improbable that little Earle ever had to threaten to take the ball and go home unless he was given his bats. Except for the question of his throwing arm, there was never any more doubt about Earle Combs's athletic prowess than about his character; of the one, Joe McCarthy, his manager in Louisville, said, "Earle Combs is the greatest gentleman in baseball"; as to the other, Gehrig moved Joe DiMaggio over to make room in center field for Combs on his all-time Yankee team.

There were, of course, hurdles, even for a youth with the reputation as "the fastest foot in the mountain country." He recalled trying for a desperation catch, the ball rolling past him, leading to a run, when he first broke in with Louisville.

"I hated to return to the bench to face the manager. In fact, I was so low I struck out." Since he was famous for his batting eye and perfect form at the plate, this didn't happen often. But on that rookie day he proceeded to repeat his error in the outfield.

"I really looked for an exit then. I felt like a telephone directory with all the Smiths and Joneses torn out.'' But after the game the manager, the same McCarthy who later would leave Louisville and take over an eighth-place Chicago Cub team and lead it to a pennant, and, still later, would put together a Yankee dynasty in the 1930s that some call the greatest of all, told Combs, ''Don't let those tough breaks worry you. That's all part of the game. I put you in center field because I know you're a good player. Just keep playing.''

He did, although one day he broke up a game with Kansas City when he dashed in from the outfield waving his cap—''We all thought you were mad,'' McCarthy said later. ''The bees! The bees are after me,'' cried Combs, among other things. Indeed, a flock of bees swarmed and darted around him until he got to the clubhouse, when they moved to the stands and dispersed the crowd.

Before that 1922 season ended, Combs was a polished fielder and a .340 hitter. The following year he batted .380, and the Yankees got him for what seemed the established purchase price, for quality merchandise, of fifty thousand dollars.

''The swamps of Florida, the hills of Georgia, the canebrakes of Louisiana and the plains of Texas are filled with busted spring phenoms,'' warned Monitor, when the rookie Combs ripped apart exhibition game pitching, ''who failed after the pitcher really began to curve the ball.''

But after riding the bench for a while because Whitey Witt ''was adjudged too valuable a center fielder to drop from the lineup,'' Combs took over when Witt failed to hit and proceeded, for fifteen weeks, to devastate big-league pitching, batting over .400, fielding brilliantly, and running wild on the bases, before breaking his ankle sliding home against Cleveland.

And by 1925 Monitor was writing, ''He has held up a sagging, shaky team of stars by his strength alone. . . . If you wish to see the Ty Cobb of 1907 in action at the plate, shifty, supple, yet sure, go to the Stadium and watch Combs against merciless big league pitching. The fielders don't know where to play for him.''

Since he didn't drink, smoke, or stay up late, Combs didn't stir

up the off-the-field attention of his free-spirit teammates, although
the presence of one complete, mature man who was not only in
control but in command of his appetites was so singular as to win
tributes like the anonymous doggerel above, titles like "the gentleman from Richmond" and recognition in *The Sporting News* as "a
ballplayer's ballplayer, a fan's idol, a manager's delight, a sportsman and a regular fellow. He never fails to bear down, he never
fails to fight until the last out."

There was concern that on the field his skills, while unques-
tioned, were of the sort—simply getting on base, covering lots of
ground—that might disappear in the fusillade that followed. Billy
Evans wrote, "When I broke in 22 years ago, the lead-off man was
of prime importance as teams played for one run. He is still important in the age of slam-bang baseball. He used to be a small man,
but Combs' crouch reduces his six feet by about six inches, giving
him many walks. He is fast, an adept bunter who can drag the ball
past the pitcher, and a .300 hitter, but he is overshadowed by the
sluggers who follow him."

"The table-setter for Ruth and Gehrig," Combs was called.
"He always seems to be on base when they belt one."

But when the Yankees welcomed the month of June by savaging
the Athletics in a double-header, 10–3 and 18–5, "dismaying the
As and 25,000 fans" with thirty-seven hits, twenty-four of them in
the second game, and including two home runs by Ruth, and one
by Gehrig, Combs's accomplishments hid under no half bushel: he
tripled, hit two doubles, and singled twice.

By the seventh inning of the second game Ruth attempted to
brighten the atmosphere by batting right-handed against the right-
hander Joe Pate. He missed a swipe at a pitch, giving the sullen
multitude a laugh, before striking out legitimately, that is, left-
handed. About the only off-notes for the Yankees were minor injuries to Meusel and Dugan.

Dugan came up to pinch hit the next day, jeered by Philadelphia's famous fans, who, recalling his absences without leave
from their club, and all that implied about the community, hooted,
"I want to go home," before he singled in what proved to be the

winning run "and retired to a quiet spot to laugh himself sick."
One way or the other, the Yankees found a way to beat you.

The great world furnished a myriad of attention-getters: Lizzie
Borden, seventy-four, passed from the scene (AX CASE FIGURE
DIES), leaving material for Sunday-supplement writers, the ballet,
and legend; Lindbergh's erstwhile rivals, Clarence Chamberlain
and Charles A. Levine, after a good deal of squabbling, hopped off
for "Berlin or Rome"—man pinpointed his destination more ac-
curately going to the moon—the *Times* reported 10,321 telephone
inquiries about the flight in its first twenty-four hours; it was a
tough week for literature in the cultural Hub of the Universe: having banned *Elmer Gantry* in the spring, Boston now faced Upton
Sinclair, who would defend his proscribed novel, *Oil,* calling on
his twenty-five-year-old son to testify that his mind was not cor-
rupted after reading a page, cited by the authorities, containing a
passage from The Song of Songs; Marcus Duffield reported in the
*Herald Tribune* that a Kremlin power struggle pitted Joseph Stalin,
"the moderate," against Leon Trotsky, "the extremist," who
favored world revolution; a wedding of London nobility was
marred by a hoax, scores of false invitations having been sent to
actors, actresses, jazz band members, and staffers from the depart-
ing Soviet embassy, leaving after a spy scare; perhaps Trotsky was
right.

But there were no surprises at the Stadium. The best the vengeful Tigers could do was one out of three. Ruether beat them with a
two-hitter, 2–0, the Yankees getting eight hits, all singles, "and
any time that happens, this team is in a batting slump."

Ruether had reason to feel satisfied. Springtime predictions,
noted the *Sun,* were that "Ruether would win his first three games
and not be heard of again. Clark Griffith and other Washington
folks heehawed over the trade of the old southpaw to the Yankees,
but they should have seen him yesterday. He won his fifth game
with as neat a shutout as any pitcher seen so far this year. . . . His
rivals were the slugging Tigers, which made the feat all the more
meritorious."

When Detroit rebounded the next day to end the Yankee winning streak at five, in spite of Gehrig's thirteenth home run, it was "not the mighty Manush, or the horrific Heilmann or the ferocious Fothergill," but "the pint-sized shortstop, Jack Tavener," who hit a home run, the second of his career, off Pennock, with two men on base, to win the game, 3–1.

A rain delay of more than an hour only stayed what now seemed to be the inevitable in the series finale. Ruth's seventeenth home run and a single with two men on highlighted a victory of the sort that so irritated Yankee-haters. New York was outhit, 2 to 1, and the Tigers managed their meager score on twelve hits, four walks, and two hit batsmen, leaving fourteen men stranded. "If they ever start hitting," observed Monitor, "it will be interesting."

Now the Yankees faced their first crucial series of the season. The phrase would assume certain comic overtones before the season was over, but the White Sox arrived in New York only one game out of first place, winners in twelve of their last fourteen, and their big three, Ted Lyons and Alphonse Thomas, both ten and two, and Ted Blankenship, were primed for the Yankees.

Manager Ray Schalk was temporarily a magician for making a star of Alex Metzler in center field, Mack having given up on him "on the grounds that he was under thirty," and so trading him. Schalk also benched himself in favor of Hank McCurdy, and the catcher was batting clean-up "and can be bracketed with hitters like Goslin, Fothergill and Cobb."

Sweeping the Red Sox, Chicago had yet to lose a game in the East. "Nobody else seems to be able to stop the White Sox," wrote Rennie in the *Herald Tribune*. "They have been breezing along at a high old rate. . . . When the Yankees were in Chicago, they shut out the White Sox twice, but that was before the White Sox started on their winning streak. They did not look so tough then, but they were making a lot of errors, and they weren't hitting. Right now, their pitching is the best in the league."

Surely it is a cliché but often overlooked or underestimated that one mark of a great team is to win a game when it has to. Teams have taken pennants picking on the little guys, but the hard marker remembers this. There is something of a bullying about it. True greatness conquers all. What shall it profit a team, it might be asked, to win the pennant and blow the big one? Pitching plays too big a part in a short series, it can be argued, or the right fielder broke up with his doxy. History only murmurs, "You're making excuses."

"The irresistible Yankees met the immovable White Sox," reflected Harrison in the *Times* the day after the opener, "and much light was shed on that scientific question. The immovable will move."

Thomas gave up only six hits, but since three of them were home runs—Ruth's eighteenth, Gehrig's fourteenth, and one by Collins—they offset the seven hits surrendered by Hoyt in a 4–1 Yankee win.

But the White Sox went to town the next day on three Yankee pitchers—Ruether, Moore, of all people, and Giard—with home runs by Clancy, Falk, and Barrett more than offsetting two by Lazzeri. They held an 11–6 lead going into the ninth inning.

As was his wont, Combs opened that inning by getting on base, this time with a single. Dugan fouled out. Ruth singled. Gehrig doubled off the right-field screen, scoring Combs. Durst scored Ruth with a single. Lazzeri, responding to the crowd "which forgot the law of averages," then hit his third home run of the day, tying the game. Only two men had homered three times in a game all the previous year, Jack Fournier of the Browns and, historically, Ruth during the World Series.

Chicago suddenly found itself "in a totally unexpected and wildly hilarious" tie game, thanks to "the wonderful Wop," which was meant to be a compliment in the pages of the *Herald Tribune*. Most of the twenty thousand fans had gone, "but those who remained will never forget the wonderful things that happened there in the twilight."

Neither team scored in the tenth. Myles Thomas was now pitching for New York. Durst opened the eleventh with a triple. Lazzeri was wisely, if unpopularly, walked to get at Morehart, who was playing because Koenig had suffered a charley horse.

Morehart, of course, had been with Chicago in 1926, "eating more regularly than he played."

And so, the eternal verity being that players come back to haunt the team that trades them, he singled in the winning run after Yankee pitching so consistently bad that it took Lazzeri and "the greatest individual batting feat of the season to save the day," 12–11.

There were times when Yankee audacity seemed unbelievable. Blankenship, "the third star in Chicago's pitching constellation," faced Pennock the next day. Pennock, who was having trouble finding himself, gave up three runs in four innings, aided by some peculiar Yankee fielding.

And so the Yankees came to the seventh inning, trailing 3–2, Morehart and Ruth having scored the previous inning on a triple by Durst. Lazzeri singled. Collins walked after Dugan flied out. Pennock, representing himself, singled, scoring Lazzeri. When Combs singled, putting the Yankees one up, Schalk replaced Blankenship with Bert Cole.

Morehart hit his first pitch down the foul line and sped around the bases while Bib Falk groped for the ball. Cole, unnerved, became more so when Ruth leaned over the plate for an outside pitch and tapped it over Falk's head for a triple. He then stole home, the wretched Cole throwing the ball over the catcher's head.

It was 8–3, final, and a shining example of what Combs called "five o'clock lightning," an apt phrase since "the team struck so often in the late innings," as Frank Graham observed. "[It] caught on, spread through the league and seeped into the consciousness of opposing pitchers. They began to dread the approach of five o'clock and the eighth inning."

Schalk, into whose consciousness had seeped questions about what his former terrors had to do to win a ball game, learned. They salvaged the last game of the series, 4–2, on brilliant pitching by Lyons, his triple also breaking a tie. Lyons threw with a peculiar, rocking-chair windup, cranking his arms three or four times before delivery, so irritating Ruth that he stepped from the box.

The losing pitcher was Shocker, back in action after being hit in the head by a pitched ball and suffering what was "diagnosed as a concussion of the brain, which many ballplayers might find highly flattering," a variant, perhaps root, of Dizzy Dean's remark that after he was beaned, "the doctors X-rayed my head and found nothing."

There were various entertaining ways for the White Sox to creep out of town, the decade being less time-rattled than the Seventies. Lots of enticing ocean voyages were advertised; more modestly, three dollars bought a ride to Albany on the Hudson River, either Day Line or Night Line, with music; it was $5.50 to Boston on the Fall River Line, "June moonlight, smooth water, refreshing breezes." "South? By sea, of course," to Miami or Bermuda. There were ten all-express trains to California, all must have looked attractive to the White Sox, battered now and further behind.

The Indians, with no such aspirations as afflicted Chicago, received pretty much the same treatment in the first game, a bit more spectacular, perhaps, since Ruth hit two home runs in a 6–4 victory, the second blow being regarded as the second longest he ever hit. Thirty thousand gasped, according to the press. Its length was not determined—the tape measure, like air conditioning, awaited invention—but this one, to center field, was so extravagant that Catcher Joe Sewell demanded the umpires check Ruth's bat, arguing that no mortal could hit a ball that far without the aid of lead in the weapon. The umpires dutifully went over the bludgeon and concluded what all the world knew. It wasn't the bat. It was Ruth.

Furthermore, he flattened himself against the fence to grab a long drive by the embittered Sewell, firing to first to double up Burns, the most valuable player having unaccountably taken off with the crack of the bat, steaming into third as Ruth caught the ball.

A Lazzeri home run "gave Myles Thomas a five-run lead to play with, and he did," allowing Cleveland to pull within three runs, bases loaded and one out, before Moore was called on. A run scored on an infield out—it usually took Moore one batter to get into the spirit of the thing—but when a hit would have meant a tie,

Moore struck out Eichrodt on three pitches. "As a three-run rally, it was perfect," Rennie estimated, "but as a winning rally, it fell short."

Lazzeri was now regarded as second only to Ruth in popularity among Yankee fans. It was an ethnocentric era. An Italian-American cabal announced that it would honor him on September 8. His presence on the team was seen as responsible for bringing new fans into the Stadium, bearing wicker baskets of fruit, bottles of wine, and Italian flags. *Time* magazine called him "the craftiest, quickest-thinking player in the major leagues," and, although only the previous year he had played in the first major league game he ever saw, he was held a settling influence on "the jittery Koenig on one side of him and the yet uncertain Gehrig on the other."

On a team that was not without its star-crossed quality, Lazzeri stood out. He was an epileptic. Koenig, who roomed with him for a while, remembers being narrowly missed by a hairbrush that flew from Lazzeri's hand as he stood at the mirror, but in fourteen major league seasons Lazzeri never suffered an attack on the field.

Perhaps the disease contributed to his reputation, even with Meusel aboard, as being "the silent man of the Yankees." Writers remember Lazzeri joining them in the railroad diner with a "hello" as he sat down and nothing more until a "good-bye" when he left. A decade later, when DiMaggio joined the team, the older San Francisco Italian took the younger one under his wing. When they sat together in the hotel lobby, "it was twice as quiet," but it was said that not even DiMaggio would equal Lazzeri's popularity with Italian-Americans.

Only a month after Lazzeri joined the club in 1926 Umpire Timmy Connelly commented, "I shouldn't say this, being an umpire, but that young Eyetalian is a ball player. When things get tough over there, the others don't look to Ruth or any of the other veterans. They look to Lazzeri."

And in 1927 he was seen as "the best second baseman-short-stop-third baseman the Yankees ever had, a fighter as well as a star and a good fellow."

He was, however, like the rest of the Yankees, with the possible exception of Ruth, only human, and they looked it, losing the second game of the Cleveland series, 8–7. It was their first Sunday loss of the year, ending a widespread belief that the hand of Divine Providence was involved in what they were up to. "Hoyt either missed the plate or hit bats, even hitting Lazzeri on the foot with a toss to second," and the Indians piled up seven runs in the first two innings. The Yankees couldn't quite catch up, even with home runs by Ruth and Pipgras.

Ruth's homer came with the bases empty. Untypically, he struck out twice at critical times and contributed a useless throw to third in the midst of an Indian rally. Did he, as rival managers instructed their pitchers, attempting to coax them back from the window ledge, really put on his uniform one leg at a time?

Even a nation that needed gods had seen nothing like the other god in action, Lindbergh. He returned to the country aboard the cruiser *Memphis* and received two freight-car loads of press clippings, 3,500,000 letters in three weeks, many of them marriage proposals. While Chamberlain and Levine landed sixty miles from Berlin, complaining that "bad weather forced them off course" and observing that Lindbergh was "lucky," his unfavorite adjective, 300,000 greeted him in Washington, no more than a warm-up crowd. He had met privately with his mother on board ship; then the President decorated him and commissioned him a colonel and, before he left for New York, Washington crowds lined the streets for twenty-five miles for his parade.

"His laundry disappeared every time he sent it out," Lardner wrote, "and he could not write checks because people kept them instead of cashing them. Of the many sentimental songs which were written about him, the most popular . . . was 'Lucky Lindy.' This was an epithet which Lindbergh hated in each of its parts and *in toto*. He set to work at once to destroy any impression that he was either 'lucky' or 'Lindy.' "

The song, with its certain bounce, fit the taste of the times, however, or lack of it, and so passed into the musical treasury along with such other 1927 hits as "Ain't She Sweet?" "That's My Hap-Hap-Happiness," "The Varsity Drag," "Sunny Disposition," and, to prove the people had a serious, not to say maudlin, side, "When Day Is Done."

Lindbergh's welcome to New York was "the greatest and most frenzied ovation in the nation's history." Four million people lining the streets, eighteen hundred tons of newspapers, ticker tape, and confetti were spilled. It took twenty-five thousand tons of newsprint for the telling of it. Governor Smith and Mayor Walker, just this side of elbowing each other, pinned additional medals on him. All of this, of course, made the receptions for participants in a far more significant adventure, the moon-walkers of the Seventies, seem no more than a weekday crowd in the minors.

There were nay-sayers even then. "Lindbergh is a work of art," argued the *Herald Tribune,* "and like a picture or a poem, he either thrills you or he doesn't."

Calling him "the Glorious Kid," the *World* conceded, ". . . still we gobble up all the papers have to tell . . . still we chuckle delightedly over some new tidbit. Why? The Evening World explains it by saying, 'This is the greatest feat by a single man in the annals of the human race.' And with one emendation, that is probably true. Instead of saying 'greatest,' let us say 'most glorious.' "

Like any editorialist or politician, when rhetoric slows, the writer turned to games, in ascending order of importance, for his analogy: "For in all truth, this flight was not great in the sense that the voyage of Columbus was great; it added little to human knowledge . . . Lindbergh did not do a service, he scored a touchdown; over the most hazardous field ever tried by man, he scooted away to the biggest touchdown of all time. . . .

"When he finally took off, we had a kind of superstition about him; he was Casey, mighty Casey, and we could not conceive how he could possibly strike out. Well, he did not strike out."

Neither, amid bedlam, did the Yankees, who staged a celebration of their own, burying the Indians, 14–6, a score that is deceptive because Pennock pitched a one-hitter for five innings before

*Ruth hitting his sixtieth home run . . . and scoring on it*

*Ruth playing first during practice*

*The Babe and his manager*

*Columbia Lou Gehrig*

*Gehrig showing off*

*Dutch Ruether*

*Robert Shawkey, Yeoman*

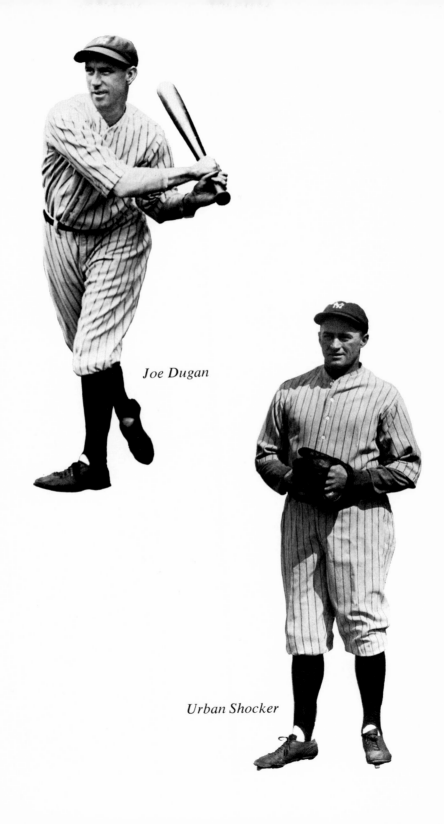

Joe Dugan

Urban Shocker

George Pipgras

Wilcy Moore

*Herb Pennock*

*Waite Hoyt before the opening game of the 1926 World Series*

*Earle Combs*

*Tony Lazzeri*

Mark Koenig

Bob Meusel

*The catchers: Grabowski, Collins, Bengough*

*Ruth signs for Ruppert. Barrow looks on.*

*Miller Huggins*

*Gehrig and Ruth on tour, Fall, 1928*

*First baseman and right fielder on "Lou Gehrig Day," July 4, 1939*

"this best left-hander in the league, wasting sweetness on the desert air with all this hitting going on," eased his grip.

Paschal contributed two home runs. "It sounds silly to say he batted in hard luck, but he did." He also doubled and tripled, and these, too, could have been home runs. At the time, only Bobby Lowe of the Braves and Ed Delehanty of the Philadelphia Nationals had hit four home runs in a game. Dugan and Lazzeri also homered, Collins hit a grand slam, and "Pretty Boy Jacobsen, traded yesterday to the Indians by the Red Sox," said the *Herald Tribune*, "must think the world is full of losers."

The Yankees now were thirty-six and seventeen, a full five games off their 1926 pace, and the *Times* pointed out that a five-game lead at the same stage of the previous season would not have been enough for the pennant "and so the team must do a little faster stepping than last year." The tougher sledding was attributed to stronger competition, a view many retroactively discarded in the rubble of autumn. The team itself was held as better balanced and better reinforced than the 1926 pennant winners, "getting stronger every day," which was not true the previous year and with improved pitching "loosening the shoe where it was rubbing hardest."

But the biggest improvement was the infield. "Gehrig, Lazzeri and Koenig," wrote Grantland Rice, "are still only a trifle more than baseball kids. Two of them have less than two years' experience under the big top. So here is three-quarters of an infield with ten or twelve more years to go, and there is no other combination so valuable to baseball in spite of their brief experience."

President Coolidge arrived in the Black Hills for his vacation; the disillusioned taxpayer of the Seventies notes that the big extra expense for this leader, as frugal with the public purse as with his own, was stocking a trout stream for his pleasure. Even this was done while he looked the other way. He netted seven the first day out. The Browns fished all day in the Stadium and caught nothing, the Yankees winning, 8–1. Ruth, fooled by an inside pitch by Zachary, pushed at the ball. It landed halfway up in the bleachers, "one of his best home runs of the year," his twenty-second. Gehrig, moments later, hit his fifteenth.

The game was delayed twenty-two minutes, waiting for Lindbergh, who did not show. By the time he actually arrived, Ruth was splashing in the shower; the two great national heroes would meet another day. Ruppert filled in, telling Lindbergh, "It's too bad you couldn't have gotten here earlier." Lindbergh, showing that he had been away a long time or was exhausted, or both, asked, "Who won?"

Harry M. Stevens, the definitive concessionaire, rushing through a darkened passageway "with his most popular viand . . . tripped and fell before he reached the gallant youth." By the time he got a new frank, the Colonel had left. A bad day for the Browns, Lindbergh, and Stevens.

Two days later seven miles of St. Louis residents roared a welcome to Lindbergh, and Gehrig saluted the Browns with two home runs and a triple, accounting for six runs, in an 8–4 Yankee victory. It was the Yankees' seventh straight over St. Louis. After the Browns sweated for a two-run lead, Gehrig hit a homer with two on, and the *Times* found Daniel P. Howley, the St. Louis manager, muttering, "This thing is an outrage and must stop, even if we have to get a federal injunction." At that, it may have been a direct quote. Dugan became the first Yankee of the year to be ejected from a game; he protested a call at third.

The Yankees then journeyed to Boston and swept a five-game series, "the Yankees looking like champions and the Red Sox like Red Sox," but the games were instructive, since they offered in microcosm the virtues of good pitching, great hitting, and, when these were absent, luck.

They opened with 7–3 and 7–1 victories in a doubleheader June 21—"Boston agreed it was the longest day and thought it would never end"—Pennock and Hoyt pitching easily, "the southpaw allowed six hits and the northpaw one less." Combs opened the game with a triple. Morehart, Ruth, and Gehrig singled for three runs as "the Boston fans sat back in amazement while Murderer's Row swung into action."

Three more runs scored in the fourth on an error, Lazzeri's single, Dugan's single, a sacrifice, and Combs's second hit. He singled in another run in the sixth.

Gehrig's eighteenth home run in the first inning of the second game started the Yankees on their way after Ruth was walked intentionally, "a quaint form of suicide Boston pitchers still adhere to."

Lazzeri, "honored by the Italian-American community of Boston with a handsome ring before the game," drove in five runs, bringing his league-leading total to seventy-six. Combs added another triple in the second game. Some attributed it to his speed. He demurred.

"You seldom stretch a double into a triple," he observed. "Where speed helps is converting a long single into a double. A triple is a triple. It's a ball that rolls to the fence."

Six in a row, eight games in front, winners in seventeen of their last twenty-one, the team was rolling, and Ruth's two home runs powered a 7–4 victory in the first game of another doubleheader the next day. The second homer, his twenty-fourth, zoomed across a vacant lot, ending up against the wall of a garage, where "six men and two boys fell on it." He was doing all this on a lame leg that interfered with his batting stance.

After the burial Red Ruffing was nibbled to death by ducks. He gave up only three hits and lost, 3–2.

Moore, "the modern Cy Young," relieved Thomas in the fifth inning of the first game, giving up three hits the rest of the way and acquiring his sixth win. He had bailed out Shocker in the opener of the series, and now had appeared in twenty games, or about a third of all the Yankee contests thus far.

Lazzeri had heard himself compared to Columbus and Mussolini at his testimonial dinner the night before. "He didn't discover America," noted the *Times*, "but Columbus never went behind third for an overthrow to cut off the tying run in the ninth inning."

The boys were back in form the next day, if that is not understatement. Gehrig became the second Yankee of the year "about the twentieth player in history" to hit three home runs in a game,

bringing his season's total to twenty-one, three behind Ruth, in an
11–4 victory. The Yankees' fifteen hits were good for twenty-six
bases, but the story now was that "the race between Ruth and
Gehrig is furnishing the greatest slugging competition in the history of baseball."

The ninth straight win, twenty out of the last twenty-four,
fanned the resentment of the Yankees that has been as much a
hallmark of American thought as the conspiracy theory of history. Monitor took note:

"What a damning with faint praise [the Yankees] are getting now
. . . the screams of anguish from the other American League
cities are joined with sneers of disdain from National League
sympathizers.

" 'The Yankees? They OUGHT to win. What have THEY got
to beat? The rest of the American League is terrible.'

"Why can't they beat that bunch of old men in Philadelphia or
those cripples in Washington? The Red Sox aren't good enough for
the Three I League. There isn't a ball club in the four teams from
St. Louis, Chicago, Cleveland, and Detroit.

"Nobody will give Miller Huggins and his sluggers any credit,
although they lead the American League in team hitting, both
leagues in home-run hitting and both leagues in team fielding.
They must have been playing tolerable baseball to do this.

"Among my letters, I find none saying that National League
pitching is poor, although the Pirates have a team batting average
of .324, which is 16 points better than the Yankees."

As conquered as the Red Sox, the Atlantic was about to be
conquered again by another intrepid American, this time Commander Richard E. Byrd and his crew. Newspaper readers of
1927, avid for details, couldn't get enough about aviation. The
*Times,* which was carrying LINDBERGH'S OWN STORY, would soon
carry BYRD'S OWN STORY, exclusively—"people were not disposed to look at themselves and their lives, in general," Lardner
wrote, "and therefore ran gaping and thirsty to look at anything
done by one man or one woman that was special and apart from the

life they knew. The farther the hero went—whether he went upward, downward, sideways, through air, land or water, or hand over hand on a flagpole, the better.'' Less attention was paid to Geneva, although it was reported extensively, where the United States, Britain, and Japan wrestled in a naval conference which did not turn out so well, and neither did the Yankee doubleheader against Philadelphia's ''old men'' when, for one of the few times that season, the team looked like just another ball club, failing in the clutch, wasting good pitching in one game, and fielding sloppily. The scores were 7–6 and 4–2, with Pate striking out Gehrig in the ninth inning of the first game with the tying and winning runs on base.

Gazella, who replaced Koenig in the third inning when Koenig's leg proved too painful for him to continue, muffed an easy fly in the ninth inning of the first game, and the Athletics piled up four runs, just enough to offset a Yankee rally. His injury is recalled by Koenig as a great bruise from a pitched ball. Doc Woods, the Yankee trainer, attempted, in the rough fashion of the day, to smooth the thing away with a rolling pin.

Sixty-one thousand, the highest attendance of the season for a doubleheader, saw the Yankees lose their third in a row in the first game the following day, 4–2, John Picus Quinn, forty-four, and a quarter of a century in baseball, outpitched Thomas and Giard, Gehrig striking out ''three times in peculiar, sickly fashion,'' with the benched Ruth ''rooting for him.'' Ruth was expected to miss three or four games now, ''and the sad part is that he was just getting a half-nelson on his 1921 record.''

Mack, hardly believing his luck, started Sammy Grey in the second game. Combs immediately walked, Morehart singled, both advancing on Bishop's wild throw. Durst singled, scoring Combs, Bishop bobbled Gehrig's grounder, Morehart scoring. Meusel doubled, scoring Durst, and Gehrig and Meusel came in on flies by Lazzeri and Dugan. The five-run lead was more than enough, but what with one thing and another, the final score was 7–3. Gehrig's twenty-second home run moved him within three of Ruth, ''but the carping critics pointed out a single in the first game would have been worth several homers in the second when the Yankees were rich in runs." Moore went all the way in one of his increasingly frequent appearances as a starter.

Combs hit his first home run of the season the next day, "a short poke landing in the right field laps," and Lazzeri contributed another in a 6–2 triumph for Dutch Ruether, winning his seventh and just missing his fourth shutout. Pennock was called on in the ninth to set down a mild A's rally as "the Yankees won in a walk after two days of stress."

There was plenty of stress in the ninth inning of the series' last game. Lamar singled. Simmons tripled. Cochrane, Dykes, and Foxx singled, and Urban Shocker, who had given up only four hits in eight innings, was replaced by Moore. Boley, "not a very good hitter," singled. Cobb, "a good hitter," singled. Pennock came in to face the left-handed Bishop, whose long fly scored another run.

Perkins walked and stole second. Morehart threw wildly on Lamar's grounder, allowing two more runs, and Simmons, the A's big man, was at bat. Huggins, it was reported, "broke the breath-holding record." Simmons flied to Combs. Cochrane, no little man himself with a stick in his hand, grounded to Morehart, "who was more careful where he threw the ball."

Eight Athletic runs. The problem was that the Yankees previously had scored nine off Walberg, Russell Johnson, Rommel, and Pate. "For eight innings yesterday, the Yankees looked like one million dollars, cash on the nail," commented Monitor. "For one inning, they looked like a not very convincing counterfeit dime. . . . The part of the 15,000 fans who walked away with the Yankees leading by 9–0 missed all the ball game."

It had been a scary series at the beginning, but the *World* observed comfortably, "If the Quakers of Philadelphia cannot overhaul the Yankees any faster . . . then the great Quakertown threat is likely to vanish in the air. Collins, Cobb and Co. started by winning three in a row, but they lost the fourth, and they lost the fifth, and the nine-game lead of the Hugmen seems hardly dented."

Before the game, fans from his hometown of Schenectady gave Grabowski fifteen hundred dollars. With the likes of Cochrane,

McCurdy, and Ruel around, with Schalk remembered and Bill Dickey waiting in the wings, it was not bloody likely anyone talked of Yankee catching in terms of the greatest of all. But it was proving more than just serviceable, which was all that was hoped for in the spring. On that other nine-man institution in American life, nine great justices never serve simultaneously, a simple majority is regarded as historic. Huggins had reason for pleasure at the way the catching was working out.

"Grabowski," it was observed, "has been a lifesaver to this team, what with Benny Bengough's arm not being so good and Pat Collins continuing to harbor the delusion he can't throw to second. John is cool. He handles his pitchers well. He has a good arm and an accurate throw. He can hit. He is fast of foot for a catcher. And he gets those foul balls. 'And that,' says Huggins, 'is what I did not think he could do.' The Yankees got something valuable when they got him."

But there was more than the pennant race to stir the blood. One of the nine Yankee runs against the As came on Gehrig's homer, which put him only one behind Ruth. Ruth bandaged his knee heavily to get into action against the Red Sox, for whom he felt sorry enough to have written, "It seems to me that if the baseball owners were wise"—surely careless writing by Ruth, of all people; perhaps he had a pressing engagement and was too busy to read the copy—"they would get together and try to build up some of the weaker teams like the Red Sox," which did not prevent him from igniting two rallies with three singles and a double.

The Yankees won, 8–2, as Boston dropped its eleventh in a row. Pipgras "pitched one of the prettiest games of the year," allowing only three hits, besides getting a triple.

But the interest was in Gehrig's twenty-fourth home run. It tied him with Ruth. Psychologically, it more than offset the Babe's absence from a couple of games.

"If I am to break my 1921 record," Ruth's column in the *World* began one day at this time, "I believe I will do it this year. I'm getting a bit older now. I figure I have about five or six more years, and then I will have to step aside and retire. Unless I can break my record this year, I believe there are only two men in baseball who have a chance to do it. One of them is Lou Gehrig and the other is Tony Lazzeri.

"So far as this year is concerned, there is just one thing that makes me think I can better the 59 mark. And that's Lou Gehrig. Having him follow me in the batting order has helped me a lot this year. For most pitchers realize that putting Ruth on to get a Gehrig is the bunk. It's just putting one more run on the path for Lou to drive in. . . ."

The Great American Home Run Derby, the likes of which baseball had never seen, would move into high now, would occupy the major part of baseball's attention, and would give the game something different from what it had ever known.

# Five

○

Joe Dugan likes a story.

The step has slowed at seventy-six, and the sandy hair is thinning over a pinkish crown above a friendly, quizzical face, but the blue eyes are keen as an eagle's and considerably merrier.

He is an elbow-in-the-ribs-at-the-punchline man—"I wouldn't walk away," he says of yesterday's girls and parties—a profferer of the rhetorical handshake. At lunch over Early Times and water with a tuna salad in the dining room of Boston's Copley Plaza Hotel, he looks as at home as the scrod; the impression is only mildly deceptive, since he grew up in New Haven, another Ivy League town.

Friends, young men, older men, interrupt lunch, ask him to join them later for a drink. The money the Red Sox paid him over the years as a goodwill ambassador clearly was not wasted. Tom Yawkey, the expansive Red Sox owner, sometimes invested heavily in infielders who couldn't go to the left and weren't too sure about the right, either, but he got full value in his storyteller, although sometimes Dugan, as Huckleberry Finn said of Mark Twain, commits a stretcher.

"My father, my mother, my seven brothers and two sisters and myself, a high school junior, were sitting down to supper in New Haven when the doorbell rang. My mother answered the door and said, 'It's for you, Joseph.' I got up from the table and almost fainted. It was Connie Mack. He said he wanted to sit down with my mother, my father and me for a few minutes.

" 'Mr. Dugan,' he said, 'I hear your son is quite a ball player.' My old man replied, 'I hear tell he is pretty good.'

" 'Well,' said Connie, 'I have a train to catch to Philadelphia, and I'll make it brief.' He reached into his pocket and put five hundred-dollar bills on the table in front of my father, a poor workingman who had never seen a sawbuck in his life.

" 'I want you to promise me that when Joseph comes of age and decides to go into organized baseball, you'll let him come to the Philadelphia Athletics.

"My father looked at the money, then glanced at my seven brothers and two sisters. He couldn't contain himself. He said, 'For five hundred dollars you can take the whole family.' "

Mack settled for young Joseph Anthony, who, it was agreed, would attend college before playing ball. After he finished high school, he tried Holy Cross, but "the money and the big league contract burned a hole in my pocket," dreams of hotels and travel were too strong, and he quit to join the Athletics. But "I never liked Philadelphia. I couldn't get used to the town, and I tried mighty hard because I wanted to play ball, and I was very fond of Connie Mack, but I could stand it just for so long and then I would have to move, whether it was time to move or not. Finally, Mack greeted my return one day by saying, 'I am going to try to figure out how to get along without you next season. Somehow I don't think it's going to be very difficult," and Dugan passed through the Red Sox pipeline before joining the Yankees.

The five-hundred-dollar bonus is as much a relic of an earlier age, of course, as the Model T. It is enough to mist the eyes of the treasurer for the sorriest expansion team of the Seventies to look at the salaries paid the greatest of all: Meusel, $13,000; Combs, $10,500, a $1,500 raise from 1926; Lazzeri, $8,000, a $3,000 raise; Koenig, $7,000, also a $3,000 raise; Bengough, $8,000;

Collins, $6,000; and Grabowski, $5,500—the entire three-man catching staff for $19,500, and—but surely no treasurer dreaming his sweetest, wickedest dreams would believe this—Lou Gehrig, $8,000, a $1,500 raise.

These were not depression dollars, either. The Coolidge prosperity roared along like the Yankees. The newspapers of July 1, 1927, reported a $630,000,000 treasury surplus, with a reduction in the national debt of one billion dollars, an accepted national concern, although by the Seventies it would be as forgotten as Marie of Romania.

"Between 1922 and 1927," wrote Frederick Lewis Allen in his classic, *Only Yesterday,* "the purchasing power of American wages increased at the rate of more than two per cent annually. And during the three years between 1924 and 1927 alone, there was a leap from 75 to 283 in the number of Americans who paid taxes on an income of more than a million dollars a year."

This is the sort of stuff called "an economic miracle," although it was powered by reasons, good and bad, which appear mundane enough. The war had left Europe impoverished and the United States richer than ever before, with apparently boundless economic resources. Advertising, now a billion dollar enterprise, and salesmanship were next to Holy Writ. The businessman was taken seriously; worse, he was regarded as seer. "The business of America is business," said the man in the White House. Stood on its head, held against the light, the sentence is a banality, but American philosophy seldom touches the first rank, and the Coolidge dictum seemed social gospel. All of this was spurred by a newly discovered, fervent belief in installment buying.

Where it all would end knew God, but in 1927 the end was two years away, and now there were more than 23,000,000 passenger cars on the road, up from 6,700,000 in one decade. The landmark study, *Middletown,* discovered that of twenty-six working-class, car-owning families, twenty-one had no bathtub. Sales of radios, the other new toy of the twenties, jumped from $60,000,000 to $425,000,000 between 1922 and 1927.

"For every $100 worth of business done in 1919," wrote Allen, "by 1927, the five-and-ten-cent chains were doing $260 worth, the cigar chains $153 worth, the drug chains $224 worth and the grocery chains $387 worth."

This made it tough on the small shopkeeper, and "the index number of all farm prices, which had coasted from $205 in 1920 to $116 in 1921—"perhaps the most terrible toboggan slide in all history," to quote Stuart Chase—regained only a fraction of the ground it had lost; in 1927, it stood at $131. Loudly the poor farmer complained, desperately they and their Norrises and Brookharts and Shipsteads and LaFollettes campaigned for federal aid, and by the hundreds of thousands they left the farms for the cities," but "the prosperity bandwagon did not lack for occupants, and their good fortune outweighed and outshouted the illfortune of those who lamented by the roadside."

Dugan certainly did not lament. He is a yea-sayer by nature, and his contract in 1927 called for him to be paid twelve thousand a year, the sort of figure which labeled him "the high-priced third baseman," and enough so that he lived in Scarsdale, one of the faintly snobbish New York suburban addresses. "Of course" he lived in Scarsdale, he says now. "I was a Yankee."

As the team rounded into July, "so far ahead, a rival manager says they should be made to play in a league by themselves," Dugan was batting only .218, more than sixty points below his then lifetime average of .281, in fifty-three games. He had ripped the cartilage in his right knee sliding in the Polo Grounds years earlier, and, although he had undergone surgery, the leg still gave him occasional trouble, and this year he had been in and out of the lineup.

But the *Herald Tribune* said, "He is still the Yankees' best third baseman, with his experience and his baseball head," and he himself once observed, "Fellows like Ruth and Gehrig can ruin an ordinary ballplayer. They win so many games by their individual efforts that you wonder why you are in the lineup."

Gehrig was leading the league with a .388 average, followed by Meusel at .385—followed by three Athletics, Dykes, .381; Simmons, .379; and Cobb, .369, proving that it takes more than hitting to win and that Mack had been overly optimistic about his pitching—nice, round figures, but, in 1927, not regarded as particularly stratospheric. More than fifty American League batters were above .300.

After forty-three hours in the air, much of it lost in a dense fog, Byrd and his crew dropped in the water 120 miles from Paris, the object of a search by more than fifty planes before they were rescued; on the Pacific front, Army fliers reached Hawaii in twenty-six hours, and 100,000 lined the banks of the Hudson River in New York City to see Columbia University win a four-mile crew race, all of these spectacles demanding so much attention that it left only 3,000 persons free to leave their radios and come to the Stadium, "2,999 of them coming out for the Great American Home Run Derby."

Gehrig hit a home run in the first inning, his twenty-fifth, going one up on Ruth, who was on base at time, along with Combs, who had opened the game with one of his triples. Ruth "trotted home ahead of Gehrig, looking slightly dejected as for the first time in many years someone had the effrontery to challenge his right to the throne." The "many years" were really two, since Meusel won the championship, but Ruth, of course, had every reason to want to forget 1925.

The Red Sox went ahead with six runs in the third inning off Myles Thomas, "who can finish all ball games except his own," but that was only enough for a one-run lead, and Gehrig tied it up in the bottom of the inning. He singled, stole second—he stole ten bases on the year, three more than Ruth—and scored on Lazzeri's hit.

Morehart singled with one out in the fourth inning and Ruth ended Gehrig's brief reign, for a time, by smacking his twenty-fifth home run. This opened the gates for an ultimate 13–6 Yankee victory, the home runs brightening "an otherwise uninteresting game [played] in an air of quiet," said the *Herald Tribune*. "No one was greatly concerned about the outcome. All they wanted to see was the home run twins in action."

It was the Yankees' fifth straight win and the twelfth straight Red Sox loss. "There are only two good players on the Red Sox," said a fan in a gag of the time. "You're seeing double," answered his friend.

Combs, who hit only six home runs all season, hit his second of the week the next day. Dugan drove in Meusel, who had tripled, and later scored after doubling, showing signs of coming out of his slump. Shawkey pitched strongly in relief of Pennock, who was not the same man after being felled by a drive off the bat of Billy Rogell in the third inning. It caught him in the stomach, dropping him "curled like a pretzel," and it was five minutes before he could resume, although shakily, but the Yankees won, 7–4.

But "the scores of these games are of little interest," the *Herald Tribune* emphasized again, "since Gehrig took to matching home runs with Ruth," and he hit his twenty-sixth, his fourth in four games. Ruth contributed a couple of timely singles, but, of course, that was not the same thing.

"I do not wish to borrow trouble for my good friend, Col. Jacob Ruppert in this serene July weather," McGeehan wrote with the deadest of pans, "while the Yankees are so far in front and while the customers are hammering the gates of the Yankee Stadium to see the neck-and-neck race between Babe Ruth and Lou Gehrig.

"But Mr. Gehrig, once a student at Columbia, is said to be of a thoughtful disposition. . . . The fact that Babe Ruth is being paid $70,000 yearly will furnish considerable nutriment of thought to Mr. Gehrig. Mr. Gehrig might pass the Babe in the matter of home runs. Then, at the end of the season, such a contingency might cause Mr. Gehrig to ask for a considerable raise.

"In baseball, athletes think along these lines when you see them sitting in the corridors of hotels. . . . I do not wish to erase the beatific smile that is on the face of Col. Jacob Ruppert . . . but all of the joys of the baseball magnate must be tempered with a little sorrow and that sorrow is usually of a financial nature."

The Yankees closed out the series the next day with a 3–2 victory, Ruether's fourth of the year over the Red Sox. Carrigan, the beleaguered Red Sox manager who had gone "from the sublime to the ridiculous with the club," from his 1918 world champions to the present group, offered a philosophy interesting, perhaps even fatalistic, in the light of shifts later designed by schemers to cut the productivity of Ted Williams and other great pull hitters. He did not move his outfielders a step when either Ruth or Gehrig batted. "If either of them hits a ball into right field," he instructed his troops, "you birds needn't worry. The bleachers will catch it."

"The Yankees had a lot of fun with the Red Sox," was the *Herald Tribune* epitaph for the series, "but today they will be in Washington, playing the Senators, who are not so funny." Not so funny, indeed. The Senators had won nine in a row, including two consecutive doubleheader sweeps of the Athletics, and, although they trailed by ten games, they were talking about the possibility of a second-half rush to a pennant.

Harrison, in the *Times,* wrote one of those cautious columns, on the one hand, on the other, which, along with tall gins and tonic, carry the sportswriter through the long, hot summer. He wondered how the Yankees could stay so far ahead "with just fair catching and pitching that does not compare with that of the great teams of the past."

He found the answer in the hitting, "which carried Dempsey and Tilden to the top and does the same for the Yankees. One home run can cover a multitude of weaknesses. . . . They are way ahead of other great teams in one department: the combination of Ruth and Gehrig has never been equalled in batting power, long distance and general skill. Add to this the bats of Lazzeri, Meusel, Combs and Collins and you have the explanation of their long string of victories."

And the questionable pitching, he conceded in a quick shift to the other hand, "came to the rescue when the Yankees aren't hitting," observing, somewhat mysteriously, that the team "has been in one prolonged slump this year."

Then he made a point which, to the old Yankees and those who saw them, cannot be overemphasized. "The Yankees are the least-

managed team in the league. The players are on their own up to a
certain limit. . . . All that Huggins asks is that they are ready to
give their best.

"On a team of ready-made stars, pampered and highly temperamental, this had doubtful success several years ago, but on a team
that he has built up himself, it works. The Yankees have their
weaknesses, but one of them is not harmony and good spirits."

"You must understand," Waite Hoyt said in conversation,
"that Huggins developed as a manager in the same way that ball
players develop as ball players. He handled each player differently, and by 1927 one of the things that inadvertently meshed
was the personalities of the fellows playing on that club. We all got
along. We had inordinate pride in ourselves as a unit. We believed
in ourselves as a unit."

The cautionary notes of the newspapers seemed justified the
next day at Washington, against an ambience reflecting the free
and joyous spirit of the times. Thirty thousand saw Ruth tie Gehrig
with a first-inning home run off the stylish Lisenbee. Goslin
tied it with a home run in the bottom half of the inning.

The Yankees went back into the lead in the third, when Shocker
singled, moved to third on Combs's double although he twisted his
ankle looking "like a slow-motion movie of an ice-berg as he
rounded the base," and managed to score on Morehart's fly.
Meusel then drove in Combs.

But because of the ankle injury, Shocker had to go out of the
game in the next inning with the tying run on first. Thomas
allowed it to score. Speaker opened Washington's fifth with a double and Goslin walked. Judge then doubled down the first base
line, scoring both runners, but Goslin had to return to third because
"the ball hit a pop salesman in fair territory. The merchant tried to
get out of the way in terror, but the ball hit him amidships. The
umpires rounded up all the pop salesmen and shooed them back
into the stands."

A few moments later, that benevolent drunk who is so much a
part of the American sporting scene wandered into the outfield and
opened the center-field gate. He sat down on the grass, waving and

smiling. When Ruth told him to clear out, the drunk stood up, turned his back on the idol of the nation and pawed the ground, going hee-haw. The police led him away.

Muddy Ruel promptly singled two runs home, putting Washington again into the lead, and this time they held it, ending the Yankee's seven-game winning streak, 6-5.

The next day, ah, the next day. Sometimes life works out, and events seem to come together in perfect commentary on a time. Out in Dakota, the President "won the West's heart, celebrat[ing] holiday and his 55th birthday in full riding regalia," a famous moment of his administration, widely photographed, the introverted little New Englander in Stetson and chaps, the least-looking cowpoke, but demonstrating that odd camaradarie between politician and electorate that would, by the Seventies, seem only memory. "Cal's our pal" was the refrain, although he drew the line at mounting a gift horse. Even our allies seemed friendly. PARIS LINKS HONORS [to Byrd and his crew] AND AMERICA, it was reported, IN ENTHUSIASTIC TRIBUTE AT FOURTH OF JULY RITES.

The numbskulls are always with us, and the Twenties were the heyday of the Ku Klux Klan, five thousand of those strangers to the dignity, decency, and possibilities of life celebrating at a meeting in Queens, New York, but this was balanced by a deed so heroic as to seem the invention of Hemingway in his dotage. A lone Coast Guard ensign boarded "a $5,000 rum craft" as she tried to slip up New York bay, knocking a crewman senseless, seizing the helm, running the ship on a reef, forcing the captain and crew of twenty-two below deck—SUBDUES CREW OF 22 SINGLE-HANDED—and holding them until help arrived.

And to further mark this most grand and glorious of Fourths, when for one of those rare moments in any nation's history, the pursuit of happiness seems won, "the world record for customers at a baseball game was broken at the Yankee Stadium," the crowd getting a spectacle worthy of the day, the date, and the record.

Seventy-two thousand, six hundred and forty-one paid, with an additional fifteen hundred employees and others in on passes. They packed themselves four and five deep in the aisles, standing on tiptoe "in the most uncomfortable positions." Thousands waited outside the gate until the last square foot of standing room was sold.

What they saw was summarized by the sentence closing a newspaper account of the games: "Let us draw a curtain over the bloody scene."

Gehrig passed Ruth with two home runs, his twenty-seventh in the first game, his twenty-eighth in the second. Pat Collins also homered in the first game, Lazzeri and Wera in the second. The Yankees accumulated the credible, but barely, total of sixty-nine bases for the day, not against the 1961 Mets or any other expansion team, but against contenders coming off a ten-game winning streak and thinking championship.

"Never have pennant challengers been so completely shot to pieces as the Senators," the *World* observed. It was Louis and Schmeling, the six-day war, the University of Michigan beating Southern California, 48–0, in the Rose Bowl, Secretariat winning the 1973 Belmont Stakes by thirty lengths. The scores were 12–1 and 21–1.

It was such carnage that fine pitching performances by Pipgras and Moore were all but ignored. Every Yankee hit. "The high and the low, from Walter Johnson to the youngest rookie of the Senators, Bob Burke, felt the flail of Huggins' threshers." The Yankees collected eighteen hits for thirty bases in the first game, nineteen for thirty-nine in the second.

The Senators didn't get Gehrig out until his final appearance of the day, and Ruth quit in the sixth inning of the second game when he was purposely walked for the second time in that inning when twelve Yankees came to bat and collected nine runs.

Johnson for a time pitched the kind of ball for which he is remembered, striking out Ruth and Gehrig in the sixth inning of the first game and Collins and Lazzeri in the second. But Combs opened the eighth with another of his triples, Morehart doubled, Ruth singled, and Gehrig hit his first home run of the day.

"There hasn't been such hitting this year or any year," commented the *World*. "It was record hitting for a record crowd." Joe

Judge, emerging from a shattered dressing room, might have said it all about the 1927 Yankees:

"They don't just beat you. They break your heart."

As developments hinted, the sentiment was more than bathos. Heartless but game, the Senators came back the next day with five runs in the first inning, then saw the Yankees creep back until Gehrig tripled and "one of the longest sacrifice flies ever manufactured" hit by Meusel tied the score at 6–all in the seventh inning.

By this time, Shawkey contributing another strong relief appearance and Lisenbee doing the same, the ending of the game must have seemed ordained, only the matter in which it would occur a matter of doubt. What happened was that, with two men out in the ninth inning, Lazzeri looked at a couple of bad pitches, swung like a top missing the third and then hit the ball out of the park, after which he was mobbed at the plate by Dugan, Collins, "and a dozen cash customers," and acclaimed in the headlines as a "diamond Mussolini," a sawdust Caesar some considered worthy of emulation, who even then was "calling on Fascists to obey his book of faith and accept the commands of history."

The Senators had picked up their early lead off Hoyt, who tried to pitch in spite of a persistent kink in his elbow, and Shawkey's reappearance in a form resembling that which won 198 games for the Yankees over nine years seems to be another attribute of the great team, which is that small things work out.

His career with the Yankees was marked by the unexpected development, which was irony itself, since he was an unspectacular personality, a good competitor but given to pronouncements of the "I like to smile. It helps a lot in life" variety. A product of Homestead, Pennsylvania, whose boyhood dream was to be a locomotive engineer, his favorite, and lifelong, hobby was hunting. Baseball was only a pastime until the manager of the Harrisburg team in the Tri-State League saw his fastball and signed him up in 1911.

Two years later Shawkey was with the Athletics and two years after that, Mack sent him to the Yankees, although he had won a World Series game for Philadelphia. He had been a first-rank pitcher, his trademark a red flannel shirt which he believed distracted the batter just enough, but Huggins had not relied on him this season, so that his coming through when Hoyt's arm hurt, Pennock still seemed shaky and Shocker's ankle was injured seemed one of those little breaks without which greatness flickers.

But any cloud was no larger than a man's hand for a team that took off for a western trip leading by 12½ games after a stretch in which it won 30 of 38.

As timeless as any other aspect of baseball are its controversies. The use of the spitter, the length of the game, the liveliness of the ball are debated as solemnly in the Seventies as in the Twenties and represent a front on which no progress has been made. In the intervening decades man has split the atom, controlled polio, and walked the moon, but he can't, or won't, do a thing about baseball's eternal arguments.

The savaging of the Senators and such improbable occurrences as Pipgras and Wera hitting home runs led to renewed charges that the ball was being doctored. Gallico took a jaundiced view:

"The jackrabbit ball is with us again. For the benefit of the uninformed, the jackrabbit is a baseball that the other side is slugging something scandalous. This felony is discovered annually by some ball club that has just been given a frightful shellacking.

"All was quiet on the Potomac this year until the New York Yankees pasted the Washington Senators, 12–1 and 21–1, when it was discovered that someone had sneaked the lively ball into the yard and that the fast-bounding pellet was once again considered a menace to the health of the infielders and the averages of the pitchers.

"To date there have been no explanations offered why it was when the Yankees hit the ball it turned into a jackrabbit, while every time the Senators touched it up it proved to be nothing but the good old-fashioned beanbag. . . . One would not like to suspect the Yankees of playing with their own baseballs and substituting nickel rockets . . . when the other side comes to hit.

"Nevertheless, while the Yankees were amassing 33 runs, the Washington club collected only two. What jackrabbiting there was was very one-sided."

In view of the meager home-run total of the era the charge of the jackrabbit ball seems inventive, but the lines already had been drawn, the fan on one side pointing to the statistics and the evidence of his eyes, the club owner on the other saying, like a President of the United States, "Trust me."

Lieb had taken notice of the alleged phenomenon two years earlier in an essay whose title is as fresh as tomorrow, SECRET OF THE "RABBIT BALL" EXPOSED. Noting the climb in major-league home runs from 1917, when there were 335, to 1925, when there were 741, and paying tribute to the influence of Ruth, he said, "Fans became nauseated with this continued home run diet. Where six years ago, they cried for more hitting and greater action, now they are frankly tired of the slugging orgy. They have asked for a less lively ball, or that the restrictions be taken away from the pitcher."

In the tradition of the great investigative reporter, which a few years earlier revealed Teapot Dome as decades later it wound up in Watergate, Lieb used his head, his legs, and his natural suspicion. He "went down into the players' dugout and asked for a ball out of the game . . . If we procured our 1925 ball from the league or the manufacturer, we might have been handed a show-case baseball."

With "the aid of a circular saw" he sliced in half a 1912 ball and the 1925 ball. "And lo and behold, so far as the eye could detect, there was not the slightest difference between them. . . .

"But there was a difference after all. The 'spring' in the jackrabbit results from the greater spring of the grade of yarn in the present ball." The 1912 ball could be placed together again "in an almost perfect sphere. The yarn stayed as it was cut, and the two parts fitted together. Not so with the present day ball. As soon as it was cut, the released yarn began to 'spring.' "

As a clincher Lieb pointed to the war years, when home-run hitting fell off, due, he said, to the fact that only inferior yarn was available. With the war's end and the availability of "the finest

New Zealand wool" home runs came in clusters. This seemed to him a happenstance, and he absolved the club owner and manufacturer of any complicity in turning out a livelier ball.

The matter, of course, does not end there. When the next Lieb will appear to discover what in the baseball turns asthmatic second basemen into Paul Bunyan awaits historic development. But there is little doubt the ball has improved faster than moral standards in government.

Hoyt, who kept in touch with the sport during nearly a quarter of a century broadcasting Cincinnati Reds' games, says today, "I think it was livelier [in 1927] than the ball of 1921 or '22 by a long shot, but I don't think it was as lively as they made it later or in this era.

"When I was broadcasting, I didn't judge by how far the batter hit the ball alone. I judged from the fact that a fellow would try to bunt the ball, and the ball would wind up in the second deck. I'm not fooling about this. They would try to bunt and the ball would wind up in the screening, or a batter would foul a ball, and it would hit on the concrete and bounce up into the second deck."

None of their contemporaries hit with the power of the Yankees, of course, and it seems likely they would have outslugged the competition if the opposing pitcher had used rocks. Now, as they headed off for exhibition games in Buffalo and Toronto to open their western swing, there was enacted in New York a sad and sordid little chapter of baseball history.

It sounds like the sort of thing engraved on the back of a watch presented to an employee who has worked too hard for his inferiors and is being retired on an inadequate pension, but no man contributed more to baseball in the early decades of the century than Ban Johnson. Simply by midwifing the American League into existence, he assured the rivalry which is the basis of the game.

But he and Landis, a former federal judge, were on collision course from the beginning. When the baseball owners moved to name a commissioner after the Black Sox scandal, there is evidence that Johnson believed he should have been the choice. He also was irritated by the fact that the new czar came from outside baseball, with no more than a fan's connection with the sport.

What the owners wanted, of course, was a man with a reputation for independence and integrity. The fact that they got one may have darkened their days later on, but that is one of life's little jokes. Presidents of the United States have been known to appoint prosecutors on the basis of a reputation for independence and then balk when it is demonstrated, and the same sort of thing undoubt-edly went on in ancient Greece.

Landis not only qualified as being his own man but possessed what is called ''marquee value,'' being a favorite of Chicago journalists and owning a somewhat overblown reputation for Solomon-like decisions which impressed the public if not his superiors on the bench.

Including the decision that made his household name, his 1907 fining of the Standard Oil Company of New Jersey $29,240,000 for accepting freight rebates. ''It landed him on the front pages for days and formed a background for everything he was to do or say,'' wrote the historian Henry Pringle in a forgotten study called *Big Frogs*.

Unhappily, the oil company turned loose its squadron of law-yers, and ''the higher courts found that [Landis] had made a number of reversible errors, and Standard Oil never paid a nickel for its sins. . . .

''The courts were destined, from that time on, to reverse him with startling frequency, so much so that he once struck back at the Circuit Court of Appeals for the Northern District of Illinois by calling it 'the Department of Chemistry and Microscopy.' But those unhappy days are over. As Czar of Baseball at $65,000 a year, his word is final.''

It was not that cut and dried, but the son of Dr. Abraham Landis, assistant surgeon of the Thirty-fifth Ohio Volunteer Infantry, who lost a leg at the battle of Kenesaw Mountain, Georgia, January 27, 1864, ''the one blunder in the drive of General Sherman from Chattanooga to Atlanta'' and named his sixth-born in commemoration of the event, now possessed "a face almost as familiar to the public as that of Charlie Chaplin. Its angular contours, topped by a shock of hair as white as the locks of David Belasco are seldom absent for long from the rotogravure sections of the tabloids. . . .

"During his years of judgeship in Chicago, Landis became a symbol to the general public for all that is good and noble, honest and wise. It did not matter that his decisions were so often reversed; somehow the reversals were seldom given prominence in the newspapers," wrote Pringle.

Neither did it matter, given the temper of the times, that he was ferocity itself toward opponents of World War I brought to his court on sedition charges. "Few men have been as zealous in the suppression of minorities, and his charges to the jury were dangerously similar to patriotic addresses," against a background of a Liberty Loan brass band blaring unceasingly under the rotunda of the Post Office building where Landis' office was located.

After handing down maximum possible sentences to four members of the American Socialist Party, he told the American Legion, "It was my great disappointment to give [them] only 20 years in Leavenworth. I believe the law should have enabled me to have had [them] lined up against the wall and shot."

Higher courts liberated the Socialists. Landis' vindictiveness seems to have stemmed at least in part from his concern for his only, cherished son, who was an army flier. Landis was "a kindly man, except when torn by patriotism," although he also was an ardent prohibitionist and handed out maximum possible sentences to bootleggers.

He was famed, too, for his profanity, once warning his wife on an icy Chicago street, "Look out, darling! You'll break your goddamned neck." All of this made good copy. So when he was appointed baseball commissioner, released from the $7,500-a-year judgeship which had presented him with persistent financial worries, he staged "a sentimental orgy for the newspapermen who suspected he was nine-tenths hokum.

" 'Oh, hell, what can I say to you fellows,' he asked them.

'These people come in and say I'm a great man, and I know you fellows made me. You printed stuff about me, and that's the reason I've got this job now. I don't kid myself.' "

But he did. There had been the day he passed sentence on a young man who stole a parcel post package and appeared in court with his wife, who held a babe in arms.

"Judge Landis leaned half over the bench and rested his white head on his hands in meditation. Profound silence held the courtroom, broken only by the ticking of the clock on the wall, an ancient timepiece brought from the judge's boyhood home . . . a typical Landis opportunity. Some minutes passed. Then the judge straightened up and stuck out his jaw.

" 'Son! You go on back home. Take your little wife and your baby and go home! In one month, come back and tell me how you're getting along. I'll not have that child the child of a convict!'

". . . An excellent actor of the old school, Judge Landis had one advantage over all other actors," noted Pringle. "Every performance was for him a first night. The critics were always in their seats at the press table. Greatest blessing of all, delicious dream of the dramatic performer, they were always friendly critics, for otherwise, they faced jail for contempt of court."

"His career," Heywood Broun wrote, "typifies the heights to which dramatic talent can carry a man in America, if only he has the foresight not to go on the stage."

But Johnson was publicly critical of Landis from the beginning, arguing he moved too slowly on the Black Sox. It was Johnson who brought the Speaker-Cobb matter to light, and it was Johnson who said neither of them would ever again play in the American League. After that he was sent on vacation for the customary reasons of health, and the magnates believed they were rid of him. But he had turned up back at his office, announcing he felt fine.

Now, this July, the owners called a league meeting in New York on pretext of amending the constitution. And there "in a darkened room on the seventh floor of the Hotel Belmont," alone, except for his secretary, Johnson wrote out his resignation, effective "November 1, or earlier," and passed it out through a half-opened door to a representative of the owners, who chose this way to part, after his thirty-four years of service to the game.

"What a pity [Landis and Johnson] couldn't have worked in better harmony," wrote J. G. Taylor Spink, publisher of *The Sporting News* and a friend of both men. "But dear old Ban; it was so difficult for him to play second fiddle."

The openness and charm of the game, it was seen again, are confined to the field.

Huggins, as the Yankees moved west, allowed that if they could finish even on the road trip, it would be permissible to talk pennant without violating nature's sacred laws, and the club split its first doubleheader in Detroit, losing, 11–8, and winning, 10–8, "to the joy of 25,000 automobile owners" for whom a tie with the Yankees was considerably more exciting than kissing a sister.

Ruth capped a five-run rally in the second game when, with Combs and Morehart on base, he hit his twenty-seventh home run, a drive inside the park so that, again destroying the stately image of legend, "he had to run for it, but he finished standing up." Of equal interest was the fact that Moore got two hits. It was recalled that in spring training Ruth studied the Moore batting form and bet him three hundred dollars to fifteen that he would not get three hits on the year. Now he had picked up two of them in one game, although as Richards Vidmer noted in the *Times,* "He must have been struck with the notion that no good pitcher should pitch that well because he quit being a good pitcher," and Pennock had to come in to preserve the victory.

The soap manufacturers of America chose the date to announce "take a bath week," claiming that "millions don't read the newspapers" so that movies, radio, and women's clubs would be called on to carry the message that it was all right to bathe in winter. A little soap undoubtedly would have helped the overflow crowd of thirty thousand that watched six hours and thirty-nine minutes of baseball the following day, the teams again splitting a doubleheader, New York winning, 19–7, before losing, 14–4.

The second game was called at the end of seven innings because of darkness, but probably also because Huggins ran out of pitchers, "using all nine of them during the past 48 hours, three of them twice." Shocker, bad ankle and all, tried to pitch the second game but left after three innings, replaced by Giard, who was replaced by Hoyt in the sixth, all to no avail. Another Lazzeri home run was wasted.

But Ruth hit two home runs to regain the lead from Gehrig, "and what matter anything as long as the king is back on the throne," a rhetorical question that washed only with twelve-game leads. His hold on people was demonstrated with an assist from the greed of the Detroit management.

"Overflow crowds seem to be handled with less skill and foresight in Detroit than in any other big league center," observed the *Herald Tribune.* "It has a disarming, free and easy touch, something after the matter of a country picnic. Patrons strolled around . . . cops squatted contentedly on the grass." Because of the overflow, balls hit into the squatters were ruled two-base hits, but "small boys dashed from their seats for balls hit down the third-base line. Ruth warned the kids to keep in their seats, but that only drew more small boys."

But when he couldn't get to a ball that went for a double, "shifting his cap to a diabolic, sidewise slant and rushing to the plate with indignation written all over his Grecian features . . . Ruth declared he could have headed off the ball and held it to a single if a fan hadn't interfered." He held up the game a quarter of an hour, arguing, then "walked over and got a drink of water, grinned at the howling fans and grinned still more widely after turning their hoots to hurrahs with a home run."

The country picnic atmosphere was further intensified when Dugan "invaded the Tiger dugout and emerged under a shower of lumber hurled by the Tigers. He came out with an ugly-looking black bat, with which he went three for three."

W. B. Hanna, writing for the *Herald Tribune,* was less sanguine about the Yankee lead than Vidmer. "One has only to remember back to a year ago to diminish any feeling of cocksureness that the Yankees will win the pennant. They are likely to, and much more likely than any other team, but they had this long a lead last year, and even later last year . . . yet found the going distressingly rough before their pennant became a mathematical certainty.''

And they were not only tamed, 6–3, the following day by Earl Whitehill, Detroit's top pitcher, "who held them to ten hits," but they saw Tavener steal second, third, and home. "He'll steal the park one of these days. Tiger runners are making bushers of the Yankees. . . . They play fiery baseball when they are ahead. The catcher's throws go straight enough, but the runners get long leads and are there when the ball arrives.''

The problem did not arise the following day when Gehrig again tied Ruth, hitting his twenty-ninth home run and "it was scarely worth mentioning that the Yankees won a ball game, 8–5.'' What was worth mentioning was that Hoyt appeared back in form, "with fine stuff as long as his strength lasted," giving up only one hit between the first and seventh innings, when Shawkey came in to relieve him. Hoyt also singled twice, driving in three runs. The scoreboard showed Washington winning its sixth straight from the Indians and now "only" six games back.

It was the Indians, "lo! the poor Indians, they are getting lower every day," the Yankees next played, handing them their seventh straight loss, 7–0. " 'Ruth will out,' '' observed Vidmer, "but it's best not to count on it." After fourteen hitless appearances at the plate, he hit his thirtieth home run in the ninth inning.

The Indians were helpless before Shocker, "who had the control of a wizard," said Hanna. "He could have driven tacks at 30 paces. The ball broke exactly as he asked it to, and he used a fast ball only occasionally. He showed he was completely back in form.''

In form Shocker was "one of the great pitchers," according to *Baseball* magazine. We are the product of accidents, and Shocker believed that a broken finger, suffered in his early days as a catcher with Windsor in the Canadian League, was an infirmity that added to his stuff, as with the great Mordecai "Three Finger" Brown, a Hall of Fame Cub earlier in the century.

"The broken finger may not be pretty to look at," Shocker said, "but it has been useful to me. It hooks over a baseball just right, so

I can get a fine break on my slow ball, and that's one of the best balls I throw.''

Combined with the spitter and a first-rate fastball, the pitch pushed Shocker to winning seasons with the Browns, an indifferent team, and with the Yankees, who were not indifferent. He used his head, too. "Pitching," he observed, with a small, eloquent waggle of his right hand, "is this and that," meaning a matter of inches.

On the last play of the game he twisted his ankle and had to be helped from the field by Lazzeri and Gehrig, a further blow to a pitching staff in delicate health. It was believed that the ankle was Shocker's only physical problem, it not being commented on that he had taken to sleeping sitting up in the Pullman.

The comment was reserved for a heat wave which hit the eastern seaboard, leaving seventeen dead in those days of no air conditioning, a homier and so more noteworthy disaster than the Palestine earthquake that struck the night of July 13, leaving four hundred dead in the ruins.

"It was too hot for much fielding practice," Hanna wrote the next day, "and it didn't take long for the players to discover they didn't need much of that. It wasn't too hot, however, for them to take every minute of batting practice." Ball players never change.

The Yankees won the next day, 5–3. Dugan, it was noted, was in "something of a batting renaissance," climbing toward the .269 he would achieve for the year. "He has rather a spare and meager frame," *Baseball* magazine noted, "when he stands with his bat poised expectantly and his thin legs somewhat apart, his body forward, he suggests a kangaroo ready for take-off.

"His antics in the field are also in character. The way he darts about, scooping up grounders with the full play of those long arms and legs of his remainds you of a toy jumping jack on a string. Not that Dugan is awkward, for he is not."

He is, in fact, remembered chiefly for his color. "They never mention Dugan as a third baseman," Hoyt said in the spring of 1973. "They mention Brooks Robinson or Pie Traynor or, once in a while, Ossie Bluege, but they never mention Dugan. To me he ranks in the first five fielding third basemen of all time, and, outside of Heinie Zimmerman with the Giants and Cubs, he probably was the greatest I've ever seen for coming in on a slowly hit ball and throwing it to first.''

The team was so good that excellence sometimes passed as routine. There was that *Times* comment about the ''season-long batting slump.'' Gehrig was at .388 for the year; Ruth, .356; Collins, .351 in forty games; Combs, .336; Paschal, .333 in twenty-five games; Lazzeri, .303; Koenig, .286; and Grabowski, .280.

Koenig doubled after a Meusel single in the fourth inning the next day, thus averting what would have been the first shutout pitched against the Yankees that season, the left-handed Walter Miller beating Moore, 4–1, as the Yankees made five errors. Both Ruth and Gehrig were hitless, Gehrig striking out with the bases full. It may have been the heat.

Bobby Jones won the British Open the next day, seven under par. The Scots attempted to carry Jones off the St. Andrews course. He was the Babe Ruth of golf, or vice versa, depending on which sport you preferred. It was a time when writers celebrated their heroes with all stops out.

''You may sing of the ancient Orioles,'' Vidmer began his story about the next game. ''You may chant of the glory that was the Cubs 20 years ago. You may harken back to the Athletics before the wreckage.

''But before anyone starts making broad statements about those famous teams of the past, let's consider the frolicking, walloping Yankees of the present. Facing the fire of George Uhle, the big Cleveland right hander . . . the Yankees entered the eighth inning six runs behind, a deficit few teams would have faced with any confidence.''

Five o'clock lightning, and it struck like this: Morehart and Ruth walked, and Gehrig singled in one run. Meusel doubled in two more, leaving the Yankees only three down and bringing in Garland Buckeye.

Paschal doubled to open the ninth, Combs grounded out, and Lazzeri singled, scoring Paschal. Ruth walked. Lazzeri stole third and scored on Gehrig's long sacrifice fly. Meusel again doubled, scoring Ruth to tie the game. And Koenig marked his second day back in action by singling in Meusel with the winning run. When the pitcher didn't pitch, Hoyt, Pipgras, and Thomas might have observed thankfully, the hitters hit.

In spite of the persistent heat that sent 700,000 to Coney Island and 500,000 to the beaches of the Rockaways in New York, and a reminder that the Twenties were not, after all, without their tensions (violent rioting broke out in Vienna, a general strike called by the Communists leaving 250 dead in the city, 100 elsewhere in the country, leading to fears that Germany might use the occasion as a pretext for absorbing Austria into the Reich), all seemed normal, in St. Louis, the Yankees touching up the Browns in a variety of ways.

Pennock won the opener, 5–2. Gehrig's thirtieth home run tied Ruth the following day, but Shocker was batted out of the game in the seventh inning, and it remained for Meusel to win it with his fifteenth home run, 5–4. Eighteen thousand watched, "a season record in St. Louis, although the crowd looked small to the Yankees." Moore retired the last eight men in a row, "all he brought with him was bad medicine," half of them by strikeouts.

"If Lou and Babe take a couple of days off," observed Lieb in the *Post,* "the pitchers turn in unbelievable performances." Allowing for the hyperbole of the time, it was fair tribute to an injury-riddled and second-guessed staff which now led the major leagues in complete games, forty-five, forty of them victories. History, like life, is unfair, and the team is remembered for scoring the most runs, not for giving up the fewest.

Gehrig broke the tie again the following day with his thirty-first home run in a 10–6 victory, as the Yankees struck in the seventh inning for six runs on five hits, a double steal, and a walk, combined with two St. Louis errors. There were 18,452 witnesses, almost 10,000 women, "half of whom didn't know the difference between a home run and a stolen base," commented the *Times,* to no recorded charge of male chauvinism.

Ruether and Moore then combined to pitch the team to a 6–1

win, closing out the series. Howley, the St. Louis manager, apparently retained his sanity with a sense of humor, telling his team as Moore walked in from the bullpen, "It's all over, boys. Here comes Frank Merriwell."

Ruth got only one hit, "but his fielding was magnificent," the *Times* observed. He handled six chances, only one of them routine, "the others the sort of plays that made Tris Speaker famous, including a running, jumping, backhanded catch off a drive by Bing Miller with men on second and third and two out in the sixth."

The Yankees were back in the lead by twelve games, the Senators having lost the ground gained by their sweep of the Indians, and it was suggested, said the *Sun*, "that the American League follow a popular minor league custom by splitting the season and starting all over again to keep interest alive in the towns outside New York." It was advanced as a humorous consideration, but it doesn't appear quite so humorous on closer examination.

The decision may have been in the works, but after the Yankees departed, Phil Ball, the St. Louis owner announced he would "wreck his present club and build an entirely new outfit before next season." Ball claimed he had lost a hundred thousand dollars thus far in the season and seventy thousand in 1926. He said the team was "loaded with players who have enjoyed long trials and failed to come through and several malcontents who do the club no good."

The Yankees had the world on a string. As a special train carried them to an exhibition game in St. Paul by way of "Hannibal, Keokuk, Burlington and other rural regions, it was met at every stop by fans demanding to see Ruth. He never failed to step out on the platform with a smile and a few words. But only when the Babe went inside and dragged him out did Buster [Gehrig] appear."

It was the same thing in St. Paul, where fifteen thousand braved threatening weather to watch Murderer's Row. "Throughout . . . Ruth, who played first base, was kept busy signing autographs and otherwise tormented by worshippers. One youth even rushed out on the diamond and offered him a bottle of soda pop, [but] Gehrig was practically in seclusion until the eighth, when he was surrounded by autograph-seekers.''

The occurrence reminded the newspaper that during the St. Louis series, Gehrig hit a home run after Ruth struck out, but ''the kids besieged Ruth at the exit gate after the game and thrust scorecards, autograph books and bits of paper with demands for his signature. Buster walked out of the gate and up the street unmolested.''

''There's only one Babe,'' the paper reflected.

The high spirits were pretty well distributed, however. Koenig, insisting he was not among them, remembers that a group of players visited a St. Paul cathouse and swiped the madame's parrot, a bird of particularly scatological tongue, appropriately, perhaps, for a bagnio mascot in a community which was first called ''Pig Eye.'' The memory still warms him.

The madame so treasured the bird as to take out a newspaper advertisement offering five hundred dollars for its return, but the polly wound up in New York, ''where one of the guys gave it to some friend of his, I don't know.'' Considering the breed's longevity, it may be squawking, ''Hello, my little shit-ass. How are you?'' to a new generation of ballhawks.

# Six

○

Dempsey knocked out Jack Sharkey in the seventh round before eighty thousand at Yankee Stadium, the gate exceeding a million dollars, as the team for which the Stadium was named rounded out the month of July by bucketing into Chicago, where they won three of four, returning home to sweep the lame-duck Browns and split a series with Cleveland.

They not only were conceded the pennant in the western cities, but the press comment developed the theme that this was more than another pennant winner or even a potential champion, that what people were looking at was something different.

"Miller Huggins has the strongest club seen in the majors for 25 years," wrote a Detroit newspaperman. "The Yankees are playing better than Frank Chance's Chicago Cubs. . . . As far as Detroit is concerned, the race ended some time ago."

"Accidents cut no figure in the Yankees' winning ways," was the somewhat murky conclusion in Cleveland. "Huggins' wonderful team holds a long lead in spite of the injuries sustained from time to time by Meusel, Dugan, Koenig and Lazzeri. The Yankees haven't even missed their star catcher, Bengough, who has been out all season.

"The way Huggins has managed Dutch Ruether illustrates how the team is directed. Ruether, once a bad actor, has pitched beautifully this year. Then look at the Yankees' new pitchers: Moore is the most valuable find in baseball this year. Pipgras and Thomas are coming along fine. . . ."

"Huggins has made Ruether," another writer said, putting it more strongly. "He hasn't pitched more effectively since he helped Cincinnati win the pennant and the World Series in 1919. Huggins deserves credit for manipulating Moore, Pipgras and Thomas with rare judgment and patience."

"The Yankees are sure champions," conceded a St. Louis writer. "A more powerful baseball machine has never been constructed. Huggins was a good manager when he led the Cardinals. Now he is in a class by himself."

And Monitor noted, "Wherever they went, [the Yankees] drew howling mobs, eclipsing the season's records . . . in Detroit, where overflow crowds sat in the outfield . . . in Cleveland, where the weekday attendance record went by the boards, in St. Louis, where the Cardinals have been submerging the Browns all season. . . . The business managers were glad to see the Yankees come and sorry to see them go, while the playing managers, gathering together the remnants of shattered pitching staffs, were sorry to see them come and happy to see them go. . . ."

Hoover reported to the President a flood-control plan costing $200,000,000, urging a special session of Congress, but, as the comic strips reported, Coolidge was entertaining Mutt and Jeff—"Eeow! boys, welcome to the wild west!" One person died and 114 were injured as The Hub's greatest crowd in history pressed in on the visiting Lindbergh, and it was announced that Mayor Walker would tour Europe with his wife and Mr. and Mrs. Grover Whalen.

But it was the old world yet to the Yankees who beat the White Sox, 4–1, after young George Connelly held them hitless into the eighth inning before eighteen thousand at the White Sox Park.

The winning streak and the heat snapped the following day as

Pennock was clouted hard in a wind so brisk that "only because they hoped Gehrig and Ruth would hit a home run did the fans shiver and shake until the last out." The home-run twins singled and doubled for one run in the eighth, and Ruth tripled with two men on in the ninth, but the rally failed to overcome an early lead—"Pennock fought the wind, cold and Sox until the sixth, when he retired trembling to the stove in the clubhouse"—and Chicago won, 7–6.

"The best-known group of girl athletes in the whole United States," Gallico wrote in his *envoi* to the Twenties, "is not made up of tennis-players, golfers, runners or jumpers, but of swimmers. . . . There have been many theories and explanations for the sudden rise of women's swimming to the tremendous popularity that it enjoys in America today. The simplest and most valid of all is that it has sex appeal."

By the Seventies, no excuses were needed and the one-piece bathing suits of the Twenties seem positively decorous compared to the bikinis and fish-nets of latter days, but there was a kind of saucy innocence, unclouded by any steam from women's liberation, in the eight-column spread of five SWIMMING NYMPHS WHOSE SPEED IN THE WATER THREATENS FATHER TIME in the *World*.

The same page revealed that it was Koenig's turn at bat, scoring twice and tripling with the bases full to account for all the Yankee runs in a 5–2 victory over the White Sox. Comiskey Park's record crowd of the season, thirty thousand, were disappointed as Ruth and Gehrig hit no more than singles and doubles.

"They say the Yankees have a great team," reflected the *Times*, "but it's been in action only two or three times. There are always replacements in the lineup. Koenig was out for nearly a month. He came back. Dugan was out with an ailing knee. Now Dugan is back, and Combs is ailing." He had been hit on the temple by a ball, but he missed only one game because of that injury; individually as well as collectively, the 1927 Yankees demonstrated that greatness handles adversity.

Fifty thousand saw Koenig win the game for the second consecutive day, his seventh-inning single scoring Collins, who walked and moved to second on Pipgras' sacrifice, but the roar was reserved for Ruth, who hit his thirty-first home run, drawing even with Gehrig, and who opened the scoring with a tremendous triple to center, driving Metzler into the exit gate, where he fell down. By the time he recovered, Ruth was standing easily on third, and Gehrig singled him home, as the Yankees won, 3–2, behind Pipgras and Moore.

"The Yankees are like the White Sox of other years," a "Chicago veteran" was quoted in the *Sun*. "They go to the ninth inning maybe trailing, but they have enough left in the batting order to bring home the victory. The Yankees never will be beaten. They will only wear out."

There were two more reminders, in addition to the swimming nymphs, of the different America in which the Yankees frolicked. The *Times* reported a threatened New York City transit strike—it would be averted—and noted, with no apparent complaints from labor, "1,500 strike-breakers here; more being rushed to the city to keep trains moving." And the *World* told about "a little cop," a boxing instructor, who happened upon a six-foot "chronic cop-fighter" on a Greenwich Village street, where he had just flattened two men. The policeman belted the cop-hater and suggested they visit the station house. The cop-hater obliged, saying, "That little guy sure can hit." No mobs, knives or guns, no charges of police brutality, or reason to make such a charge, bare fists only, man to man, and the lawbreaker went along quietly.

So did the Browns. Ruth and Gehrig made themselves at home, back at the Stadium, Ruth hitting two home runs, Gehrig one, as the Yankees' "cyclonic slugging" featured 15–1 and 12–3 victories, although it was only St. Louis. Both of Ruth's home runs came in the first game, when he also singled twice. He singled three times in four at-bats in the second game. Gehrig added a double and two singles to his home run. Every Yankee scored at least once in both games.

"Ruth is only one-ninth of the Yankees, but he is one-third of their home-run hitters," noted the *Times*. "His thirty-third was the Yankees' one hundredth. In addition, he breached 100 runs scored, the first of the Yankees to reach that total."

In all of the hitting, it was mentioned in passing that Hoyt and Ruether pitched good games. And it was reported that Huggins, "usually cautious and conservative," admitted that "the flag is as good as clinched." He hoped for an even break on the road, considering the shaky state of his pitching staff when the team left. He got thirteen of eighteen games. The second-place Senators won nine of eleven and went nowhere. "We win and we win," said Judge, "but they don't even pause for breath. How can you jump a club when you can't even catch up with it?"

Pennock retired the side in order in seven of the nine innings the next day, allowing only three balls hit out of the infield and three hits, as Gehrig again tied Ruth, hitting his thirty-third home run, and Lazzeri added another in a 4–1 victory that was a pitching duel between Pennock and Win Ballou until the sixth inning.

Americans, who seldom do anything in an uncomplicated way, set aside the glasses of prohibition gin to walk the sawdust trail for Billy Sunday, affirm the Four Square Gospel for Aimee Semple McPherson and read about Elmer Gantry, and baseball felt the old-time religion as the Yankees again hammered the Browns, 9–4, in 87-degree heat that left three dead in New York City.

"Just as the strains of 'Revive Us Again' floated across to the Stadium walls from the campfire meeting tent of Uldine Utley," said the *World*, "Babe Ruth came to bat in the eighth inning.

"The game needed reviving, for it was a slow, one-sided contest, devoid of feature. So the Babe revived it by hitting his thirty-fourth home run of the year into the sloping terrace of seats in right center. . . .

"Lou Gehrig came next and, although the orchestra played and the choir sang, 'I Need Thee Every Hour,' Lou couldn't do anything about it. He fanned. . . .

"Moore, that rock in a weary land, warmed up, but he was not needed . . . the music from Miss Utley's tent was a great help to the boys. When the band played softly, 'There's Sunshine in My

Soul Today,' Mike Gazella hit one of the loudest three-baggers of the year, his third hit of the afternoon, and he made a sweet single in the fifth to the strains of 'Shall We Gather by the River?' ''

Baseball players, of course, generally a fun-loving group, tended, like a good many others, to opt more for the hedonistic side of life in the Twenties. Out in St. Louis, Flint Rhem, who lost a Series game to the Yankees the previous year, took brief leave of the Cardinals on July 27, upset over being fined $2,000 for breaking training. He admitted it but said, "There were others. . . . I don't see why I should be the only one to be penalized for enjoying myself." He was the only one, Sam Breadon pointed out levelly, because his contract stipulated "a $2,000 salary reduction if he violated training rules."

Like so many Americans of the middle Twenties, Rhem's finest drinking hours lay ahead. John Lardner's essay, "They Walked by Night," concerns ballplayers "with a single-minded thirst and feet that point away from home" and commemorates such heroes as Shuffling Phil Douglas, "the only man in baseball history to have a detective all to himself for a whole season," and Big Ed Delehanty, "the Babe Ruth of turn-of-the-century baseball, who had once hit four home runs in a single game, and who fell off a train as it was crossing the Niagara River. He was drowned in the rapids above the Falls. Ed had been drinking. Baseball fans, as they mourned his death, were aware that he usually had been."

Lardner gave Rhem highest honors for imagination when "after he had been missing from the sight of man for forty-eight hours, [he] reported back . . . pale and shaken, with the story that he had been kidnapped by gangsters, locked in a hotel room and forced to drink great quantities of liquor at point of gun."

"You couldn't disprove his story by the way he smelled," said Branch Rickey.

Night baseball put a crimp into that kind of heroics, cutting into man's traditional drinking hours, but the fun-lovers on the Yankees and other clubs in the Twenties were only conforming to the spirit of the times. In his "Drinking in America, An Unfinished

History," Lardner noted that "by 1927, the national death rate from alcoholism had risen by 150 per cent since 1920. In Kansas, which had been dry before Prohibition, the death rate was only 60 per cent, indicating that two laws are twice as good as one."

The Yankees lost a game to Cleveland, but the derailment proved nothing serious, as Gehrig hit two home runs, moving ahead of Ruth again on the following day, and the Yankees won a doubleheader, 7–3 and 5–0. Gehrig's second home run, it was pointed out, "barely got into the left field sun section, and then only after taking a hop off the running track," while the forty thousand fans saw Ruth hit two towering drives that were caught by "outfielders playing somewhere in the next county."

Languid Bob, who had been faulted for failing to hit at crucial times the previous day, hit a home run in the second game, and Ruether, winning his twelfth victory of the season, drove one out with Lazzeri on second in the first, but not even Gehrig's slugging took away notice from Hoyt's shutout.

Hoyt was "supreme, allowing only one hit per inning," noted the *Times*, "and doing his best pitching after his worst, which was not at all bad. . . . In the eighth, with the bases filled and one out, he forced Burns to pop and struck out Fonseca." It was the only time he was threatened. Only one other Indian reached second, four reached first and Hoyt gave up no walks.

"Hoyt's pitching," reflected the *Herald Tribune*, "has been a treat—a treat for those who can see something other than murdering the ball. Such control, such transition from one speed to another, such art in the pleasure of his slow curve. There isn't a better right-handed pitcher in all baseball than Hoyt as he is at present and has been since he got rid of his latest kink. The refinement of skill."

"A man of many parts," a sportswriter called Hoyt, who was "handsome, a beau ideal" of the team, who had studied to be a mortician, who, in October 1921, appeared at Reisenweber's cabaret in baseball uniform with the entertainer Sally Fields and, before an audience of six hundred, including a half dozen Yankee teammates, did "the shimmy, Chicago, the toddle and other steps," then introduced his father, the minstrel Ad Hoyt, whose song was "On the Old Fall River Line." It was one of those magical night-life nights, and the father offered a gracious little speech: "It was not long ago when I was fortunate enough to have my name in electric lights, and very often I would take this youngster with me to the theatre. Then I'd hear someone say, 'There goes Ad Hoyt and his son.' But how different that is now. Today I was coming here with Waite, and I heard someone say, 'There goes Waite with his old man.' " He obliged with "The Old Fall River Line," and how the wine must have flowed, and the emotions!

Hoyt was twenty-eight in 1927, but already a ten-year veteran of the major leagues, having signed a contract with the New York Giants after pitching six no-hitters, winning thirty-one of thirty-three games and once striking out twenty-four men in a single game for Brooklyn's Erasmus High School.

He partied as well as anyone on a team of individuals dedicated to studying the sunrise, but after going eleven and fourteen in the dismal season of 1925, when he lost eight in a row and "ballooned like Ruth," he lost twenty pounds over the winter, and Lieb said, "Full of the exuberance of youth, Waite's training trips in the past were more or less of a frolic. But this spring finds him one of the most serious athletes in camp." He won sixteen games in 1926 and broke even in two World Series appearances.

Hoyt's competitiveness was of the hair-trigger kind. It might be measured by incidents that more or less bracketed his playing career. Although he signed with McGraw, a friend of his father's, he balked when McGraw wanted to send him to the minors, "fought with the Little Napoleon and defied him, something few ballplayers dared to do," went so far as to leave organized baseball and pitch with the semipro Baltimore Dry Docks, then was picked up by the Red Sox before joining the Yankees. And when he was with Pittsburgh in the twilight of his career in 1933, he walked over to a dugout of jeering Cubs, who had been traumatized in four straight World Series games by the Yankees two seasons earlier, and said, "If you guys don't shut up, I'll put on my old Yankee uniform and scare you to death."

The 1922 World Series earned-run average of .000 in three games is not the only mark he will leave: he is a gifted painter, described by an art professor friend as "one of the most talented amateurs around—largely, I think, because he is very perceptive and sensitive to his environment." One of his paintings, "Retired," hangs in the Hall of Fame, along with Hoyt's plaque. After twenty-four years of broadcasting Cincinnati Reds games, Hoyt is called by another friend "one of the most lovable men I ever met. If you collected a dollar from everyone who's been influenced favorably by Waite Hoyt, you'd be a millionaire."

"The thinking man's big leaguer in every facet of his life," he is called by *Cincinnati Magazine,* something more than just another baseball announcer, given to midnight reading. "Now that I'm coming to the small end of the funnel," he says, "I find myself more and more reviewing my life and asking myself whether I'm justified in believing I was a success. I find myself in the quiet of night . . . thinking, 'Could I have done this? Could I have done that? Would it have been commensurate with my character to do it?' Sometimes I think, well, what am I? Now that it's nearly over, what am I, really? And that's the goddamndest question you can ask yourself."

A cab driver, recognizing the address, says that for years the rain delays were the best part of Cincinnati baseball games because Hoyt would call on a prodigious memory, and there is a phonograph record of some of those moments, "Waite Hoyt in the Rain," recalling the victory he lost when Ruth came in to pitch with an eight-run lead, and the consequences of tossing a melon rind out of a New Orleans hotel window.

At seventy-four, he is so compatible with the years that the old nickname "Schoolboy" obviously was appropriate, although he carries a certain presence as a member of the Hall of Fame Old-Timers Committee and chairman of the Powell Crosley, Jr., Amateur Baseball Fund. The old ballplayer and the young are equal interests to the man who was seen five decades ago as "a man of many parts."

In a sunsplashed den he recalls that 1927 pitching staff, one-two-three in earned runs—Hoyt, Shocker, and Moore—on "a team that didn't often beat itself. Most baseball is a play on errors. In other words, the pitcher looks for the deficiency in a batter. And he works on that, he tries to capitalize on the weakness of his opponent. So many times you beat yourself. Once in a while, you take a walloping, but the 1927 Yankees probably beat themselves less than any ball club that ever lived."

This was partly because, as the *Herald Tribune* said, "The pitchers are going smoothly, and Hoyt and Pennock as double-header workers lately have been wonderfully effective." The two men were in many ways studies in contrast, beginning with Pennock's left-handedness and reputation as "the silent man of the pitching staff," but they shared common backgrounds with the Red Sox—"like all successful Boston players, Pennock was traded to New York," it was bitterly observed—and a standard of excellence that put them in the Hall of Fame.

Pennock broke into baseball in 1911 as a mediocre first baseman with the Atlantic City Collegians at a hundred dollars a month. Not long after, he switched to pitching and threw a no-hitter. His catcher was Earl Mack, who recommended him to his father, and it was with the Athletics, from one of Mack's great pitching staffs, that he learned his trade—Chief Bender was there, and Eddie Plank and Jack Coombs. Having learned to use his head instead of his arm, he came to be "a poet of pitching who works without apparent effort," even "the greatest left-hander of all time because he is the smartest. He has the ideal disposition for pitching under pressure and the heart of a lion."

Great men also make mistakes, and Mack traded Pennock to the Red Sox "because he didn't seem to have any ambition." He won more than 60 games in six seasons, but Huggins was scoffed at for buying him in 1923 because "he is not worth cash and three players. His best years are behind him." Huggins only saw him as a stopgap, but Pennock led the league in won-loss percentage that year, going 19 and 6, won 2 games in the 1923 World Series and 2 more against the Cardinals, and would win 115 games for the Yankees in his first six seasons with the club.

He was, like Hoyt, a thoughtful man, of similar pitching philosophy. "If you don't pitch bad balls, you do not have to pitch so much in nine innings. The first commandment is observation. Look around. Notice the little quirks in the batter, and notice your own quirks. Your doctor never stops learning. The great pitcher imitates him."

He was struggling in August of 1927, but he was winning. His earned-run average was seldom impressive, but he figured that the team would get runs for him and, when it was necessary, he could pitch low-run games, so much so that Ruppert once criticized Hoyt, "What's the matter with you? Other pitchers win their games, 9–3, 10–2. You win your games 2–1, 1–0. Why don't you win your games like the others?"

To these mainstays of the pitching staff it was noted that "Pipgras has finally arrived this season and is now a regular member . . . He is 5–1, including a two-hitter over the Red Sox. His fast ball is probably faster than that thrown by any other Yankee. He has a fair curve and a 'sailer,' a ball that has a big break to it and is both hard to hit and to control. . . . His inability to control his fast ball and his 'sailer' kept him in the minors for years."

Pipgras traveled a hard road common to the era, from his birth in Denison, Iowa, to a farm boyhood in Slayton, Minnesota, where he got up at four thirty to feed 150 head of sheep and milk cows and curry horses. He believed his time at the south end of a horse headed north helped build the physique responsible for his "Danish Viking" nickname. At seventeen he went overseas with the Army engineers during World War I, returning to pitch for a Woodstock, Minnesota, semipro team that owned one complete uniform.

They looked so ragtag that it was believed a big-time team from Jasper, Minnesota, which was fully uniformed, "would bat until twilight" against them, but Pipgras only lost, 2–1, on a ninth-inning run, and the Jasper manager offered him $350 a month to change sides. While Pipgras was thinking it over, a Fulda, Minnesota, team offered him $400, proving again life's first law: it pays to procrastinate.

His talent was counterbalanced by his wildness. He was released after two weeks with a Saginaw, Michigan, team by manager-catcher Red McKee "to save McKee's life." In five innings Pipgras once walked fifteen men. "I had poor McKee black and blue," he once said. "No wonder he fired me."

Bob Conery, then head scout for the Yankees, discovered him with Madison in the Dakota League, where he was twelve and six. Pipgras signed with the Red Sox, however, in one of the Yankee-Red Sox *quid pro quos* common when Frazee owned the Boston team. Pipgras came up to Boston after going nineteen and nine with Charleston but sat on the bench, a position he continued to hold after coming to New York with Pennock in 1923. After two seasons Huggins sent him to the minors to learn control. "I knew I was terribly wild," Pipgras admitted, "but I pitched so seldom I had little chance to improve."

The wildness that was still with him at the beginning of 1927 now seemed curbed. Bengough, who believed any pitcher could be cured of wildness by throwing fifty or sixty times a day at the stationary target of a catcher's mitt, claimed he helped Pipgras, but the pitcher said that Huggins came to him before he went against Detroit in July "and suggested I do more of a pivot. It seemed to do the trick. Almost overnight, I found I could pitch the ball where I wanted to," a statement that proved selectively inoperative.

Admirable as the pitching proved out, it was the home-run derby that demanded most of the attention. The *Herald Tribune* pointed out that Lazzeri, with 15 home runs, attracted almost no notice for his hitting, although only two batters in the other league, Williams, 22, and Hornsby, 19, had hit more than the diamond Mussolini. He was simply lost in the cannonadius conducted by his towering teammates. It was noted that the National League led in home runs, 326 to 305, the sort of statistic favored by National League fans during the years of Yankee dominance as indicating something called "better balance through the league," although it also could mean worse pitching. In any case, since the comfortable assertion usually followed some slaughtering of the innocents by the Yankees in a World Series, it was suspect.

The intellectual twists of the fan's mind is as worthy of close study as the game itself, and in August 1927, a Temple University psychologist revealed that BASEBALL FAN LACKS MENTAL POISE, asserting that "a man who would stand in line for hours for a bleacher seat and shout himself hoarse for his team is not well-balanced. . . . He may not be abnormal, but . . . the well-balanced man will not become fanatic. . . ." If he does, said the savant, he suffers from "a mental hypertrophy."

Professors frequently make such excited discoveries, which are then ignored, and the hypertrophic fan read eagerly that Babe and Buster "cheer each other's success as merrily as they cheer their own. When Ruth hits a home run, Gehrig is waiting at the plate with a smile and a quip. When Gehrig hits one, Ruth and he walk to the dugout arm in arm. It is all very spontaneous and not rehearsed."

Ruth was quoted as calling Gehrig "one of the greatest fellows in the game and a real home-run hitter." Gehrig said, "I'm just fortunate even to be close to him." They even were bridge partners, it was pointed out, a circumstance which has shattered more friendships than matching home runs.

The age encouraged the dramatic gesture. "It was a good time to have a good time," in Hoyt's phrase, and something more than that. On August 3, Coolidge announced from the Black Hills, "I do not choose to run in 1928." That was all. The twelve-word, typewritten announcement handed to newspapermen in a Dakota schoolhouse shocked both his party and the opposition, jolted the bull market bearing the President's name, and remains a hieroglyphic for which no Rosetta Stone has been overturned.

In Boston, Governor Alvan Fuller upheld the jury and the findings of a board headed by the president of Harvard University and set August 10 as the execution date for Nicola Sacco and Bartolomeo Vanzetti, the shoemaker and the fish-peddler, convicted of the murders, in April 1920, of two shoe-factory employees. It was widely believed that the accused were condemned for their philosophical anarchism and their ancestry rather than for the crime, and, as what has been called "their six-year Golgotha" neared its end, the capitals of the Western world were shaking under demonstrations and the fear of demonstrations.

Having dropped his bombshell and as telegrams and letters protesting his decision poured in, Coolidge, who earlier in the summer challenged belief in a cowboy suit, now "donned full Indian regalia" and became a chief of the Sioux.

And that slump predicted all season long by the fan-manager, who is as devoted to trends as the politician, finally hit the Yankees. It began with a split of a doubleheader with the Tigers, 6–5, Detroit, and 8–6, before thirty thousand.

Gehrig clouted two home runs and moved ahead of Ruth, 37–34, but a four-run rally by Detroit won the first game, in spite of Moore, who allowed only three hits in five innings after he relieved Shocker, and a similar four-run outburst in the ninth inning of the second game knocked out Pipgras and brought Detroit within two runs before Moore made his second appearance of the day a success.

When Owen Carroll held the Yankees to five hits, the Tigers clustered groups of three runs in the first and ninth innings the following day, and the *Herald Tribune* commented, "The Yankees, to tell the truth, have lost some elan lately, and the team is in a slump."

Three Tigers singled off Hoyt in the first inning and added a sacrifice fly for two runs the next day, but this time the Yankees rebounded on Koenig's single, his force by Ruth, a walk to Gehrig, a single by Meusel, scoring Ruth and sending Gehrig to third, and a single by Lazzeri, which scored both Gehrig and Meusel. Meusel scored all the way from first and it was noted that "because he takes such long strides, some think he is not fast, but when he scored today, he was off before the ball was hit, rounded second like a whirlwind and raced home."

But after leading, 3–2, the next day, the team lost to the White Sox, 6–3, their fifth loss in nine games, and, worse, Ruth struck out his first two times up, fouled out, and dribbled a grounder about two feet in front of the plate—"as Ruth goes so go the

Yankees," it was recalled sardonically. Gehrig twice grounded to second, bounced to the pitcher, and struck out; Meusel struck out with the bat on his shoulder, completely fooled by Lyons ("anyone would have fanned on that ball, if not that badly," said Hanna; "it had a shoot on it which would have eluded a shovel"), Pennock, Moore and Shawkey gave up a dozen hits and, finally, Huggins was thrown out of the game for arguing with an umpire.

"The Yankees didn't show anything to warrant a bulletin to the effect they are out of their slump," it was reported the next day, but one big inning and Moore's relief of Shocker held up for a 4–3 victory. Ruth hit two drives that might have been home runs "but weren't. One was too straightaway and Metzler caught it on the warning track; the other wasn't straight enough and landed foul in the right field bleachers." Shocker bunted home the winning run. "He deserved credit for the victory," said Vidmer, "but he earned it with his bat, not his arm."

Bengough's appearance in the lineup and his bases-loaded triple before Shocker's bunt demonstrate that fortuitous circumstance that so often accompanies greatness. After missing all season, he became fit just as Grabowski sat down for two weeks with a split hand. Bengough is remembered by later generations of fans as a fat, bald coach, rather a clown, with the Phillies, but in 1927, he was called "the Peter Pan of baseball," a slim, dark-haired, fun-loving young man, "nothing more than a big kid in the big leagues." Christopher Morley's lines, "Dreams full dreamed/ Always come true, come true," suited him, according to the *Evening Graphic*.

When Bengough was a boy in Niagara Falls, New York, he would go to Buffalo and watch the great Hank Gowdy catch. "My eyes were always glued on Hank, and I'd dream of the day when I'd be there myself." This happened after he made a reputation as a catcher with Niagara University and local semipro teams. He was signed by Buffalo and, after warming the bench, got his chance when his mother called the manager angrily and said she was tired of making the trip from Niagara Falls to watch her son sit.

Bengough came to the Yankees in 1922, but after Uhle hit him on the arm, he seldom made an appearance until after midseason when the sun and various nostrums brought the arm around. Whenever the team was in Cleveland, for instance, he visited a self-made specialist named Bonesetter Reese in Youngstown. Reese had a reputation among ball players as a magician with what were called "atrophied soupbones."

"In those days, Bengough roomed with Lou Gehrig on the road," Joe Williams recalled in the *World Telegram*, "and the two players got into a motorcar and drove to Youngstown to see the Bonesetter. There was nothing wrong with Gehrig's arm, but he was fond of Bengough and liked to drive. They'd get up at 5 a.m., drive from Cleveland to Youngstown and return for the game."

The treatment sometimes helped for a couple of weeks. Bengough also visited a New York eccentric with a magic liquid. "I laughed when I stepped into his office. He had a big bucket of smelly stuff on the table and a paintbrush in his hands. He told me to strip. 'This is going to burn a little, but don't let that alarm you.'

"Well. This fellow took a brush and painted me from the waist up. He was right about the stuff burning. But, strangely, it helped. For two or three days, I could throw all over the park. Then it passed, and the flame died out. The only way I could keep catching regularly would have been to have the guy with the paintbrush work on me between innings. There is nothing so dead as a dead arm."

Almost nothing. Bengough later claimed that he woke up one morning and found he was bald. Once more he became the target of healers. "Not long ago," he would say, "I passed a man with a long white mane in a hotel lobby. He was carrying two green bottles under his arm. . . ." Within a short time, Bengough said, "I think his stuff works. Every time I use it, I get a headache. I think that means that hair is trying to break through."

He was the liveliest of the Yankee catchers, on and off the field. "Sure we liked to go out at night," he once said of the '27 team. "But we all went out together." He was adept at distracting batters. "I try to get their minds off their work," he said. "I tell the new players what a spot they're in and how I feel sorry for them. You can talk to the veterans about their families, their autos, anything like that. Funny. The wise ones don't pay any attention to you.''

The Yankees left town after beating the White Sox. It was their longest road trip of the season, and it worried Hanna in the *Herald Tribune*. ''They won't be back until September. . . . It is a soul-searing trip the schedule-makers have visited on the Yankees, case-hardened though ballplayers are to such experiences.''

The Senators, for one, were still playing good baseball, and, although they were twelve games back, ''one must remember the immortal Braves. If anyone can do it, the Senators can.'' Huggins was reported worried, although if the Yankees played no better than 50–50 baseball, Washington had to win thirty-seven of forty-nine games remaining to tie.

Rube Walberg held them to six hits in their opener at Philadelphia, Gehrig's thirty-eighth home run preventing a shutout as they lost, 8–1. The As simply poked away at Ruether until they knocked him out in the seventh. Huggins was so upset that only an umpire's warning kept him checked. Ruth was hitless for the third straight game, and it was the Yankees' sixth loss in their last eleven.

The crowd demonstrated in matters great and small, even as in the Sixties when the occasion might be a war protest, a civil-rights march, or the appearance of a rock star. Sacco and Vanzetti won a stay on the eve of their scheduled execution, as a group of New York writers, including Dorothy Parker and John Dos Passos demonstrated at the Massachussetts statehouse. This followed by less than a week the bombing of a Presbyterian church in Philadelphia, vigils at various American embassies, a meeting of 500,000 in New York City, nationwide ''Sacco Must Not Die'' gatherings, and the journey of thirty busloads of protesters from the Apple to the Hub.

At the same time more placid thousands were on hand as Coolidge dedicated a memorial at Mount Rushmore in North Dakota, and the sculptor Gutzon Borglum carved out the first lines of the profile of George Washington. The temper of a Washington crowd was somewhere between the bomb-throwers and the monument-watchers. Police were called on to protect Umpire Clarence "Pants" Rowland when the Yankees beat the Senators, 4–3, after Ruth hit his thirty-sixth home run.

The fans believed Rowland was responsible for the Senators' defeat, Vidmer wrote in the *Times,* "in what they have kidded themselves is a crucial series. There hasn't been any such thing in the American League all this year, but you can't convince the natives, who are known for their imaginations."

Combs opened the game with his triple. Speaker started in the wrong direction, reversed himself but let the ball fly over his head. Ruth singled Combs home. After the Senators tied the score, Combs and Koenig singled and Ruth hit a home run off Tom Zachary, recently acquired from the Browns, not for the last time that season. Rowland called one Washington batter out on a marginal pitch, and when he refused to believe that Hoyt hit another, the true believers started out of the stands. The police dispersed them, but it was reported that "the throngs reassembled after the game and searched for Rowland far into the night."

A triple by Judge decided a pitchers' duel between Lisenbee and Pipgras the next day, 5–2, Combs acquiring half of the Yankees' eight hits, as the lead plummeted to eleven games. But the Yankees then destroyed even the most hypertrophic fans' belief that the series was crucial with a 6–3 victory the following day. Although Moore gave up his first major-league home run, to Goslin, Bump Hadley issued a half dozen walks and Bengough contributed a bases-loaded single that put New York ahead to stay.

The getaway game was played in conditions that warranted a postponement, but Griffith was not called the Old Fox for nothing, and, "because this was the last visit by the best-drawing team in the American League this year, refused to let the cash customers escape." The game was more like a naval engagment, the *Times* reported, but it convinced twenty thousand that "the Yankees are the best on land and sea," as they splashed to a 6–2 victory. Balls sank from sight. "A few more inches and there would have been breakers, but no one was drowned."

After pausing for an exhibition game in Indianapolis during

which Ruth hit a home run that "came down in a railroad yard half a block away," the Yankees beat the White Sox, 8–1, collecting thirteen hits.

Playing for real, Ruth became the first man ever to hit the ball out of the White Sox park, "one of the hardest he ever hit . . . it was last seen clearing the roof of the doubledecked right field stand with never a hint of slowing up, soaring in the general direction of the stockyards, where it may have dropped on a startled steer, although its distance will never be known."

He was beyond belief, all right. He also doubled, singled twice, and prevented a first-inning score with a perfect throw to the plate from deep right field on a hit with the bases loaded. Five thousand boys surrounded him after the game, pounding him black and blue to get his attention, and it required a police escort to separate him from what it required no press agent to discover were his favorite fans.

Mayor Walker opened his European tour with a night on the town in London, so that he had to be awakened to meet his official visitors, greeting them in his pajamas. Coolidge addressed ten thousand Sioux, who were accustomed to the forked tongue, "telling them what the government does to aid their problems." The third national hero may have had the best day, however, Ruth beating the White Sox with his thirty-eighth home run in the ninth inning, 3–2. Twice Connelly struck him out with a change of pace, delighting the hometown crowd, but Moore held the tie after Pipgras left for a pinch-hitter, until Ruth demonstrated the danger in tampering with a natural force.

Moore won his second game in two days the following day when he relieved Shocker in the ninth inning of a 4–4 game and Gazella pinch-hit in the winning run with the bases loaded. But the team was not yet straightened out. Chicago won the last game of the series on an unseasonably cold day, if that can be said of the Windy City, in spite of Gehrig's thirty-ninth home run, which put him one up on Ruth.

Hoyt's personal winning streak ended at seven. He and Blankenship each gave up eight hits, but half of Chicago's blows were infield scratch hits that might have been handled on a warmer day, and the Yankees were reported "more intent on keeping warm than sweeping the series. They didn't seem worried by the fact that they only held a 15-game lead. . . ."

Even after international protests, including Walter Lippmann's masterly editorial in the *World,* "Doubts That Will Not Down," Edna St. Vincent Millay's "Justice Denied in Massachusetts," which first appeared in the *Times,* and Vanzetti's eloquent statement from his cell: "Our words—our lives—our pains—nothing! The taking of our lives—the lives of a good shoemaker and a poor fish peddler—all! That last moment belongs to us—that agony is our triumph," SACCO AND VANZETTI PUT TO DEATH EARLY THIS MORNING/ GOVERNOR FULLER REJECTS LAST-MINUTE PLEA FOR DELAY was the *Times* headline August 23. But life goes on, as Miss Millay remarked in another bitter connection, and in Dublin Mayor Walker fought back tears as the folk sang "Come Back to Erin."

His European tour was a smash—in Paris, where he said, "It's not hard to understand the French people if you have an ear for music"; in Berlin, where his slim and youthful form was favorably contrasted with the stern, bearded mayors of the fatherland; in Rome, which he called "an earthly paradise"; in Venice, which he found "absolutely ideal"; in Baden-Baden, which he called "so lovely it should be called 'good and gooder.' "

And the Yankees moved to Cleveland, where they dropped the series in a sweep, the only time that had happened that season. The reasons were ascribed to the fact that "the Indians are not going any place, but they seem to take an impish delight in keeping the Yankees from clinching the pennant," a feeling that "the World Series is just a few weeks away, and the team doesn't want to get tired," and a belief in Cleveland that the locals played their best against New York. Ruth did, however, hit his fortieth home run in the series, going one ahead of Gehrig.

The long lead precluded panic, but the Tigers were next, and they had climbed into second place on the basis of a thirteen-game winning streak, the longest in the history of the club. However, as

Hoyt recalled forty years later, the '27 Yankees "were an exceptional team because they met every demand. There wasn't any requirement that was necessary at any particular moment that they weren't up to."

A great team doesn't stay untracked long: The Yankees trailed by three going in to the seventh inning of the opener but tied it up then, 5–5. There matters remained until the ninth, Moore producing his usual wonders in relief. Combs opened the inning with a walk. Koenig sacrificed him to second. Ruth flied to deep center field. Gehrig and Meusel walked to load the bases. And Lazzeri hit a home run.

"Yankees end Tiger threat," it was reported, apparently seriously, the next day when an 8–2 ball game extended the lead to 14½ games. Gehrig hit his fortieth home run, tying Ruth, and drove in four runs, bringing his total to 147, only 23 short of Ruth's major league record with 33 games left to play. Pennock outpitched four Detroit pitchers, and only a double play ended a fifth inning in which the Yankees batted around on two singles, three walks, a sacrifice fly, and another single, so that Huggins "toyed with the idea of sending Moore in as a pinch hitter before the athletes ran themselves to death."

A triple by Ruth with the bases loaded made the difference in the last game of the series, 8–6. Moore achieved his third hit of the season. It wasn't exactly a scorching drive, a little roller down the third-base line, but he had bet Ruth he would get at least three singles. "This is just an easy park to hit in," he was reported saying modestly after the game. The story grew that he sent Ruth a telegram from his Oklahoma farm saying that he had bought two mules with the three hundred dollars naming one "Babe" and the other "Ruth."

This is the kind of thing that fires the photographers' imagination during the easy days of spring, and the following year, so many requests came in for pictures of the beasts that Moore had to go out and buy a pair.

The Yankees left town with a 15½-game lead, as big a margin as they had enjoyed all season long "and worth more than it was two-and-a-half weeks ago.'' They break your heart, Judge had said. It would be noted shortly that ''The Senators haven't won a game since the Yankees killed their pennant chances in Washington, and the Tigers haven't won since the Yankees silenced their guns last week.'' As the Senators lost 12 games in a row and dropped to fourth place, the desperate Harris chose his lineup and batting order by lot.

The Browns, like the sacrificial lambs they were, welcomed New York and absorbed a first-game loss, 14–4, as Ruth, Meusel, and Combs hit home runs, for Hoyt's eighteenth victory. It was Ruth's forty-first home run. ''Only seven players have hit more than 40 home runs in a year,'' it was noted, ''and Ruth is five of them, the other two being Rogers Hornsby and Cy Williams.''

Ruth went two up on Gehrig the next day in a 10–6 triumph, St. Louis closing the gap at one point to a single run, ''but that may be as close as they'll ever get. Then Gehrig hit his forty-first with two on the following day in a 8–3 win, the team's eighteenth straight from St. Louis.

''When we were challenged,'' Hoyt says of the '27 Yankees, ''when we had to win, we stuck together and played with a fury and determination that could only come from team spirit. We had a pride in our performance that was very real. It took on the form of snobbery. We felt we were superior people, and I do believe we left a heritage that became a Yankee tradition.''

With no team left to challenge them, there were records to break. The team would have to sweep its remaining 29 games to tie the Cubs' major leag record of 116 wins set in 1908, but the American League record of 106 was within reach. The Yankees could revenge themselves with the Red Sox, who won 20 of 22 games from New York in 1920. They could beat the Browns in a season's sweep. Gehrig could break Ruth's runs-batted-in total.

The big record, of course, his own, was Ruth's to shoot for.

# Seven

○

I have no boudoir secrets . . . beyond the fact that, in that particular aspect of marriage, I envy no woman in the world.

—*Mrs. Babe Ruth*

The Babe is a superman. He can derive more nourishment from a piece of bread than the average man can get from a whole loaf.

—*Arthur P. McGovern*

Some 20 years ago, I stopped talking about the Babe for the simple reason that I realized that those who had never seen him didn't believe me.

—*Tommy Holmes*

To understand him, you had to understand this: He wasn't human. No human could have done the things he did and lived the way he lived and been a ballplayer. Cobb? Could he pitch? Speaker? The rest? I saw them. I was there. There was never anybody close. When you figure the things he did and the way he lived and the way he played, you got to figure he was more than animal even. There was never anyone like him. He was a god.

—*Joe Dugan*

Obviously a national monument, off the field and on.

There was a keeper-of-the-flame mentality toward Babe Ruth in 1973 that stretched almost from the date of his death exactly a quarter of a century earlier, but what is ultimately the single most impressive fact about him is that contemporary judgment, which held him every bit as great as the memories of those who played with him, wrote about him, and saw him.

It took a lifetime to build what is, unvarnished, a legend, although the Babe had a pretty good stranglehold on it young, but if one month could summarize the prodigies of that career, even with more than three hundred home runs left in his bat, it would be the month of September 1927. It is almost as though what came before was preparation, rich enough in comedy and drama though it was, plenty for a good story right from the beginning when, with an ironist's art, there was confusion over his birth date. Late in his life, Ruth learned that he was a year younger than he thought and had celebrated the wrong day, too, the proper date being February 6, 1895.

He was the eldest of eight children. The family name, contrary to some accounts, was Ruth, all right, not Gerheart or Erheart. His parents didn't want him. "His nursery was his father's saloon," in the words of one biographer, "and his kindergarten the slums of a large city." He was seven when he was first placed in St. Mary's Industrial School for Boys of the City of Baltimore, operated by the Xaverian Brothers of the Roman Catholic Church, and, although he was sometimes furloughed to his parents, he spent most of his youth in that refuge for what were then called underprivileged boys of any race or creed—"orphans, boys with sketchy home lives, bad boys, whatever," including, among others, the boy who would become Al Jolson.

Ruth received his first baseball the year he arrived at the school, the young Mozart presented with his first harpsichord. There were forty-three teams for eight hundred boys, arranged according to age and size, and he immediately was a star catcher.

"We played most of the time it seemed," Ruth once recalled. "Maybe 200 games a season. Most days we played two games and three on Sunday."

"It was a fortunate and historic circumstance that a boy who had such a natural aptitude for the game should have spent his boyhood at a place where it was part of the roots of living," wrote Martin Weldon.

Brother Matthius, Prefect of Discipline, was so much the surrogate father, "a man who loved and helped you," that Ruth adopted for life his peculiar, mincing gait. In the school Ruth built cabinets, rolled cigars, worked as a shirtmaker, but there was not long any doubt about his real trade.

At seventeen he was the star pitcher of a team undefeated against Baltimore high school and athletic-club teams. Through the body-building years while most boys his age spent their youths, in the phrase of another eminent Baltimorean, confronted by chalky pedagogues, he absorbed the discipline of the diamond, a wiry kid until the food got to him.

"The boy was a natural," said Brother Herman, who offered him some early throwing and hitting hints. "He was born for the game."

"The last item on my record," Ruth recalled of February 27, 1914, "was a single sentence, written in the flowing hand of one of my teachers, 'He is going to join the Balt. baseball team.' "

He was recommended to Jack Dunn, manager of the Orioles in the International League. "The Babe could hit a ball right from the start," in the recollection of an aide to Dunn. "As a pitcher, he had a fast ball, curve and control—all good. He was all the ball player in the world, right then and there."

Dunn took him south to Fayetteville, North Carolina, for spring training. Ruth was the definitive greenhorn, dazzled by the train, riding the hotel elevator all night, demolishing twenty-five griddle cakes at breakfast. He also demolished the pitching.

"Who's that?" a sportswriter asked in one of those historic moments that sometimes actually happen.

"That?" said a Dunn coach. "That's Jack's baby."

The nickname was born. Dunn tried him as a pitcher and outfielder. One look was enough for Connie Mack. "You don't expect to keep that boy long, do you?" he said to Dunn. "No," Dunn replied. "Frankly, I don't."

He sold Ruth to the Red Sox for two thousand dollars. Boston farmed him out to Providence. There were easily fifty minor leagues in 1914 and, as Mrs. Ruth observed in *The Babe and I:*

"The International League was right behind the majors, filled with men of major league caliber who were only a year away from the big leagues, coming or going. It was a league not one in 500 professional baseball hopefuls could achieve after years in lesser leagues. Yet a 19-year-old kid, fresh from Babe's weird background, won 22 and lost nine, which made him the International League's best pitcher."

It was, indeed, "ridiculously easy for Babe to achieve success in baseball." He won eighteen games as a Red Sox rookie, twenty-three his second year, then twenty-four. He pitched 29⅔ consecutive scoreless World Series innings, a record that stood for forty-three years until Whitey Ford of the Yankees broke it.

But on a spring day in 1919, in Tampa, Barrow, then the Red Sox manager, stopped a couple of newspapermen and said, "I have a piece of news for you. Starting today, the big fellow is an outfielder."

"But he's the best left-handed pitcher in baseball."

"So he is. But he can also hit the ball farther than anybody I ever saw. Great a pitcher as he is, he can be of more help to us by being in the game every day."

"That afternoon," Frank Graham wrote, "two reporters sat in at the beginning of a tremendous story, although they didn't know it at the time."

Ruth, who had tied Tilly Walker of Philadelphia with eleven home runs the previous year, now hit a record twenty-nine, although he also managed to win nine games as a part-time pitcher.

Then, in 1920, he came to New York and hit an unheard-of fifty-four home runs. He hit the record fifty-nine the following year, inspiring a belief that the mark would no more be equaled than man would walk on the moon, and, although the home runs continued—thirty-five in 1922, forty-one in 1923, forty-six in 1924, twenty-five in the disaster year, forty-seven in 1926, that record seemed secure enough until he responded to Gehrig's challenge and the interior call of genius.

All of this was accompanied by appropriate salary increases. His first baseball wage was $18 a week, quickly upped to $600 a season. It was $3,500 his first year with the Red Sox, $10,000 when he became an outfielder, $20,000 his first year in New York, $30,000 after the 54-home-run year, then $52,000 through 1926.

His standard of living kept pace. He bought a bicycle with his first baseball money and was a menace on the streets. By 1924 he estimated in a public confessional through the offices of *Collier's* magazine that he had squandered half a million dollars on bad investments, bad bets, and nine shiny motor cars, still a menace on the streets.

Christy Walsh not only showed Ruth how to make more money, but managed it for him. This was a good thing. Dugan recalled approaching Babe in a hotel lobby one evening and asking him for a loan to entertain some friends. The figure in the polo coat casually reached in his pocket and handed Dugan a bill. Joe, thinking it was a fifty, pocketed it, took his friends to dinner, and, when the waiter brought the check, gave him the money. The waiter's eyes popped. So did Dugan's, when he saw what he had handed him. It was five hundred dollars. When he repaid Ruth a few days later, Ruth was grateful. "Jesus," he said. "I thought I blew it."

In 1914, with a note of permission from his father, since he was a minor, Ruth had married a tiny, eighteen-year-old waitress from Texas named Helen Woodford. By 1927 the formerly devoted couple had drifted apart, and Ruth, a man of many women, had met Claire Hodgson, who would become the second Mrs. Ruth. Hoyt once wrote about Ruth's home life during these years:

"Ruth lived at the Ansonia Hotel in New York. It was rather a Bohemian existence. His suite was shared with the first Mrs. Ruth and an adopted daughter and anyone who cared to drop in. It was constantly crowded with visitors, strangers and friends. Babe didn't know one from the other, as Babe rarely recalled meeting people. A room service waiter had a path worn from the kitchen downstairs to the Ruthian throne room. Babe was paying all the checks.

"Little Dorothy hardly slept, and Helen could hardly keep track of the new arrivals. Ruth wandered about, making promises he never kept, entering into business deals he forgot ten minutes later.''

On the road, Ruth seldom went out with his teammates. There was no snobbishness involved. ''Ruth was too much in the public eye,'' according to Hoyt. ''We couldn't keep up with the Babe. We didn't have the money in the first place, and we couldn't stand the strain and still play ball.''

Herb Pennock once recalled, ''One night he and Helen were out riding when they ran out of gas. Babe had to walk five miles to get home. He didn't get to bed until five in the morning. Then he pitched the first game of a doubleheader and won, 1–0. The next time my wife saw Helen, she asked, 'What do you feed that man?' ''

Dugan remembers Pennock taking a group of Yankees to a Masonic festival in Kennet Square, from which all hands returned sated. ''The next day I felt ill. Hoyt looked green. The Babe drove a couple of long ones out and added a pair of doubles.''

Estimates of Ruth's drinking vary widely. Hoyt said in the spring of 1973 he saw Ruth dazed by liquor ''only two times in my life, and then not drunk but what we called 'under the influence.' You must remember that even on the road, he was treated like royalty, like a visiting movie star, with people by the dozens passing through his suite, so there was always liquor available. That doesn't mean he was drinking it.''

The second Mrs. Ruth noted ''liquor in his talk'' on their first date, after they were introduced in Washington, by James Barton, the actor.

''But there was no drunkenness. The Babe was not then, nor was he ever afterwards, either a drunk or a teetotaller. The Babe drank like a man and a gentleman.'' He never drank bourbon, she has recalled, sometimes scotch. But he preferred beer.

''I never saw anyone drink beer like Babe,'' Bengough remembered. ''But he always got to the park the next day.''

The spirit of the age encouraged exaggeration when it came to liquor. The Eighteenth Amendment saddled the country like a bad

President, and public challengers to it were regarded, in some thoughtful quarters, as knights.

To Heywood Broun, Ruth ''was a liberator who endeavored by personal example to show that no fun ever hurt you and that a bold spirit walks through the gloom ignoring old signposts, following instead his nose,'' a man ''uncorrupted by good living.'' Irritated when the head of the Anti-Saloon League singled out Bill Tilden, the tennis star, as exemplary because he didn't drink or smoke, McGeehan rooted for Babe to break his own home record partly ''because I am quite sure that Mr. Wayne B. Wheeler will not point him out as an example of what total abstinence will do. . . . I am not out to prove anything, but I am quite sure that statistics will show that the greater number of successes have been scored by those who have led moderately dirty lives.''

Even the matter of his eating is in some dispute. The second Mrs. Ruth challenged the story of the twelve hot dogs and eight bottles of soda pop. ''The Babe had a very delicate stomach, probably from not having too many square meals as a boy, and he had to be very careful about eating.'' But Weldon wrote, ''He was the most cheerful kind of hypochondriac. He ate ten times a day and complained that his stomach was a worthless sack, requiring endless doses of bicarbonate of soda.''

''Before changing clothes'' in the clubhouse, Red Smith wrote, ''the Babe would measure out a mound of bicarb smaller than the Pyramid of Cheops, mix and gulp it down. 'Then,' said Jim Cahn, 'he would belch. And all the loose water in the showers would fall down.' ''

Sometimes Ruth combined appetites, as Marshall Hunt told Jerome Holtzman in *No Cheering in the Press Box*. In Hot Springs, he said, he and Ruth would ''play golf every morning, and then we'd get tired of the food in the hotel, and I'd hire a car and we'd go out in the country looking for farmhouses that said, 'Chicken Dinners.' What the Babe really wanted was a good chicken dinner and the daughter combination, and it worked out that way more often than you would think.''

Dugan told Roger Kahn that Ruth was both god and animal.

Hoyt, who cherishes the memory of Ruth, said in 1973, "He was a juvenile, there was no doubt about it. We used to kid about Ruth being like a big dog, an airedale. He'd run hard all day with the other dogs, and then he'd come home at night, and you'd pet him on the head and tell him what a nice dog he was. He was sort of like a big animal in that way, but he never hurt anybody else—the ballplayers, the owner. Jesus, the fellow was beyond—the fellow was a whole ball team in himself."

Much of this is unimportant to the central proposition, which was, as Hoyt saw it in a memoir called *Babe Ruth As I Knew Him:*

"Ruth won for baseball the number one position in American sport. He did it all with a large bat, a homely face, a warming charm, a bad boy complex, an inherent love for his fellow man, an almost legendary indifference to convention and a personal magnetism more irresistible than the flute to the cobra."

The *Times* called him "the most popular man in the land." He signed his name more "than any ten movie stars combined," according to Weldon. He received thousands of letters a year. He usually tossed aside requests for money or other personal favors, unless charity was involved, and then he nearly always responded, no matter what the trouble was.

"Signing bats became an industry, although the profit was not his but others'." When the Indiana Knights of Columbus asked him to sign bats which it could use to raise money for homes for delinquent boys, "he lined up dozens of bats and signed them industriously." He did the same for the Masons of Oklahoma and the Elks of Nebraska.

His bedside visits to ailing youngsters dated back to the early twenties, but the most celebrated instance occurred during the 1926 World Series, when he received a request for an autographed baseball from eleven-year-old Johnny Sylvester of Essex Falls, New Jersey, critically ill with a mysterious blood ailment. From St. Louis Ruth promised the boy he would hit a home run for him.

"Do you really think he will do it?" the boy asked his father.

That was the day Ruth hit three.

And the day after the Yankees lost the Series, back in New

York, Ruth took a train to New Jersey. "It was God himself who entered [Johnny's] room," wrote Gallico, "straight from His glittering throne. God dressed in a camel's hair polo coat and flat camel's hair cap, God with a flat nose and little piggy eyes and a big grin and a fat, black cigar sticking out of the side of it."

The boy, as in story books, recovered. It is generally agreed that Ruth was happiest around children, most relaxed with them. Gehrig said he once had a date with Ruth in Chicago. "When he failed to meet me in the hotel lobby, I became alarmed. . . . However, he had left an address in case of emergency. At the end, I found him in a shabby apartment with a crippled Negro boy, telling the little fellow how to hit."

His failings were instantly recognized as human. He could not remember names, famous or otherwise. He broke a date with "that guy and girl from the movies" to go out with Pennock. The people from the movies were Douglas Fairbanks and Mary Pickford, the very clout of Hollywood in the twenties. Introduced to the French hero, Marshal Foch, Ruth asked politely, "Were you in the war?"

"To him, Urban Shocker was Rubber Belly, Pat Collins . . . was Horse Nose. All redcaps at railroad stations were Stinkweed and everybody else was kid," Red Smith wrote. "One day, Jim Cahn . . . watched two players board a train with a porter toting the luggage.

" 'There go Rubber Belly, Horse Nose and Stinkweed,' Jim said."

By the Seventies there were other professional team sports competing for attention. Even in the Twenties, there were other gods— Dempsey, Jones, Tilden, and Red Grange. But:

"My God, major league baseball was such a big thing then, occupying a third of the front page of the final editions of the New York, Boston, Philadelphia and Chicago papers," Hunt told Holtzman. "Politics, everything else, was pushed aside. . . . Ruth was getting daily perhaps twice as much publicity as the President."

As September rolled around, the musical, *Good News,* opened at the Forty-sixth Street Theatre in New York City, with songs like "The Varsity Drag" and "The Best Things in Life Are Free," so much a part of the national musical treasury that, in its search for happier times, 1973 would see a revival of the show. Good news, however, is what the other teams in the American League looked for without result.

The cry, "Break up the Yankees," which would bounce around baseball for the better part of four decades was given its first soundings: RUNAWAY RACE STARTS TALK OF YANKEE TRADES TO OTHER TEAMS was the *Times* headline. Gehrig was going to Detroit —where it was felt that Ruth and Gehrig were too powerful to play on the same team—Meusel to the White Sox for Willie Kamm, Lazzeri would be leaving.

Moriarty, the Detroit manager, called the Yankees "the baseball trust," and the *Times* noted that every time the team faced a critical series, they eliminated the threat and so destroyed the race, the most recent examples being the three-of-four sack of the Senators, the three-game sweep of Detroit.

"My good friend, Col. Jacob Ruppert . . . seems to be a very unreasonable man," McGeehan wrote. "It has been suggested, since the Yankees are so far out in front of the other teams . . . that the rest seem to be in South America, that Colonel Ruppert ought to break up the machine next season. . . .

"The argument for this is that it would make a better baseball league. . . . But as yet the Colonel has not shown any signs of getting ready to take off for the jump. . . . Somehow he does not see why he should pass around baseball players any more than Mr. Rockefeller should pass around oil wells or Mr. Ford automobiles. . . .

" 'When the Yankees were last, did anybody give me players?' demanded Colonel Ruppert. 'Maybe they did give me a couple of lemons, and now I should give away Gehrig or Ruth or Lazzeri?' "

McGeehan nailed the thing down with a comment on his town's

notorious appreciation of excellence: ''The sight of the Yankees winning baseball games may be monotonous to the customers of other cities, but it does not seem monotonous to the customers of New York, where they only have use for winners.''

As if to punctuate the argument, the Yankees demolished the Athletics, who had won twelve of fourteen games in the West, 12–2, on two home runs by Gehrig, one by Ruth. Combs collected four hits, including one of his triples; Koenig also hit safely four times, and Lazzeri added a double and two triples to the Yankee total of twenty hits.

But Yankee hopes for one record, which truly was more a matter of concern to the newspapermen than to the players, something to write about on a rainy day, ended in the next game when Grove, ''tall and slim and striking out nine,'' handed them their first shutout of the season, 1–0. Moore, who also pitched well, was the loser. Twenty-five thousand turned out for their last look at the home-run twins that season and, given a pleasant and unexpected surprise by the team so many had favored for the pennant, let loose a roar when Grove struck out Meusel, Lazzeri, and Dugan on ten pitches in the second inning.

Gehrig tied Ruth with his forty-fourth home run the next day, before Fenway Park's largest crowd of the season, thirty-six thousand, but the Yankees, after struggling back to tie the game in the ninth, lost the first half of a doubleheader, 12–11, in eighteen innings, before taking a 5–0 game called after five innings on account of darkness.

Interest in seeing the deadlocked Great American Home-Run Sweepstakes so gripped the Hub that an estimated fifteen thousand had struggled to get in after the gates were shut. The start was delayed twenty minutes while the outfield was roped off. Ruffing went fifteen innings against four Yankee pitchers—Pipgras, Giard, Shawkey, and Moore, who lost the game when he could not hold a three-run advantage his teammates gave him in the seventeenth.

Gehrig moved in front of Ruth the next day with a fifth-inning home run in the first game of a doubleheader. This was his last, brief threat in the home-run derby. He had pushed Ruth all season long into this final month. Koenig still remembered in 1973 Gehrig's habit of taking a great gasp of air, filling the bellows in his chest, before he addressed the pitcher, and he remembered the explosion as Gehrig swung, letting it all out, as it were, so that in terms of the infielders' physical safety, he was feared more than Ruth. Through the years Gehrig's uniform number, four, would be called by rivals "the hard number." But September, like the headlines all along, belonged to Ruth.

For the Babe demonstrated why he got more publicity than the President of the United States by hitting in the very next inning after Gehrig's home run "one of the mightiest of all Ruthian smashes, clearing the outfield wall," running up on a slow pitch by Tony Welzer and smacking it to dead center for "what all agreed was the longest blow ever hit at Fenway Park."

He hit another home run in the seventh inning and returned in the second game to hit yet another, amid such wild excitement that it was noted more or less in passing that the teams again split the games.

When he hit two more the next day, number forty-nine increasing his margin over Gehrig to four, the 12–10 Yankee victory was clearly an incidental. Five home runs in three consecutive games, the *World* noted, tied a record first set in 1887 by Michael Muldoon of the Cleveland Nationals, tied two years later by Mike Kelly of the Chicago Nationals, by Ken Williams of the Browns in 1922 and, a year earlier, by Ruth himself.

That was the Yankees' last road game of the season, and the *Sun* pointed out that this appeared to benefit Gehrig, who "liked to hit in the arena on the east bank of the Harlem River, while Ruth avers he would rather do his hitting almost any place else. Their attitudes toward hitting in the Stadium is reflected in the fact that the Babe has hit the majority of his home runs on the road, and Lou has made most of his at home."

As the Yankees returned, Thomas Cook and Sons advertised a package for another great event, a "Sport Airplane Cruise from Garden City, New York, to Chicago," 8 A.M. departure to "early evening arrival" for the Dempsey-Tunney rematch. Ringside seats were included along with a room in the Hotel Stevens, and the return flight with "comfortable chairs and observation windows from which to view landscape, clouds and strange lighting effects." All this for $575.

Along with the gelt, a certain *sangfroid* was a requisite for the trip. A Los Angeles-to-Hawaii air race had ended with six missing planes; a plane from Europe carrying a princess was lost; *Old Glory,* another plane, was missing on September 7. There were calls for an end to transoceanic flights. The Chambers of Commerce of Boston and Philadelphia withdrew offers of prize money for flights from Europe, although Cleveland still offered twenty-five thousand dollars to the pilots of the first plane to make that destination from abroad on the grounds that "mastery can be gained only by excellence."

The diamond Mussolini, as he was more or less routinely called in some of the press, hit the sacrifice fly that beat the Browns for the Yankees' nineteenth straight over the St. Louis club, 2–1. This was only appropriate, since Lazzeri was honored with a floral horseshoe from Italian societies before the game, and he had struck out twice before driving in Ruth, who scored "with an amazing spurt of speed and an amazing slide at the plate," proving "it is impossible to keep Babe out of stage center, no matter what the occasion is."

Hoyt's four-hitter was hailed by the *World* as "the pitching masterpiece of the season," but it was bettered the following day when Shocker allowed only three hits. Ruth, hugging stage center even without a home run, drove in three runs that started the Yankees rolling for the twentieth straight time over the Browns, 9–3. "While it is not likely that Babe Ruth will break his 1921 home run record or that the Yankees will set a new mark for winning games in the American League," Hennigan predicted in the *World,* "there is a good chance of the American League champions going through the season without losing a game to St. Louis. . . ."

Miss America was crowned before fifteen thousand at Atlantic City, Elenor Delander, her only revealed statistic her age, sixteen and a half. The fourth-place Senators, once a great threat, eliminated themselves as a pennant possibility in a loss to the White Sox. The Yankees set an American League mark by edging the Browns, 1–0, making it twenty-one in a row over St. Louis.

Moore was the winning pitcher, and Huggins took the occasion to point out that but for the old rookie, the team might be battling for its life, since his fifteen victories were just about the margin of the Yankee lead. He had only pitched four complete games, but he had worked in forty-five, and with his reputation as "the lifeguard of the staff," it became one of Barrow's fondest boasts that "I got him out of the record book," that is, with no personal scouting reports. Moore's salary was twenty-five hundred dollars with a five-hundred dollar bonus if he lasted the season, but now he felt secure enough to ask timidly if he did not deserve more money, and the club gave him a bonus variously estimated at twenty-five hundred or five thousand dollars.

In his column Ruth said that he looked forward to watching Moore work in the World Series. He was "the type of pitcher who's a mystery to any club the first time they face him. He's different than anyone in either league. For a single game pitcher, I'd rather see old Cy out there than any pitcher I know of."

Turning aside from his typewriter, Ruth hit his fiftieth home run, but this did not avert the Browns escaping the ultimate baseball indignity of losing in a season-long sweep. They closed out accounts by finally beating the Yankees, 6–2, although it is Dugan's recollection that the team had trouble concentrating on its work, having been entertained the previous night by his brother Elks of White Plains, N.Y., whose band serenaded them before the game, perhaps adding discordant effects to katzenjammers Dugan recalled almost fifty years later as monumental.

"As the ball landed in the bleachers," the *World* reported about Ruth's home run, "there was the best shower of straw hats seen at the Stadium this year. They came from all sections of the grandstand, and the game was halted while the field was cleared."

Among Ruth's foibles was a widely publicized set of superstitions—he always touched second base coming in from the outfield, he believed a yellow butterfly meant big news, good or bad, an empty barrel seen on the way to the ball park presaged victory—but he chose the thirteenth of the month to hit two home runs in a doubleheader defeat of Cleveland, that, it was noted without great excitement, clinched the pennant for the Yankees, who had been in first place all season.

Twenty-five thousand saw Hoyt, the league's leading pitcher, do the honors in the decisive second game, although "there was no celebration by either the fans or the players, who seemed to take the pennant for granted." The Yankees trailed, 3–1, in the seventh inning of the first game, when Ruth hit his first of the day's home runs with Koenig on first to tie the score. A few minutes later Meusel crossed the plate with the run that put the home team ahead to stay, while the Indians were engaged in trying to run down Lazzeri.

Again in the second game the Yankees trailed, 2–1, when Ruth's fourth-inning home run not only brought them abreast but signaled a four-run outburst that won the game. He was of definite value to the team.

"When the Yankees left on their final western trip," the *World* reflected, "Huggins was a bit doubtful about his team finishing in front and declared he would not smile until the pennant was won. He started smiling after the second game."

The dancer and international *amoureuse,* Isadora Duncan, whose celebration of free love titillated an age not without its hypocrisies, was killed when her scarf caught in the spokes of an automobile wheel. HAD PREMONITION OF DEATH was the revelation. In what might have been a cheerful episode from a Scott Fitzgerald novel, more than forty thousand saw the U.S. polo team retain the International Challenge Cup, defeating Britain, 8–5, in snooty surroundings on Long Island.

Showing no signs of easing up, the Yankees again defeated Cleveland, 4–1, moving within one game of a hundred victories, as Ruether allowed no Indians as far as third base until the ninth inning and so enhanced his chances of pitching in the World Series.

But "the principal event of the day was the failure of Ruth to hit a home run," the *Times* declared.

George Uhle pitched Cleveland to a 3–2 win the next day, in the year's final meeting of the teams, the sixth-place Indians losing the series by a narrow 12–10 margin, which was the best showing of any 1927 Yankee opponent. Ruth again demonstrated his talent—like Sherlock Holmes's dog that didn't bark—to attract attention when he *didn't* do something. He doubled, struck out, and twice flied out to deep right field. His sixth-inning out attracted the notice of the Ruthologists:

"It had all the earmarks of a home run, and the crowd let out a yell as the ball left the bat," the *World* reported. "Ruth trotted down to first base with a smile on his face.

"Homer Summa, who was standing on the embankment in right field when the ball was hit, rushed up against the bleachers and put his back against the screen. As the ball descended, Summa leaped up in the air and caught it in his upstretched, gloved hand. It was a spectacular catch, and the crowd cheered."

In other words, a long out. It was further noted that Ruth's double, which hit the top of the screen, narrowly missed being a home run.

The punchless White Sox came to town, murmuring, "Do with me as you will," and the Yankees swept a five-game series. They won the opener, 7–3, as Ruth collected his fifty-sixth homer and Moore, perhaps now seeing himself as some kind of hitting fool, shocked everybody, not least the proud Chicago pitcher, Ted Blankenship, by also hitting a home run.

"Ever since he became a member of the Yankees, Moore's greatest ambition has been to hit the ball into the bleachers and jog slowly around the bases, a la Babe Ruth," the *World* reported, "while the crowd cheered wildly.

"After Ruth's home run, Moore said, 'You know that I have spent all of my energy on pitching, but now the Yankees have clinched the pennant, I am going out and getting a few home runs.'

" 'I'll buy you the best box of cigars in town if you do,' said

Ruth. . . . In the fourth, Moore hit an outside pitch into the bleachers. 'That don't go,' Ruth objected. 'You had your eyes closed when you hit the ball.' ''

Meusel, the secret sharer, was the hitting star of the day with a homer, double, and single. Perhaps his uncommunicativeness made him slip by almost without notice, even when he did important things with his bat. Forty years later Hoyt wondered why Meusel was not in the Hall of Fame. "He was as good a ball player as I've ever seen," said the teammate of Ruth and Gehrig, the foe of Cobb and Speaker, the observer of Mays and Mantle.

More than a dozen years after Meusel starred for the greatest of all, a writer, searching for a comparison that would adequately capture the marvel of a throw by Joe DiMaggio, called it "one of the most remarkable . . . since the days of Bob Meusel."

But his silences matched those of Coolidge in duration and mystery. " 'Good morning' might be the day's conversation," Hoyt remembered. Daniel cited a time when Meusel, who was rooming with his brother Irish, the Giant outfielder, rose from the chair silently after Irish returned from a long road trip, went into the bedroom, packed his suitcase, and departed, without a word, on a long road trip of his own.

Nothing pathological or even grouchy was seen in any of this during the Coolidge administration. "It was only a characteristic of the man," Daniel said. And it was not that Meusel opted for the ascetic life. He was a companion of Ruth's.

He liked to call himself Ruth's manager after he booked them on a western tour following the 1922 World Series. "Ruth said I was the greatest manager he ever worked for," Meusel said proudly. "Why? I only had one rule. Ruth had to get to bed the same time I did. And I never did get to bed."

But the final word is a contemporary assessment: "A strange, cloistered gentleman is Mr. Meusel, impervious to gibes, threats or criticism. He moves through life in solitary splendor."

The scores of the next games were 3–2, Shocker beating Urban Faber, in a battle of lawful spitball artists, and 8–1, Pennock beating Connelly's curve-ball pitching, which was baffling only to the extent of sixteen hits.

The *World* reported an outbreak of infantile paralysis in the United States and Canada, although it did not appear as severe as the 1916 epidemic, which affected millions, hundreds dying, a reminder that the Twenties were not all bathtub gin and vo-do-dee-yo.

Where Combs was concerned, however, there was a touch of class not often emulated since. Between games residents of the bleachers presented him with a $125 gold watch, a condition being that the ceremonies take place at the bleachers, where all of them got to know each other, so to speak, rather than at home plate, traditional site for such affairs.

Combs expressed his appreciation with a home run.

"I hit a homer for them that day," he later recalled, "and my home runs weren't too frequent. I had only fifty-eight in twelve years, but if I could have limited it to one, I would have hit it then. Can you imagine them putting together nickels and pennies to buy me a watch?"

Thirty-five thousand were on hand, and the mood was not entirely one of good fellowship. Ruth was walked three times in the first game, inspiring un-Christian comment about Schalk. Ruth singled three times in the second-game romp, but he got no cigar, although he was swinging freely each time he came to bat, as long as the pitcher kept the ball inside city limits.

The race was long since decided, the pennant safely packed away, the remainder of the season could be viewed as preparation for the World Series, but forty-five thousand were on hand the next day "apparently for the sole purpose of seeing Ruth hit one." In the first game it was Gehrig, now hopelessly out of the Great American Home-Run Derby, who came closest with a sixth-inning triple that landed near the flagpole in center field. Fast fielding by Metzler kept him from scoring until Lazzeri brought him in with a single, but it was the margin, as Pipgras beat Al Thomas, 2–1.

In spite of the importuning of the crowd, Ruth failed to hit a

home run in the first game. In the fifth inning of the second, however, he caught a Ted Lyons curve and drove number fifty-four
into the right-field stands. He now had equaled his 1920 home-run
total, his second best year.

The warmth of the cheers gave even the Babe pause, although
he was used to them. What appeared to be the last straw hats of
summer—five of them—floated to the field. When Ruth returned
to the outfield at the end of the inning, a fearless ten-year-old boy
dashed out to greet him with pen and paper, and there were more
cheers when Ruth obliged him with a signature. The Yankees, it
was noted for the record, won the game, 5–1, Hoyt's twenty-
second victory of the season.

Five special trains carried New York-area fans to Chicago for
Dempsey versus Tunney, at prices ranging from $125 to $2,000.
Almost predictably, Thomas Cook reported only one of its thirty
special sports planes sold out. Infatuation with the toy of aviation,
however, continued, from the safety of the ground. More than
"20,000 aviation-hungry men and women" crowded the Spokane
airport to see the winners of derbies from New York and San Francisco.

In spite of Huggins' announced intention to keep the Yankees
geared up for the Series, however, only Ruth's fifty-fifth home
run, which gave him his second best season total ever, prevented a
Yankee shutout in the opener with Detroit, which they lost, 6–1.
Sam Gibson pitched well enough, but the two teams committed ten
errors, six of them by the Yankees. The small crowd was "first
shocked and then amused by Yankee ineptness. . . . A couple of
more days' rest, and they might fall completely to pieces." All
told, said the *World*, a demonstration "of how terribly a championship club can play."

But Ruth's fifty-sixth the following day, the afternoon of Tunney's long-count triumph, epitomized one of those magical days in
the Golden Age of Sport. The Yankees tied the record of 105 victories set by the Red Sox in 1912. Ruth hit the home run with
Koenig on base to win the game, 8–7, and "jerked the handful of

O

customers who remained out of their seats, yelling and cheering."

Millions listened to the fight on radio that night. Promoter Tex Rickard claimed this kept the gate below two million dollars, setting an example for squadrons of sports entrepeneurs through the ages. The medium was novel enough so that sophisticated, not to say jaded, hosts invited friends to listen at radio parties. Among the hosts were Edna St. Vincent Millay at her Fifth Avenue Hotel, the Maharajah of Rajpulpa at the Savoy Hotel in London, and the captain of the Cunard liner *Berengaria,* who ordered a special radio setup for 563 passengers.

Only fifteen thousand, one of the smallest Stadium crowds of the year, saw the Yankees set an American League record of 106 victories the next day, beating Detroit, 6–0, behind a three-hitter by Pipgras. The only extra-base blows were doubles by Combs and Lazzeri, and, although he contributed two singles that aided the scoring, Ruth was homerless, striking out twice, once with such force that he wrenched his shoulder.

He failed to hit a home run again the following day, to the dismay of thirty-five thousand as the Tigers made their last appearance of the season at the Stadium a 6–1 victory for Earl Whitehill, "who has been beaten by the Yankees many times [but] had them ducking and dodging a roundhouse curve." The fans, who stuck around for Ruth's last bat in the ninth inning, left muttering after he grounded out.

"If the manager of the winning team in the National League cares for a World Series' tip," offered the *World,* "it is to shoot left-handers with wide, sweeping curves at the Yankees. In their present condition, they can do little with such pitching."

More importantly, the *Times* pointed out, with four games remaining, Ruth would have to average a home run a game in order to break his record. "For one of Ruth's capabilities," it added presciently, "this is not altogether impossible."

As if to get the maximum effect as well as drama from his effort, Ruth waited until the bases were full in the sixth inning the next day, and then hit the sixth grand slammer of his career, beating

Grove and the Athletics, 7–4. The four runs gave the Yankees 952 for the season, breaking the record of 948 they had set in 1921. Gehrig also homered, his first since September 6, when he had moved ahead of Ruth for the last time. "Considering the day, which was cloudy and not too cool, and the state of the league race," the *World* noted, "there was a surprisingly large crowd on hand. The only answer appears to be that they came to see Ruth."

He gave them something to see when the Senators came to town, hitting two home runs to tie his old mark. The *Sun*'s headline writer made a judgment: RUTH'S EQUALLING HIS 1921 HOME RUN RECORD DECLARED BABE'S GREATEST FEAT IN BASE-BALL. But that was only a temporary opinion.

The first home run, in a 15–4 slaughter, came in the first inning off Lisenbee, the best non-Yankee pitcher in the league that year. Ruth hit a curve, low and outside. In the second inning, Lisenbee still pitching, Ruth crashed a drive to center which would have gone into the bleachers if it had been pulled a trifle. Instead it hit the barrier and went for a triple.

In the fifth inning, he hit number fifty-nine off a rookie named Paul Hopkins. The bases were full as Hopkins worked the count to three and two, and Ruth judged correctly that the young pitcher "would have to come through" with a fastball down the middle.

"What did you say his name was?" Ruth asked after the game. "Hopkins, eh? Very good."

"Hopkins should be grateful," the *Sun* noted. "Less than twenty-four hours ago, he was unknown. Now he is celebrated as the young man who pitched the ball Babe belted to tie his record. . . . Even the Babe knows his name, a distinction that can't be claimed by numerous players who have been in the American League a good deal longer than Master Hopkins."

This was a newspaperman's point of view, not, as it would soon develop, a pitcher's, but it was not just an effort to give the Babe another folksy failing. "After the game, a tall, good-looking chap, his black hair shower-plastered, shouldered his way into the Yankee clubhouse," Weldon wrote. " 'Autograph this for me, will you, Babe?' he asked Ruth. 'It was one of the home run baseballs.'

Ruth signed the ball, and, after the visitor left, asked, 'Who was that?'

" 'That was the guy you hit the first one off today—Horace Lisenbee.' "

Although only seventy-five hundred attended, the *Times* reported "the roar they sent up could hardly have been equalled by a capacity crowd." It was only the seventh grand slam of Ruth's career, "but his second in two days. That seems to be the way with this amazing infant. He makes miracles seem commonplace."

It was after the following day's game, one of the glories of baseball history, that John Kieran in the *Times* resorted to verse for the second time that season to ask the rhetorical question to which the whole world knew the answer:

> You may sing your songs of the old, old days
> till the phantom cows come home;
> You may dig up glorious days of yore
> from many a dusty tome;
> You may rise to tell of Rube Waddell and
> the way he buzzed them through,
> And top it all with the great fast ball that
> Russie's rooters knew;
> You may rant of Brouthers, Keefe and Ward
> and half a dozen more;
> You may quote by rote from the record book
> in a way that I deplore;
> You may rave, I say, till the break of day,
> but the truth remains the truth:
> From 'One Old Cat' to the last 'At Bat' was
> there ever a guy like Ruth?

BABE CARPENTERS NUMBER SIXTY! the *News* front page exclaimed. BABE CLOCKS NO. 60! echoed the *World*. BABE RUTH HITS 60TH HOME RUN, headlined the *Herald Tribune*, AS YANKS BEAT SENATORS, 4–2.

"Triumphing over age and veteran craft as on the day before he triumphed over youth and blazing speed," Monitor reported, "Babe Ruth yesterday set a new home run record. He clipped his sixtieth four-bagger of the year. . . . He did it off a slow ball as the day before he made number 59 off a blazing fast ball. He is hitting, and when he is hitting, nothing stops him. . . .

"I saw the Pirates acclaimed when they drove through the mist and rain to overcome the Senators to win a world championship two years ago. I saw Matty borne off in triumph after defeating Chief Bender in one of the greatest Series games ever pitched, and I saw Walter Johnson serenaded to the skies when he turned back the Giants in the twelfth inning at Washington in 1924, but I have never witnessed a heartier, more joyous scene of honest-to-goodness happiness than greeted the Babe as he trotted around the bases yesterday, 20,000 fans standing and paying tribute.

"Twenty thousand! The Yankees 'in' weeks ago, the Senators out of the running, nothing to draw anyone to the place to see the last few, flickering embers of a dying season. Nothing to draw them but the Babe, and when he came through, they gave him all they had. . . ."

If this was hyperbole, it was shared. "While the crowd cheered, and the Yankee players roared their greetings," said the *Times,* "the Babe made his triumphant, almost regal tour of the bases. He jogged around slowly, touched each base firmly, and when he embedded his spikes in the rubber disk to record officially Homer 60, hats were tossed in the air, papers were torn up and tossed crazily, and the spirit of celebration permeated the place."

That wasn't all. "Nobody ever got a livelier reception per capita than the Babe did," said the *Herald Tribune.* "When the Babe crossed the plate, he lifted his cap high and with the other hand waved a salute. He held his hand there in mid-air. 'Well, folks, here we are. How about it, folks?' . . . The Babe's stroll out to his position was the signal for a handkerchief salute in which all the bleacherites to the last man participated. Jovial Babe entered into the carnival spirit and punctuated his kingly strides with a succession of snappy military salutes."

Even so sardonic an observer as Paul Gallico joined in. AND HE

DID IT! ran the headline over his column, and he wrote, "They could no more have stopped Babe Ruth from hitting that home run that gave him a new world record than you could have stopped a locomotive by sticking your foot in front of it. Once he had that 59, that Number 60 was as sure as the rising sun. A more determined athlete than George Herman Ruth never lived. . . . He is one of the few utterly dependable news stories in sports. . . .

"A child of destiny is George Herman. He moves in his orbit like a planet. . . . I even recall writing pieces about [Gehrig and Ruth] and saying that Gehrig would soon break Ruth's cherished record and feeling kind of sorry for the old man, having this youngster come along and steal all his thunder, and now look at the old has-been. . . .

"Think of the eye, the coordination, the rhythm and strength it takes to hit sixty baseballs. . . . Succumb to the power and the romance of this man. Drop your cynicism and feel the athletic marvel that this big, uncouth fellow has accomplished. . . . I get a tremendous kick out of that egg. I like to have illusions about him. I like to believe that everything about him is on the level. I don't trust many things in sports, but Ruth I do, and I still get that silly feeling in my throat when he conks one, and I'm tickled silly. . . ."

The pitcher was Tom Zachary, "as wise and wily a lad as ever spun a roundhouse curve," according to Monitor, "a master marksman." He walked Ruth in the first inning, waking the beast in the crowd. Ruth singled in the fourth. Only a single, was the feeling. Again in the sixth, he singled, producing a run.

The eighth inning presented him his last chance. "All present knew it would be the last chance." The score was tied, 2-2. Koenig smacked a drive past Goslin, the ball taking a high hop and going for a triple. Ruth took a strike, "a beauty, slow and sinking." Another pitch, "beautifully placed, just outside the corner." He half swung at the next pitch, then pulled back.

"And then came another wobbling curve, and on this he swung," said Monitor, "and the ball went away, away up in the right field bleachers. Power did it, the power of the greatest slugger of them all. No other man could have driven as slow a pitch half the distance.''

In the hurly-burly of modern life is it remembered that the ball was caught by forty-year-old Joe Fornier of 1937 First Avenue, Manhattan, a fan for thirty-five of his years, who brought it to Ruth to be autographed?

Zachary pitched in the major leagues from 1918 to 1936, working for Philadelphia, Washington, and St. Louis in the American League, Boston and Brooklyn in the National. He came to the Yankees in 1928 and won a World Series game for them. He was, in point of fact, three and nothing in World Series competition. But he would be remembered only as the man who gave up Ruth's sixtieth home run, and Hoyt recalled an Old Timers banquet at the Plaza Hotel in New York when Zachary, introduced that way— ''the man who gave up''—pushed back his chair, got to his feet and stalked from the room. He deserved to be remembered for something other than his party-of-the-second-part role. He won 185 major league games, after all—and lost 191—and the respectful adjectives describing him the day he let loose a pitch he quickly wanted back indicated that he was something more than fortune's fool.

Through the years, including 1973, there has been a good deal of conjecture about Zachary's pitching to Ruth with one out and the lead run on third. A walk, it is argued, would have been more prudent. This is hindsight of the highest degree. No one questioned Zachary's strategy at the time. All season long, some pitchers had deliberately walked Ruth to their regret. Writers made fun of them after Gehrig hit a home run.

What Zachary was trying to do was both elementary and possible—get Ruth out. ''I gave him a curve, low and outside,'' he said. ''It was my best pitch. The ball just curved into the seats. Instinctively, I cried, 'Foul!' '' Even when he joined the Yankees, he said, he and Ruth never agreed on that point.

Once he added, with the smoldering resentment of the pitcher wronged, ''I'd rather have thrown at his big, fat head.''

There was the last game of the season to be played. Twenty

thousand turned out to see if Ruth would hit another home run, but with his fine sense of literature, he did not add an anticlimax. The Yankees won, 4–3, after Combs singled and Koenig tripled. Bob Burke walked Ruth, the prudent move some argued Zachary should have made the previous day.

Gehrig hit the ball, and the ball game, into the right-field seats.

And now the great waiter of life presented the bill, the final standings:

| New York | 110 | 44 | .714 | |
|---|---|---|---|---|
| Philadelphia | 91 | 63 | .591 | (8–14 with New York) |
| Washington | 85 | 69 | .552 | (8–14) |
| Detroit | 82 | 71 | .536 | (8–14) |
| Chicago | 70 | 83 | .458 | (5–17) |
| Cleveland | 66 | 87 | .431 | (10–12) |
| St. Louis | 59 | 94 | .386 | (1–21) |
| Boston | 51 | 103 | .331 | (4–18) |

The team had set all sorts of records, which are made to be broken—most games won by an American League team, 110; most runs scored, 971, most home runs, 158. In the cannonading it is all but ignored that Hoyt led the league with his 22–7 record. He was followed by Shocker, 18–6, Moore, 19–7, and Pennock, 19–8, before a non-Yankee, Lisenbee, 18–7, entered the lists.

Above all, there were Ruth's shining sixty home runs, which have not been improved on in the span of 154 games, although one day they will.

But all of that is bookkeeping and asterisks. At the beginning of the season only nine experts polled by the Associated Press picked the Yankees to win the pennant. Twenty-nine picked the Athletics.

There was still a World Series to play. But the man who asked "Was there ever a guy like Ruth?" now apotheosized the team:

> There were mighty men in the good old days,
> When you and I were young.

They were there with the skillful fielding plays
And there with the wagon tongue.
Yes, the Cubs were great in Chance's time
And the Pirates great in Wagner's prime
But I'll lay five bucks to one thin dime
There was never a team came crashing through
Like Ruth and the rest of the Yankee crew.
Like Combs and Lazzeri and Buster Lou,
The battering boys from the Harlem banks.
What ho! The Yanks!

# Eight

○

Two comfortable American fictions, out of similar psychological roots, died hard and painful deaths in the late Sixties.

One was the myth of the Yankee pinstripe. The other might be called the Truman effect. Put simply, this last stated that the Presidency ennobled a man. Through some confusion of the office and the individual, always a problem in American thought, it was held that merely by accession to the White House, a man became stronger, wiser, better.

Never mind Harding and what Mencken called his cutie in the broom closet, or Pierce lapsing into alcoholism, or the whole string of sorry specimens following Andrew Johnson. The American boy learned in civics class or history courses that the Presidency touched a mythic chord and improved a man, like the love of a good woman or the confession of sin.

And this became something more than another half-digested, pleasant teaching of grammar school, the belief was given flesh by the example of Harry Truman. He was maligned in office, but it was apparent almost immediately that his Presidency was sound, not free of error, but impressive enough so that historians gave him high marks, a good Presidency, almost a great one. Never mind the revisionists, they are always with us.

The Truman effect, then, for a euphoric period seemed to rein-
force the schoolboy's belief in the almost mystical, ennobling
powers of the highest office in the land. But by 1973 it was clear
that far from ennobling, or even improving, a man, the Presidency
could diminish him, could isolate him and feed his pettiness, his
paranoia, and his vindictiveness.

And so it was with the myth of the Yankee pinstripe, which held
that simply by putting on a Yankee uniform, a ball player became,
not nobler and wiser, but steadier, more talented, possessed of un-
suspected or renewed talents. The Sains, Mizes, and Country
Slaughters found new lives as Yankees after being apparently worn
out in the service of other teams.

But by 1973 that fiction, too, was dead, one more assumption of
American life in the dust. The Yankees, like the Republic, lapsed
into mediocrity, and retreads couldn't help them, not even by the
familyfull, like the Alous. The Truman effect was of the great
world, of course, and affected the destinies of millions; the myth
of the Yankee pinstripe was only part of sport, a toy department in
American life, but the collapse of those legends in the convulsive
Sixties symbolized the changed and diminished view a nation took
of itself.

Not that the slaughtered mythologies meant an end to romanc-
ing. Other legends died harder. There were still, in 1973, New
Yorkers who identified in complicated ways with the Giants and
Dodgers, more than a decade after the teams fled the city, finding
them somehow forever lovable, forever New York.

A corollary to all this, in baseball, was a hatred of the Yankees,
not so much based on identification with one of their victims, but
expressed in the easy wisecrack, "Rooting for the Yankees is like
rooting for United States Steel." Now all front offices in baseball
are conducted along the lines of that board-room philosophy
which regards life as a bookkeeping, but comparing a ball club that
produced, through the decades, Babe Ruth, Lefty Gomez, and
Yogi Berra to United States Steel is simple-minded.

Since Americans like to think rooting for the underdog is so
American that it should be included in the citizenship require-

ments, it can be argued that it was no more than good old underdog-loving to hate the Yankees as they piled success on success in the Twenties, Thirties, Forties, Fifties, and early Sixties—a standard of excellence no other team in professional sport even remotely approached.

But there was an ingredient less pleasant and more unmanly (if the word is sexist, so be it). By 1973, as a television critic called Cyclops pointed out, self-pity had been injected into the national bloodstream, into entertainment as exemplified by Jack Paar and into politics as exemplified by Richard Nixon. The anthem of a nation which once prided itself on its courage and self-reliance became a great whine, its chorus swelled by women, blacks, hardhats, Wasps, ethnics of all sorts. And, at the end of what is in the main a marvelously funny book about the team that lost more games than any other team in major-league history, Jimmy Breslin asked:

"So the Mets are a bad ball club. All right, they're the worst ball club you ever saw. So what? . . . The Mets lose an awful lot? Listen, mister. Think a little bit. When was the last time you won anything out of life? "

With a little catch in the throat, then, the fan in the Seventies departs for the ball park, set to cheer the fellow who drops the ball, preferring parody to the game as it should be played, secure in the knowledge that in that other area of life, to which he gives so little thought, the Presidency enshrines and ennobles, as sure as the Giants are the team of his childhood and the Dodgers remain Brooklyn.

But the bottom line is this: For a consideration, to be sure, but for a consideration modest by the demented standards of the Seventies, the Yankees stayed. While other teams went west or followed the fans to the suburbs, deserting the great cities which made them rich, but which are now riddled with hatreds and poverty, while other teams put off the problems by avoiding them, like the alcoholic who changes mates, jobs, locations, but keep drinking, the Yankees stayed.

Other, more lovable teams—why shouldn't they be lovable?

they were losers, losers like yourself, mister—fled with the dollar on its suburban course.

The Yankee success was so constant. it was monotonous. For the better part of five decades, the Yankees won. So, even though it was simple-minded, it was easy to see them as the soulless corporation.

But the bottom line remained.

The Yankees stayed.

The Stadium was surrounded by a wire fence, which served as a moat, in the post-season fall of 1973, effectively shuttered for the first time since it opened as "the House That Ruth Built" in 1923. It was guarded over one leaden afternoon by a blustering fellow, swollen with authority, who gave life to the old saw about what happens to some men when they put on a uniform.

It stands in a polyglot, deteriorating neighborhood of the kind encouraging other teams to put on the snoot. Near the main gate, which echoed through decades of autumnal afternoons to the scuffle of feet at World Series time, there was only a whistle of wind. Lined in serried rows were the uprooted seats, repositories once to elegant or plebian rumps whose owners bore witness to any of a thousand afternoons and evenings of what was once the sunshine game. At twenty dollars each, the seats were being sold by the Inivrex-Cuyahoga wrecking firm, which demolished the Polo Grounds and the Metropolitan Opera, and which was involved in renovation of the Stadium.

("The Stadium isn't really being destroyed," a company representative told Larry Merchant of the New York *Post*. "The changes that will be made will be for the fans' comfort." The changes include destruction of the rooftop façade, the outsize gingerbread facings which should have been designated historical landmarks. "Additionally," Merchant said, "the magnificent sweep of the Stadium's shell will be broken up by three modern escalated towers that will be grafted onto it, like milk containers stapled into a Henry Moore nude.")

For the fans' comfort, too, the seats were being sold.

O

"There'll be new seats going in," a workman said this fall afternoon. He lit a cigarette. "Probably plastic."

The day, with its lowered, faintly threatening sky and the sparse landscape—a couple of workmen, a visitor, the uprooted seats, the bounce of a subway train—embodied the gulf that separated the team in 1973 from the greatest of all.

In 1927 the Yankees faced the Pittsburgh Pirates at World Series time. The Yankees were modest favorites, although it was noted that they had lost three of four previous Series. "It was just as well the Giants had not won," the *World* observed, "for half a Series is enough to make us balmy in the head," although "seeing the Yankees win is the most monotonous thing we know of, save seeing Gene Tunney get the decision over Jack Dempsey."

The Pirates had wrested the National League pennant after a season-long, fang-and-claw struggle with the Cardinals, winners of the pennant the previous year; the Giants, winners of three pennants earlier in the decade; and the Cubs. It was "the greatest race in league history," according to John Heydler, the circuit's president in 1927, a genuine race between four complete baseball teams.

The Pirates were true champions, all right. Paul Waner, in his sophomore season, was already called, with good reason, "Big Poison," having won just about all the league offensive championships—batting .380 on 237 hits, driving in 131 runs—and Lloyd Waner, "Little Poison," hit .355 in this, his first big-league season, and collected 223 hits, a record for a rookie. According to Lieb, their nicknames derived from being identified by someone with a Bronx accent as "the big person" and "the little person," and so with unconscious art, that simple identification twisted into the fearsome tag opposing pitchers found appropriate.

Manager Donie Bush in midseason benched the third outfielder, the enormously popular Kiki Cuyler, who had batted .357 and scored a record 144 runs in the Bucs' pennant year of 1925, and replaced him with the pedestrian Clyde Barnhart. Cuyler had complained about batting second or third, but the specific incident that caused his banishment was failure one day to slide in an attempt to break up a double play. Some Pittsburgh columnists, and a good many fans, sided with Cuyler, but Bush, a former player with Detroit and Washington, was running a tight ship. He kept Cuyler in the dugout and, in the off-season, would trade him to Chicago, leaving him to reflect, "I played between the two Waners, the greatest outfielders I ever had the good fortune to be with. We weren't together long, but I believe that if I hadn't been traded to Chicago, there is no telling what records this trio might have made."

Since all three are in the Hall of Fame, there is no telling, indeed.

Most experts gave Pittsburgh an edge over the Yankees on the left side of the infield, with the storied Pie Traynor, .342, "playing third as it was seldom played before," and Glenn Wright, .281, at shortstop. George Grantham, .305, was at second and at first was Joe Harris, .326, a purchase Pittsburgh owner Barney Dreyfuss made after remembering Harris hitting .440 for Washington against his club in the World Series.

The catching was divided between Johnny Gooch, .258, and "Silent Earl" Smith, .270, and currently in bad odor for flattening Boston's Dave Bancroft earlier in the season with a sneak punch to the jaw. He was no stranger to the Yankees, having caught in the World Series against them for the Giants, once riding Meusel so hard that Languid Bob warned him as he took first on a walk, "If I get around to third, I'm stealing home. So be careful." Meusel did take third and did steal home. There was no collision at the plate because Smith dropped the ball. He was bigger than Bancroft but considerably smaller than Meusel; it is instructive how these things work out.

Pirate pitching, it was felt, would give the Yankees trouble. Ray Kremer, 19–8, was regarded as the ace of the staff with his league-leading 2.47 earned-run average, although the bespectacled Carmen Hill, 22–11, was the club's biggest winner. Lee Meadows, 19–10, also wore glasses, and much was made of this in 1927. Vic Aldridge, 15–10, rounded out the starters. Kremer and Aldridge won two games apiece in the 1925 World Series. John Miljus, a hometown Serb, won eight games in relief, including the pennant-clincher, and was a World War hero besides, with "sixteen or seventeen wounds."

All were right-handed, which was a problem, since most managers liked to think that left-handed pitching was harder for the Yankees to hit, but Meadows and Aldridge were curve-ball pitchers, which also was supposed to trouble the Yankees, and Bush said flatly, "I spent the greater part of my career in the American League and believe that National League pitching is better."

Hornsby, who had managed the Cardinals to victory over the Yankees a year earlier, predicted a Pittsburgh victory. "The Pirates will outhustle the Yankees," he said, "just as all National League teams always do . . . with American League teams. That hustling and fighting spirit cause the breaks that mean so much in a short series like this one." It was a speech which was copied and widely used, futilely, against the Yankees for four decades.

Pittsburgh's team batting average of .305 was only two points below New York's, but the entire club hit only fifty-four home runs, and when Ruth and Gehrig, who had 854 total bases between them, took batting practice in Forbes Field, Hennigan noted, "Ruth's mighty drives caused shivers to run down the backs of Pittsburgh fans, and Lou's terrific clouts—the broad-shouldered first baseman sent the ball into the grandstand—put the followers of the Pirates into a coma."

The story is disputed that the Yankee cannonading took the starch out of the Pittsburgh team before the first ball was pitched, although the Pirates played some innings like a team intimidated. One reporter swore he watched the Yankee wrecking crew in the company of the Waner brothers and heard one of the poisons say to the other, "Jesus, they're big," and the other reply, "Let's get out of here," although Bush, combative since his playing days, announced, "The heck with that demonstration. Let's show 'em we have a few hitters ourselves."

Ring Lardner, covering the games for the *World,* suggested, "It would be clearly unfair to pit these two teams versus each other on even terms. The Yankees won the pennant the day before the season opened, and the only thing they had to worry about since was the remote possibility that one of the other American League clubs would trade itself in bulk for Casey Stengel's Toledo club [which had just won the first American Association pennant in that city's quarter-century of trying] and thus introduce an element of competition.

"Whereas on the other hand, the Pirates are nervous. If they ain't nervous, they ain't human. I don't mean to imply that they are scared. If they were the kind of boys that get terrorized, they would have jumped right out of the league just listening to the Giants talk."

Whatever the state of the Bucs' nerves, their fans were fearless in their curiosity. Forty-one thousand, four hundred and eighty-seven of them filled the park "and would have filled it once more if there had been room," said the *World*. "As it was, there wasn't room in the whole ball park for an extra pocket flask. They say tears rolled down the cheeks of Uncle Barney Dreyfuss the size of little green apples at the size of the turnaway. He had done his best by Pittsburgh, his country and himself by building extra bleachers out by the center field fence. Row A began at the top . . . and the ringside seats extended back beyond the Monongahela River. . . .

"Forbes Field opened its gates at 10 A.M. Hundreds stood in line all night for bleacher seats. They slogged in tiredly. By noon, the lines stretched clear down Sennet Street. . . ."

With Ruth on base in the first inning, Gehrig hit a lofty fly, on which Paul Waner, "anxious to impress in his first World Series," attempted a shoestring catch. The ball rolled past him for a triple. Since Meusel followed with the third out, the mistake was obviously costly.

The Pirates grabbed the run back immediately, when Lloyd Waner was hit by Hoyt's pitch, moved to third on brother Paul's double and scored on Wright's fly to Combs.

The third inning produced the kind of action Yankee-haters tell their children about, to pass along the disease. Grantham fumbled

Koenig's grounder. Ruth singled. Gehrig and Meusel walked, sending Koenig home. Lazzeri forced Meusel at second, Ruth scoring, and Gehrig moving to third. Smith threw down to Traynor, catching Gehrig off base, but Gehrig scored when Smith, perhaps recalling the Meusel caper, dropped the ball.

In the fifth inning Koenig doubled and scored on an infield out and a sacrifice fly. That proved to be the winning run. The Pirates pecked away at Hoyt, who was pitching with a stiff neck, and Moore came on in the eighth inning with the winning run on base. He allowed one score but that was all, and the Yankees, outhit, nine to six, won, 5–4.

After the game Huggins praised Kremer but added, "He is the type of pitcher who is easy for my batters. I don't think we need fear him any more." He also praised Ruth, who singled three times, and Gehrig. "As long as the pitchers pitch to them, they will make runs, and Pittsburgh pitched to them."

If Monitor missed "the pitching wizardry of the Benders, the Joe Woods . . . the crashing deeds of Home Run Baker and Cobb and Speaker," New York City demonstrated that its sophistication was inches deep. Fifteen thousand fans stood in City Hall Park and watched the game played on the *World*'s scoreboard in front of the Pulitzer Building. "Men in shirtsleeves and caps, men in well-cut suits and gray felt hats, messenger boys and portly old bankers from Wall Street, they all stood shoulder-to-shoulder with their eyes glued to the board." It was further recorded that "every radio shop in town had its quota of fans" and "every radio . . . in Bellevue Hospital was tuned on the Series."

When Bush noted that the team which won the first game of the 1926 World Series did not win the championship, FPA growled in "The Conning Tower": "We have no more desire for immortality than the next fellow, but we would like to live long enough to read the statement of the manager of the team that lost the first game of the World Series which would not be to the effect that the loss of the game was the most encouraging thing that could have happened, and that it was a sign his team would win."

The fan-manager exercised the unlikely option of criticizing

Huggins *before* the event, questioning his choice of Pipgras to start the second game. It was held to be too important a contest for the relatively inexperienced Viking, and Bush said, "George has got a lot of stuff when he gets it over, but he's hot-headed, and when he gets sore, he loses control." He expressed "all the confidence in the world," in Aldridge, the Hoosier schoolmaster, his starting pitcher for the second game, and uttered other managerial sounds: "Then we have Meadows and Hill to follow up. I can't see where New York is nearly as well-fixed in the pitching department."

The doubts about Pipgras seemed well founded when Lloyd Waner scored after opening the game with a triple, but that was about the extent of Pipgras' problems. He was "the sensation of the Series thus far," according to the *World*. "He allowed only seven hits and these were scattered over as many innings. Never once was he in trouble, and he gave up only one base on balls." Bengough said, "Pipgras pitched one of the best games that I ever caught. Never did he give me any worry, and the Pirates were helpless before him after Waner's triple."

The third inning again unhinged the Pirates. Combs singled to right to start things off. Koenig singled over second, and Lloyd Waner misplayed the ball, Combs scoring and Koenig racing to third. Ruth sacrificed Koenig in. Gehrig doubled. Meusel singled him to third, and he scored on Lazzeri's sacrifice. Three runs would have been enough, but the Yankees added three more to win, 6–2.

"They simply outclassed the Pirates in the second game. It looks now as if they are not only the best team in the American League but in the National League and any other league which may be invented. Nothing short of the League of Nations, if it goes in for baseball, can stop the Yankees."

Ruth was uncustomarily hitless in the game but customarily irrepressible afterward, cavorting for the newsmen in the shower with the cheerful chant, "It's just a breeze now, boys." Aldridge had struck him out, to the wild delight of the fans, and, said the *World,* "The star of all time dropped his head, sensible of his shame. That's the glory of Ruth. He takes his job seriously . . . . Like the famous Casey, he makes a strikeout more exciting than the three-base hit of another man.'' And, in spite of his hitless day, ''he fielded spectacularly'' and drove in a run with a sacrifice fly.

Lazzeri announced that the team should be shot if it returned to Pittsburgh, the action switching to the Stadium for three games, if necessary. The Pirates, who had feasted on left-handed pitching all season long, announced they could hardly wait to get at Pennock, a feeling that lasted until his first pitch.

The highly touted National League pitching, meanwhile, didn't seem particularly different to the Yankees from what they had been looking at all year long. ''Wow! The first real shout from the crowd of more than 60,000 comes when Earl Combs whistles one over the bespectacled dome of Master Meadows,'' wrote Hunt in a play-by-play account as exuberant as the era. ''A fine beginning, Earl . . . A hit! A hit! Koenig pops a bouncer over the box. . . . Woe settles over the field. Your hero, George Herman Ruth, has done nothing more then raise an easy pop to Master Wright.

''Woe, hell! Whoopee! Three whoopees! Columbia Lou Gehrig smites one of Master Meadows' offerings out to center field, the longest and most thunderous hit of the Series, which was pursued furiously by Messrs. Barnhart and Waner. Around the bases raced Combs and Koenig and Gehrig, and the first two scored.

''Hurry, Lou, hurry! Now Barnhart has tossed the ball to Waner and Waner to Wright and Wright to Gooch, and bless us if Mr. Gehrig isn't absolutely out at the home plate, trying to stretch a mammoth triple into a home run.''

Meanwhile, no Pirate was reaching first base. ''One of the choicest bits of misinformation about the current World Series,'' Will Murphy wrote in the *News,* ''had to do with the murderous deeds the Pirates performed on left-handed pitchers.

''Yes sir, the Pirates just laid them waste when they threw from the first-base line. This seems to be slightly erroneous.'' The crowd hushed as Pirate after Pirate, wagging heads, returned to the dugout. These were not the foul weeds of expansion baseball, either, but a lineup laced with Hall of Famers, ''The Waner boys, Wright, Traynor, Harris and the rest of those vaunted Pirate clouters were made . . . to appear like .250 hitters on a high school scrub team.''

Not until twenty-two men went down in a row did Traynor single. By that time, the proud league champions were in disarray. ''Crash! That was a good one! Lazzeri peeled a nice single to center'' to open the Yankee seventh. ''Dugan slapped one at Meadows, and Lee pivoted to get Lazzeri at second, but Tony was too fast and beat the throw,'' wrote Hunt. ''Durst batted for Grabowski and was retired. Pennock was next and was given a great reception by the customers.

''Now, this is something like it! Pennock slapped one to [second baseman Hal] Rhyne, who winged to the plate to get the onrushing Lazzeri, but the signor slid under Gooch as though he were greased, and the Yankees had another run. Of course, Dugan took third on the play. . . .

''Whee! Wotta sock! Professor Combs slammed a nice single to center, leaping Dugan scoring and Pennock legging for third. . . . O! O! What was that? Why, Kid Koenig slapped a beautiful double off the face of the right field bleachers, Pennock scoring and Combs shagging for the third with alacrity. Then it was the Lee and his spectacles went far away, and in came Michael Cvengros, a very left-handed young man. . . .

''Now came the great song of joy, a deafening, cheering cry of delight, a sustained chorus of rejoicing. You guessed it! That incomparable person, George Herman Ruth, dug his cleats into the soil, took a few practice swings, and then it happened—the greatest thrill in baseball, a home run by the game's most ferocious player.

''O, a home run is a home run, but none is quite like one from the bat of G. Herman. . . . Far into the right field bleachers the ball carried its course, a he-man sock, indeed!

''Torn score cards floated like snow from the upper tiers of the vast Stadium as the illustrious one stepped on first, turned his head to assure himself that the ball had found safe haven, then on to second, third and home, and ahead of him danced Professor Combs and Marcus K. The Series is now a complete success. . . .''

The Pirates added a couple of hits to score a meaningless run in the ninth inning. The final score was 8–1. "Offhand, I cannot imagine any championship team being more thoroughly steeped in disgrace than the Pirates," reflected Murphy, in phrases applied earlier to the mighty Athletics, the mighty Senators, to any team that crossed the path of the greatest of all.

"Of course the Yankees won. It was a typical Yankee game, the kind that Stadium fans have been used to watching all year . . . perfect fielding and two innings of berserk slugging, winding up with a terrific slam by George Herman Ruth."

But "the town is talking of only one thing today. Not about the Yankees winning their third straight game from the Pirates . . . not about the local heroes scoring eight runs to Pittsburgh's one; not about the massive home run . . . No, wherever you go, you hear only, 'What a pity!' 'What a shame!' They are referring to the beautiful thing that was Pennock's game for seven innings. . . . Who has not dreamed of a perfect ball game pitched in a World Series?" But that, of course, was down the road, for another Yankee to accomplish.

At that, Pennock might have been the man if he had been entirely healthy. He had been "half-killed by a line drive in batting practice on Tuesday, if you can believe what you hear. One of his knees was practically shot out from under him." So he pitched only seven and a third innings of perfect ball. It was his fifth straight World Series victory. There were no losses. And the old words of consolation were hauled out for the Pirates, the southpaw-murderers, "That wasn't a left-hander you faced. That was Herb Pennock."

The story circulated that a West Virginia mountaineer ripped apart his newfangled crystal set, muttering, "Something is wrong with this damned thing. Not a Pirate hit comes out of it."

But the Pirates did not fold. They hopped on Moore, who was a surprise choice to start the fourth game, with a first-inning run on Lloyd Waner's single, followed by Glenn Wright's hit. The Yankees immediately came back on singles by Combs, Koenig, and Ruth.

The score remained tied until the fifth inning. Then Combs singled, Koenig struck out, and Ruth smacked the 426th home run of his career, his tenth World Series home run, causing Grantland Rice to reach into his memory book:

"There was a sausage-shaped balloon swaying against the gray October sky. Ruth's wallop almost hit the balloon. It sailed up far and high in a mighty arc, and when it fell, it was many, many yards beyond the reach of anyone except the spectators. . . . Paul Waner in right field and Lloyd Waner in center each took a couple of steps in the general direction of the ball's skyward path. Then the two Waners stopped dead. . . ."

That would have been the ball game if the Yankee defense, flawless to date, did not unravel in the seventh inning. Smith tapped the ball to Gehrig, but Moore, covering first, dropped the throw. Lazzeri then fumbled Fred Brickell's pinch-hit grounder.

"The ground was soft and slow," he later explained, "and I expected a hop that never came. Geez, it almost ruined everything."

With two men on base who should have been two outs, Lloyd Waner sacrificed them along. Barnhart singled in one run. Paul Waner's sacrifice tied the score.

Miljus, the pennant-clincher, came on in relief of Carmen Hill, for whom Brickell had batted. Combs walked to open the ninth. Koenig's pop fly sacrifice bounced off the ankle of the usually sure Traynor. Ruth, amid bedlam, came to the plate. "Miljus in his eagerness dumped a wild pitch beyond all reach," moving Combs and Koenig along. Miljus then walked Ruth deliberately.

McGraw and Wilbert Robinson, who were in the stands, called Miljus' next moments "one of the greatest exhibitions ever seen." With the bases loaded, looking into the very muzzle of Murderers' Row, he struck out Gehrig and Meusel. He now faced Lazzeri, who must have been swept with a wave of *déjà vu,* since he batted against Alexander in similar circumstances just a year earlier.

The stands and the dugout were full of advice for Huggins. The players urged a squeeze play on him. The gray-faced little man was firm.

"Listen, we don't have to take a chance at all," he said. "That fellow is bearing down too hard. It isn't in the cards for him to get away with it. If Tony doesn't hit one, he'll wild pitch."

The words were barely out of his mouth before Miljus threw a "sailer" that didn't drop but kept rising, like the daffodil to the sun. Gooch couldn't reach the ball. Combs, "a mighty happy Kentucky boy," raced for the plate and crossed it with the winning run, 4–3.

"The most dramatic battle of the brief series was thrown away at the most dramatic moment of the afternoon," Rice wrote. "The final game carried more high spots than the other three put together."

Miljus was disconsolate. "If only it had ended any other way. If they had knocked the ball out of the park—anything but a wild pitch. That's terrible."

Some felt it was a passed ball, and Gooch tried to take the blame. "It was my fault," he said. "I should have had it."

"No," said Miljus, "it was mine. I threw the ball too high and too hard."

Huggins, bone-weary after the long season, received visitors almost mechanically, slumped at his desk, but his first words demonstrated his thoughtfulness, class, as it came to be called.

"Say something nice about the Pirates. Don't be hard on them. It was tragic to lose a ball game that way, and they were a much better ball club than they showed in this Series."

But "Pittsburgh was badly outclassed" in Rice's eyes. "The weary-looking Pirates were outbatted, outfielded and outpitched. They were badly outfought. For three days that Yankee juggernaut had rolled in ruth and Ruthless fashion. . . .

"When the Yankees broke the American League record for victories and Ruth set off 60 home runs, there was the old cry that the curve-ball pitching from the National League would tell another story. But Pittsburgh pitching could not stop either the Yankees or Babe Ruth. The Yankees were never crowded until the final game, and then it took two simple errors in a row to haul the Pirates within reach."

It was the second four-game sweep in Series history, the only other being the Braves' triumph over the 1914 Athletics. Two other teams, the 1907 Cubs and the 1922 Giants, won four games, but each also tied one.

Having got the hang of it, the Yankees again swept the Series in 1928, beating the Cardinals after finishing two and a half games ahead of the As, although Ruth limped through the Series on a bad ankle, Combs, a finger broken, managed only a pinch-hit appearance, Pennock was out with a lame arm, and Lazzeri played with one; in 1932 and 1938 the Yankees swept the Cubs, in 1939, the Reds, and, in 1950, the Phillies. Those were only sweeps. There were six other Yankee world championships between 1927 and 1950.

Were the 1927 Yankees, then, the greatest of all, not just the greatest of Yankee teams, but the greatest team of all times, although it can be argued that one is the same as the other? It is customary to fudge, or even to cop out, at the questions, explaining that the game has changed, that it is comparing apples and oranges or even to choose the obvious retreat into banality: "We will never know."

But that would be the easy way.

Baseball players and their wives are notably loyal to the memories of their teams. Bengough might have spoken for all the greatest of all when he called the 1927 team "the greatest combination in the history of the game." The second Mrs. Ruth said flatly, "The 1927 Yankees were the greatest baseball team that ever played, and my husband was the greatest player on that team."

Dugan, standing in the clubhouse of the 1939 Yankee team that had just won the world championship for the fourth straight time, said, "This Yankee club may be greater than the 1927 team. I doubt that very much. Let that go. But we certainly had a lot more fun," pointing to "a quiet and sober group of players sitting in front of a Yankee locker."

And in 1973 he recalled saying years later to Red Ruffing, who pitched against the greatest of all and then for the dynastic Yankees of the Thirties, "You probably had a better team than we did." Dugan was just testing, of course. "And Ruffing said, 'Yeah? Let's see how many of our guys could take your guys' places.' That's all he said." Calling off the names of fine old wines, Dugan intoned, "Ruth, the greatest ball player who ever lived. Combs, a star of the first magnitude. Meusel, the greatest thrower who ever lived. The three of them and Lazzeri each knocked in 100 runs that year.

"Gehrig, a superstar, one of the greatest. Lazzeri, a star, a great thrower, good hitter. Koenig, erratic but he made it up with his hitting. Dugan. Ah, one of the lesser lights, but yes, I'll go for this: I could field as well as anybody in those days. The catching, ordinary. Hoyt, a star. Pennock, a star. Pipgras, a good pitcher. Moore, the best relief pitcher I ever saw."

The old Yankees are modest. Dugan, answering Ruffing's question, would surely have excluded himself at third base, choosing Red Rolfe, say, of the Thirties team. Similarly, Koenig said of the 1952 club, which also had won a fourth straight world title, "This New York team is good, but they couldn't have handled us over a season. Heck, there isn't but one guy here who could crack that outfit. That'd be Rizzuto. He'd beat me out at short." He reflected, a judicious man. "Maybe Mantle in a few years and Berra. Well, I guess Raschi and Reynolds might make it. But then, we had Hoyt, Pennock, and Pipgras."

Combs, who served as a coach with the Yankees and Red Sox after ending his playing career, said of 1927: "It was the greatest year I experienced personally. Ruth broke the home run record. Gehrig led the league in doubles, and I led in triples and base hits. The team averaged better than six runs a game.

"The '27 team was the greatest I ever saw while playing. I've been out of baseball since 1954 and haven't seen too many games, but I read a lot, and from what I can tell, it was the greatest team ever."

Pennock, a thoughtful man like Hoyt and Combs, and, like them a professional observer of the game—he was general manager of the Phillies when he died of a stroke in 1948—was firm on the matter to the end. "Our outfield was marvelous, our infield great, our pitching fine. Our catching was secondary, but it was the best ball club ever."

The arresting fact, of course, is that similar judgments were being made during the 1927 season. People who saw the Yankees play that year did not wait for memories to fix things up. So persistent was the claim that these players were the greatest of all, that the Pirates had barely joined the Athletics, the Senators, and the Tigers in the oblivion which engulfed impertinent challengers, when *Baseball* magazine undertook, in three monthly issues, to answer the question: "Were the 1927 Yankees The Greatest Baseball Team of All Time?"

J. Newton Colver asked of history's great clubs "How far did they exceed the pace of their day?" How many more runs did the team score than its contemporaries, for example, how many bases did it steal, how did its fielding compare and so forth. It is weighty stuff to read, freighted with statistics, fever charts and tables, a noble effort. Colver's conclusion was that the Yankees ranked after Chance's Chicago clubs of 1906–10, Hanlon's Orioles of 1894–96, the Boston Nationals of 1891–93, Mack's Athletics of 1910–14, and Fred Clarke's Pirates of 1901–03.

But there comes a cropper at the very end of the articles. Alas, Colver acknowledges, these sixteen "greatest of all teams" performed indifferently in the World Series, winning 20 of them, losing 17, winning 129 World Series games, losing 124. It says here that great teams do not lose championship series. It can be argued, of course, that a seven-game series can be won by some such accident as the ball hitting a pebble. It can also be argued that a great team doesn't let the series go seven games and, additionally, sweeps out its infield.

Uncle Wilbert Robinson, who played for the Oriole team Colver ranked second and competed against the others, attended the 1927 World Series. Before things got under way he said, "The Pirates could be trouble. The Waner boys and all that pitching."

"Do you think they can beat the Yankees?" he was asked.

"Don't be silly. The Yankees are the greatest team that ever played."

And whenever the matter is put to a formal vote, the verdict is the same. Thus, in 1944, *The Sporting News* polled 140 baseball writers. Seventy-one chose the '27 Yankees as the greatest of all. Fifteen chose the 1919 White Sox. Thirteen voted for the 1928 Yankees, essentially the same club as the greatest of all, giving it 84 votes of 140 cast by notably idiosyncratic observers.

More recently—it was in 1963—a vote of the American Academy of Sports Editors, based on a hundred newspapers with circulations of 100,000 or more, voted the 1927 Yankees the number-one team of all time, with 84 percent of the vote. The 1929–31 Athletics finished second.

These are largely the testimonies of men accepting the evidence of their eyes, although it is always possible in such things that striplings of fifty years or thereabouts, who did not witness the 1927 season, voted on the basis of what their fathers told them. The vast resources of the Hall of Fame library in Cooperstown turn up no election for a team to challenge the greatest of all. There have been other great teams. But it is not recorded that there are any electoral contenders for the title.

The results were even the same in a lighthearted approach taken by the National Broadcasting Company in 1970 on its televised pregame broadcasts for "The Baseball Game of the Week." Through Computer Research in Sports, Inc., which is two brothers in Princeton, New Jersey, the network conducted a season-long tournament "aimed at uncovering the best team in the last 50 years as the computer sees it."

Since organized sport takes itself as solemnly as organized religion, Baseball Commissioner Bowie Kuhn and American League President Joe Cronin turned up on the show reading killjoy sentences like, "I'm pleased about the way these games have been handled—the fact that it has been made clear from the start that the idea of the computer series was not to decide the best baseball team in major league history but rather to have some fun matching them up."

But the press, in its shameless way, continued to talk of the tournament as an "all-in-fun venture designed to settle once and for all the argument over what team is the greatest in baseball."

That same computer that audits all our tax returns and prepares all our bills assimilated statistics comparing players and performances for a given, high-spot year and printed out a play-by-play which was then edited down with accompanying film clips. It was an imaginative idea and drew howls from stick-in-the-muds.

Funny things happened. The computer credited Sandy Koufax, whose genius fled when wood was pressed in his hand, with a home run. The organizers, with an eye understandably on the nation's largest market, entered as the first two teams in the eight-team tournament the 1951 New York Giants and the 1969 New York Mets, both of which were blessed with miracles rather than genius.

A panel of such stars as Joe DiMaggio, Ted Williams, and Stan Musial selected the tournament's other six teams, based on voting by some seven thousand fans. The greatest of all "easily led in votes gathered." The other teams were the 1929 Athletics, the 1942 Cardinals, the 1955 and 1963 Dodgers, and the 1961 Yankees.

As might have happened in real life, the tournament wound up as an all-Yankee finale, 1927 versus 1961. The championship was won when Lou Gehrig hit a tenth-inning, two-run homer off Whitey Ford. "In the final analysis," it was said, "the games will not really settle much, but it will take us one small step beyond opinion."

In every vote taken among those at least theoretically qualified, then, the 1927 Yankees are the greatest of all, and their talent is such that even the computer marvels. Now the nation has almost doubled in size since the 1920s, and since "more" means "better" in the old American credo, it follows that there are more and better baseball players.

And if sport mirrors life, baseball in the 1920s reflected the great wrong of American civilization—the systematic exclusion of black athletes from the game. Not that it was then a burning question.

Lorraine Hansberry wrote that prejudice produces results that are both silly and unspeakable, and in a year in which there were sixteen recorded lynchings, the exclusion of the black man from what is called the national pastime hardly qualified as top priority.

The game has gained immeasurably through the black's talent. But the gains realized by opening the sport up may be offset by other factors. In the 1920s, baseball was the only professional team sport in town—football and basketball did not offer serious competition for the talent pool. It is argued today, in the specious manner of the times, that colleges are baseball's new minor leagues, as if springtime seasons for athletes burdened by their studies of philosophy and biochemistry equal the years of painful trudging along through the minors.

The old Yankees are cautious to the extreme lest they fall into the caricature of the old-timer who sees everything as better yesterday, the girls were prettier and it snowed more. But there are times when a point must be made.

"The players were more dedicated," said Hoyt in 1973. "They weren't as educated as the men today, and they didn't have a briefcase with stock market reports, and they didn't worry about other jobs. It's a pity they didn't. They probably would have been better citizens and done more later in life.

"I'm not saying they were better people. But they were better ball players. They were uncouth, many of them, but all they did was work at baseball, and this made them better players."

Dan Daniel, who believes the 1927 Yankees were the greatest of all after seeing every team since 1903, wrote, "writers who saw the 1927 team know that subsequent years have not seen its equal. . . .

"This does not betoken discouragement with current baseball quality, nor does the writer believe that baseball has been slipping in technical quality. However, that amazing combination of conditions, including high acumen in the Yankee front office, headed by Ed Barrow, and spectacular leadership in the field, by Miller Huggins, will not again favor construction of a similar machine."

With their rather naïve faith in progress, Americans believe that because athletes are bigger and faster, it follows that baseball teams and prizefighters, for example, move onward in a more or less steady line. But, in whatever field of human endeavor, it is possible the thing already has been done better than it ever will again.

Genius flowers inexplicably. Why did it happen that Shakespeare, Marlowe, Jonson, and the rest of the Mermaid Tavern gang should come together at that particular moment?

Americans, of all people, should understand this. Suppose Nixon, Carl Albert, Gerald Ford, and Lyndon Johnson had been our Founding Fathers. What then? All else is equal in this little flight of the imagination, Columbus, the Pilgrims, the vast, rich continent blessed by two oceans serving as moats against our enemies. But Nixon, Albert, Ford, and Johnson instead of Jefferson, Madison, Hamilton, and Franklin.

One of the Nixon group is given the assignment, "Look, we want to explain why we seek our independence. Go home tonight and think about it, and see what you can come up with on the basis of all your reading and deepest convictions. Give us good, ringing stuff. And see if you can keep it inside 2,000 words."

Who would write the Declaration of Independence?

Without plundering poetic resource, it seems that the 1927 Yankees, a team so favored by destiny, paid a price in later life beyond the law of averages.

Shocker was the first to die.

Not long after the World Series, in February 1928, he announced that he was "voluntarily retiring from baseball for the future of my business interests at home." He was involved in a fast-growing radio-shop business in St. Louis, he said, emphasizing he was not a holdout.

"The end of my career will come eventually, so why not resign while I can leave a good record behind me? I feel that my work with the Yankees is the best-selling record I have."

But then, mysteriously, he turned up with the team in the late spring. Only long enough, it turned out, to collect some money.

"When Huggins got me from the Browns," Shocker told Hearst's Bill Corum, "he promised me $1,500 for moving expenses. But he couldn't get it from the front office"—the Yankee-haters sometimes have a leg to stand on—"Barrow hadn't authorized the payment. Hug wanted to pay me from his own pocket, but I wouldn't take it. I wanted it from the club. Well, it took nearly four years, but I've got it. My July first check squares the promise. Hug and I had a good laugh when we said goodbye this morning. Now I'm going to Denver to fight this thing."

"This thing" was an internal ailment that reduced Shocker to 115 pounds over the winter. He worked out to build himself up before seeing Huggins, but he was a shell. He passed out while pitching batting practice in Comiskey Park. Questioned by the writers, he said only, it was "a fainting spell" and asked them to keep it out of the papers so that his wife wouldn't hear of it.

But he told Corum, "I've had a bum heart for some time now. You've seen me sitting up late at night in my Pullman berth. I couldn't lie down. Choked up I was. I've slept sitting up three years now."

He was always a baseball player, always looking for an angle: "But I used the time reading the papers from the next city on our schedule, and that way, I could keep book on the streaky hitters. Gave me a little edge. Sometimes, I needed it."

He went off to Denver and died in midsummer. HE PUT TOO MUCH IN GAME HE PLAYED, said *The Sporting News,* reflecting the latest judgment of advanced medical science. Death was "due to what physicians call 'athletic heart,' meaning effects of over-strain on that organ through physical endeavor." An autopsy showed that Shocker's heart was "half again larger than normal, five inches across, weighing 16 ounces, rather than the normal 11."

Huggins did not outlive him long. He led the Yankees to another pennant in 1928, his sixth, and his third world championship. But there remained something wistful about the little man with the stub of a pipe in his mouth.

"Do you know this team doesn't play my kind of baseball?" he once told a writer. "By that, I mean the kind I played myself and liked to direct with the Cards. But a manager has his cards dealt to him, and he must play them. A team is like a bridge hand. You've got to get up your strongest suit. My strongest suit is a slugging attack.

"And it's the kind of baseball New York likes. New York is a home run town. It likes to see home runs sail over the fence, so now I play that kind of ball."

Arthur Mann argued, "If such was possible, he was the team." There was something to the greatest of all beyond the hitting, fielding, and pitching. "It was upon this unseen power the Yankees fed and thrived."

His way with rookies was pointed out: Gehrig, Combs, Koenig, and Meusel. Pennock, "a veteran, blossomed into real stardom under the Little Manager," said the *Times*. "Ruth's rise to the very pinnacle was due in no small part to the leadership of Huggins, even though the two clashed often until Huggins' personality overcame Ruth, and the latter was willing to serve in the army with his leader."

Still, the wistfulness remained. Not long before his death, the lifelong bachelor said, "If I had a boy, I could send him to Yale or Princeton or some other great university and he could play just a little second base or halfback. I'd be the happiest man in the world.

"Because I could do so much for him, so many things I longed for when I wanted to study law at some outstanding university and couldn't. But I guess nobody is supposed to be as happy as I would be if I had a boy like that."

His health, always delicate, suffered under the stress of the pennant race in 1928, and it collapsed as the team, failing to respond to the challenge of the great Athletics, surrendered to age and injuries in 1929. "Baseball is my life," he explained to worried friends. "Maybe it will get me some day, but as long as I die in harness, I'll be happy."

One September day when the team played Boston, Huggins told Coach Arthur Fletcher, "Take the reins, Art. I'll be back tomorrow." He never returned. A boil under his left eye hospitalized him with an infection that spread through his body. The little man who had built up his young body with weights and pulleys had nothing left to fight with, and, in the Twenties, there were no miracle drugs.

The players dressed for the game knowing he was desperately ill. Midway in the third inning, the flag at Fenway Park crept to half-mast.

"Finally, they were told," reported the *World*. "A shudder rippled along the bench. A choked voice, a sound in the throat that might have been the start of a nervous cough, a tightening of toughened, sun-bronzed jaws . . . The Yankee bench remained inarticulate.

"Then Earle Combs broke down unashamedly and wept. The Babe waved away a questioner in scowling silence. The silence was finally broken with nothing more than a prosaic, 'Well, we'll have to finish the game. Let's get it over with.' "

The Yankees won. They were, after all, playing the Red Sox. "Save when the action called for words, they went through the game in the same tight-lipped silence that first gripped them on the bench."

Stories were told of how Huggins handled his players with an individual touch. In the dugout, chewing his leaf tobacco and spitting, he might indulge himself in conversation with the third man on his shoulder:

"That Lazzeri. He's no good. Can't do nothing."

Lazzeri, overhearing, would bear down, hit a home run, steal a base, and return to the little manager.

"Well, how do you like that?"

"Routine."

But he called in Lazzeri after the 1927 World Series and said, "You'll be getting a good-sized check. What are you planning to do with it?"

"I haven't given it a thought."

"Turn the check over to me. I'll make this series worth a lot more money to you. If there was any doubt about it, I wouldn't suggest it, but I know."

Three weeks later, Huggins asked Lazzeri if he still held the stock. "It's in the middle eighties now. It will go beyond a hundred. That World Series will keep on making money for you for a long time."

But Lazzeri, after the funeral at the Little Church Around the Corner in New York City, the tall ball players carrying the coffin of the little man who had improved the conditions of so many of them, after the largest funeral crowd since the death of the screen idol, Rudolph Valentino, Lazzeri had more than money in mind when he said of Huggins:

"He made me. That's all."

It would be misleading to overemphasize the mortuary aspect of the Yankee destiny. A glorious career awaited Gehrig, for instance, although his hitting tailed off at the end of the 1927 season, dragging his average down to .373, because he worried about his mother, in the hospital for another operation. And, although he danced a public dance of joy just before the World Series, hearing that she had survived surgery, he picked up only four hits in the Series—two doubles, two triples, driving in four runs. He was voted Most Valuable Player for the first of four times. He was more than that.

"Lou was not the best player the Yankees ever had," Stanley Frank wrote. "Ruth was number one by any yardstick, DiMaggio a more accomplished performer. Yet Lou was the most valuable player the Yankees ever had because he was a prime source of their greatest asset—an implied confidence in themselves and in every man on the club. Lou's pride as a big leaguer rubbed off on every one who played with him."

That was an ultimate irony, that this shy, good-looking, muscular, even mighty man with the engaging grin, so lacking in confidence in himself, haunted by the fear that his one talent might leave him, gave such confidence to others.

"There is no greater inspiration to any American boy than Lou Gehrig," Gallico wrote. "For if this awkward, inept and downright clumsy player that I knew in the beginning could through sheer drive and determination turn himself into the finest first-base-covering machine in all baseball, then nothing is impossible to any man or boy in the country.''

Work, work. "In the beginning, I used to make one terrible play a game,'' Gehrig told Quentin Reynolds in 1935. "Then I got so I'd make one a week, and finally, I'd pull one about once a month. Now I'm trying to keep it down to once a season.''

Four times he was runner-up to Ruth in home runs. He tied him with forty-six in 1931, a year he was, typically, robbed of the title when he hit a home run that teammate Lyn Lary inexplicably thought had been caught and so left the base paths, becoming the third out, and erasing the run that would have pushed Gehrig ahead of Ruth for the only time.

On June 3, 1932, Gehrig hit home runs in four consecutive at-bats against Philadelphia, something not even Ruth managed to do, and he was robbed of a fifth on a great catch by Al Simmons. "Kid,'' said Ruth, "that was the greatest I ever seen.'' Gehrig won his first home run title, with forty-nine, in 1934, when Ruth made only token appearances, and he also won the league batting championship with .363, after years of missing it by a couple of points or so.

He hit a record twenty-three home runs with the bases loaded. He led the league four times in runs scored and runs batted in, and he scored more than a hundred runs a season for thirteen consecutive years. He quit with some twenty-five major-league records.

And yet he was never long out of Ruth's shadow. And when Ruth left the Yankees, the charismatic DiMaggio eased into stage center. Gehrig marched along, setting his record of 2,130 games, in conditions he never bothered to complain about. Late in his career, X rays of his hands revealed seventeen fractures he had let heal by themselves. He had broken every finger in both hands, some twice, and didn't mention it. Hit by a pitch that gave him a concussion that should have put him in bed for a week, he came to the park the following day and got four hits.

The Yankees did not reward this devotion with showers of gold. His lifetime earnings with the club were estimated at $316,000, his highest annual salary, $37,000 in 1937, not half of Ruth's $80,000 top. This may have contributed to a tension that developed between the two men.

The frugal Gehrig husbanded what he earned, acquiring something of a reputation as a pinchpenny. But he didn't spend much of it on himself. For a brief, embarrassing period, he decided to open up, be a little more like the Babe, horse around with the writers, stand them to drinks. It didn't work.

With his World Series money he bought his parents a small, comfortable house in New Rochelle, a New York City suburb, in 1928. In 1933 he married Eleanor Twitchell, an effervescent, auburn-haired woman from a social background. He knew her for four years before they married. He would sit for long periods, tongue-tied, unable to think of anything to say.

She worked him around to proposing, she once explained. "It began with talk about baseball. Even when proposing, in stating his qualifications as a potential husband, Lou spoke disparagingly of himself as a player. It finally got around to my asking him if what he was trying to say was that he wanted to marry me. He nodded his head, and told me that was it. Then he kissed me and ran for the door."

He hit a home run for her the next day. Although he did not bow and doff his cap, "it was one of the happiest days of his life, and, for once, nothing happened to jinx it." Eleanor worked hard to build up his confidence. She gave him little parties, kidded him, praised him. She undoubtedly gave him happiness. But nothing could shake for long his feelings of failure.

In 1938 the Iron Horse, the indestructible, began to falter. He dropped things, his hands sometimes shook when he held a coffee cup. He lost his great energy on the field. He forced himself to continue playing, even though he told a teammate he felt that every fan in the Stadium could hear him creak when he went to bat. Still, he hit .295.

He played in only eight games the next year, hitting .143. But it was left to him to take himself out of the lineup, the Yankees would not break that imperishable record. On May 2, after waiting for an hour, the ashen-faced Gehrig stopped Manager Joe McCarthy in a Detroit hotel lobby and said, "You'd better take me out, Joe. I guess that's it."

A famous photograph appeared in the newspapers the next day, showing Gehrig leaning on the dugout ledge, thinking God knows what thoughts, as Babe Dahlgren took over first base. A month later, on his thirty-sixth birthday, Gehrig left the Mayo Clinic with a sealed report, diagnosing him as suffering from "amyotrophic lateral sclerosis. This type of illness involves the motor pathways and cells of the central nervous system. . . ." It is known familiarly today as Lou Gehrig's disease.

On July 4, 1939, 61,808 fans and, on the field, the greatest of all, gathered to honor Lou. Dan Daniel, who presided, wrote:

"Baseball today had in its treasury of rich memories the story of a gesture that grew into the most dramatic demonstration in the annals of the sport. What started out to be just a pat on the back for Lou Gehrig, the greatest first baseman the game has developed, became a stirring testimonial which, in its manifestation of loyalty and appreciation and its emotional aspects, never before had been approached in any league.

"This afternoon, which pulled at the heart-strings, centered around a man who for 15 years had been the endurance king of sport for all time. As the tribute approached its climax, it left Gehrig with tears rolling down his face. . . .

"It was left for the greatest showman of baseball history, Babe Ruth, to come forward with a much-needed tension-breaker. Before the biggest crowd of the baseball year, Ruth and Gehrig, who had quarrelled before the Bambino left the Yankees, became reconciled. With his face wreathed in the old Ruthian smile, the Babe posed with his right arm around Lou's neck. The old king and the crown prince had become reconciled at last.

" 'I say the 1927 team was the greatest the Yankees ever had,' shouted the Babe into the microphone, as he pointed to the graying heroes of the club which twelve years ago established the Stadium's Murderers' Row as the most formidable machine in major league drama."

Gehrig's words are legend. "Two weeks ago, I got a bad break. Yet today, I count myself the luckiest man on the face of the earth. . . . To leave this game, to leave these kids would be oblivion."

It was not quite oblivion. Mayor Fiorello LaGuardia appointed Gehrig a member of the New York City Parole Commission. He worked with a good many young men who, like himself, grew up in poverty, unlike himself did not possess the skill to lift them from it. "He knew the cause of most crimes," a biographer wrote. "Few men so well understood frustration and loneliness and deprivation."

At that, it is well Gehrig served when he did. Time changed his world in incomprehensible ways after he died. Warren Miller, writing of the Harlem street world in 1959, said ". . . many years ago I lived near East Harlem—at the realtor's frontier, 96th Street—and saw gang fights from my window, boys killing under a street lamp, in front of the house where, a bronze plaque attests, Lou Gehrig was born. Lou would not recognize the old neighborhood; nor even, perhaps, understand the language of the boys. It is American, it is comprehensible, but it is not easily understood."

Gehrig stayed at his desk until he could no longer move. Then he retired to the apartment on Riverside Drive, where his wife read to him because he could no longer hold a book in his hands. He was without self-pity. His wife threw parties, inviting Broadway stars and athletes to the apartment, to keep things gay. She was sure that he did not know his disease was fatal. She was with him when he died, June 2, 1940.

Ruth came to the funeral home, uncharacteristically brushing aside the kids and autograph-seekers. By that time, of course, he himself had been out of baseball five years.

What Babe Ruth meant to the sport cannot be measured. When the Yankees bought him, "they had never won a pennant, had never amounted to anything but a poor relation to the glorious and beloved first team of New York City, the fabulous Giants," Mrs. Ruth wrote. "The Yankees were eventually to chase those entrenched Giants right out of town."

That isn't a wife's fond exaggeration, and it speaks of Ruth's mark on only one team. "He made the salaries possible," an old-time player recalled in 1973, during celebrations for the fiftieth anniversary of the House that Ruth Built. "He made them possible because of what he did, and to ball players that may be his greatest meaning."

No player matches Ruth's legend. He joined the team in time for a western swing in 1920, and his roommate was Ping Bodie, the first of the San Francisco Italians to grace the Yankees. (A monograph awaits the scholar wishing to trace the symbiotic relationship of the two cities. A man who likes one generally likes the other. Each, of course, is given over to romance, fine food and drink, the arts, sport, and skullduggery. Except for the last two, these are un-American interests, which is why San Francisco, and, especially, New York, are so often attacked by demagogues as being outside the mainstream.) Bodie, on his return, was asked who he roomed with and answered, "Babe Ruth's suitcase," and the legend was off and running.

Ruth needed no help, of course. He hit the longest home run in just about every American League ball park, usually under the most dramatic possible circumstances. When he hit a particularly long drive off Walter Johnson, it would be before the largest crowd in Polo Grounds history, on a day when Man o' War ran the fastest mile ever recorded for a horse in the United States. Ruth rose to all occasions. "When it was realized he was writing new chapters in baseball history, all by himself," his biographer noted, "a kind of fever ran through the nation."

None of this ended in 1927. Ruth kept on hitting home runs and for average—54 and .323 in 1928, 46 and .345 in 1929, and so on, until it began to tail off in 1933 and ended two years later. It was never just what he did on the field. Hoyt said that if Ruth had never played a game of baseball in his life, "you would turn and look at him if you passed him on Broadway."

His first wife burned to death on January 11, 1929, freeing Ruth—who had seen himself as "a Catholic with a wife and a kid"— to marry Claire Hodgson. They chose a place and an hour designed to escape great notice—5 A.M., April 17, in St. Gregory's Roman Catholic Church on West 91st Street in Manhattan—and found the church jammed, five thousand people milling around outside.

That was to be the opening day of the season, but the rains provided the happy couple with a one-day honeymoon. The next day, with Mrs. Ruth in the Stadium, he hit one out for her, stopping on his rounds to bow and wave his cap. There was never another like him.

He desperately wanted to manage the Yankees. He never got the chance. They sold him out of the league, to the Boston Braves in 1935. He served one year as a coach for the Dodgers. That was as much as baseball could do for the man who saved it. He was never offered any kind of responsible job in baseball, the old excuse being that he couldn't manage himself, the old suspicion lingering that the man who did more for the game than any other individual did too much in the matter of players' salaries.

He didn't need the game to remain a legend. In *A Farewell to Sport,* Gallico wrote:

"The last time I saw Babe Ruth was at Jones Beach State Park on Long Island, where I was putting on a water circus for my paper. Ruth, finished as an active ball player, had been brutally discarded by the game and its operators, for whom he did so much. It made me angry to see this glamorous figure completely neglected and out of the picture. I invited him to come down to the beach as the star of the day's show.

"It was a warm, bright sunshiny seashore afternoon in August, a Saturday, and there were some seventy-five thousand people jammed around the flat, sandy area of Zach's Bay, many of them standing waist-deep in water to see the fun. Midway during the program, Ruth was led out from the show control station, down the aisle bordering the bay, and out across the catwalk that led to the big water stage. No announcement had been made or was to be until he reached the stage and the act then going on was completed.

"But as we walked, a murmur began in the vast crowd as they recognized the big, burly man with the ugly face, blob nose, curly black hair, cigar stuck out of the side of his mouth. There were individual cries of 'Hi, Babe! Oh you Babe! Hey, Babe, look up here!' The name passed from lip to lip. The crowd caught fire like a blaze running over a dry meadow, and the murmur swelled and rose, gained and grew and took on volume, until by the time he reached the stage it was one thundering, booming roar, drowning out the pounding of the surf on the beach a few hundred yards away. It shook the stands and the glassy surface of the water. It shook Ruth a little, too, the man who had heard so many of these crowd roars. He stood facing into this gale of sound, grinning, his little eyes shining. The ringmaster had a stroke of genius. He dispensed with his microphone and simply swept his arm in Ruth's direction. The greeting redoubled.

"And this was not a baseball crowd. Many of the people there had never seen a major league baseball game. They were simply Mr. and Mrs. Average Citizen out for a day's fun at the beach. But they all knew Ruth and loved him.

"A few minutes later, Ruth began to hit fungo flies out into the bay. 'Hitting fungo flies' is the baseball term for the act of throwing the ball up and out in front of you a little way and then hitting it with a specially constructed bat. . . . A most curious sight followed.

"The first three baseballs had hardly splashed into the bay, the fourth was still in its arching flight, when the shoreline—a half-mile or so of it—suddenly became frothed with white. The line of foam extended around the U of the bay and grew in width, white splashings in which dark heads bobbed, the beginning of one of the strangest and most exciting races I have ever seen. More than a thousand youngsters, girls as well as boys, with one sudden, simultaneous impulse, had taken to the water and were threshing out towards those tiny white baseballs bobbing on the blue surface. . . . Many of them were competitors who had been waiting for their swimming races to be called and who should have been resting and husbanding their strength. They didn't care. There was but one goal for that army of splashing, water-churning youngsters. It seems that there was magic in those baseballs.

"There has always been a magic about that gross, ugly, coarse, Gargantuan figure of a man and everything he did. . . ."

That was in the late thirties. Years later, Breslin wrote, ". . . the only sports legend I ever saw who completely lived up to advance billing was Babe Ruth.

"It was a hot summer afternoon, and the Babe, sweat dripping from his jowls and his shirt stuck to him, came off the eighteenth green at the old Bayside Golf Club in the borough of Queens and stormed into the huge barroom of the club.

" 'Gimme one of them heavens to Betsy drinks you always make for me,' the Babe said in his gravelly voice.

"The bartender put a couple of fistfuls of ice chunks into a big, thick mixing glass and then proceeded to make a Tom Collins that had so much gin in it that other people at the bar started to laugh. He served the drink to the Babe just as it was made, right in the mixing glass.

"Ruth said something about how heavens to Betsy hot he was, and then he picked up the glass and opened his mouth, and, there went everything. In one shot, he swallowed the drink, the orange slice and the rest of the garbage, and the ice chunks. He stopped for nothing. There is not a single man I have ever seen in a saloon who does not bring his teeth together a little bit and stop those ice chunks from going in. A man has to have a pipe the size of a trombone to take ice in one shot. But I saw Ruth do it, and whenever somebody tells me how the Babe used to drink and eat when he was playing ball, I believe every word of it."

Riddled by cancer, Ruth was given a day at the Stadium. Microphones carried his voice to ball parks around the country. His voice was awful. One of his visitors in his last illness was Johnny Sylvester, now grown to manhood. This time it didn't turn out the way it does in the story books.

Ruth died August 14, 1948. No one has come close to him.

There remained survivors of the greatest of all in 1973. Hoyt, Combs, Dugan, Shawkey, who managed the Yankees in 1930, Meusel, a former shipyard guard, restaurant employee, and baseball player, and, although life had treated them variously and they changed uniforms, conversation made it clear that the team remained with them.

Koenig, for example. In the odd thinking of the time, he "was spotted wearing glasses, which hastened his departure from the Yankees." He was traded to Detroit in 1930, where they tried to make a pitcher out of him. Then he was sent down to the Pacific Coast League, where he played a lot of night ball and batted .333, proving he could still see.

The Cubs brought him back to the majors. It proved "the happiest purchase by a National League club in some time." He batted .353 for Chicago in thirty-three games, hitting .400 during a fourteen-game stretch that clinched the pennant. He was rewarded with a partial share of the Series money. "Cheapskates," is how he remembered Chicago.

This slighting of their old teammate led to a lot of jockeying by the Yankees when they met the Cubs in the Series that year. The Cubs jockeyed back. Ruth did, or did not, point to the fence with two strikes on him. It is now part of legend.

But 1927 remained something special to Koenig. "That Koenig gets a lot of knocks," a rival manager said early in the year, "but one season and a tough World Series will make a man of him."

The words were prophetic. The failure of the 1926 Series was the most brilliant performer of the four-game set just a year later. He led both clubs with a .500 average. He figured in every run the Yankees scored, except in the fifth inning of the fourth game. He fielded brilliantly, handling fourteen chances without error.

"Every time you looked up, there was Koenig on base or driving a man over the plate," J. Roy Stockton wrote right after the Series. "The goat of 1926 was the ball hawk of 1927. Far to this side, far to that he ranged, cutting off potential Pirate safeties. The greater the pinch, the greater Koenig . . .

"There were several brilliant plays by Koenig and many a throw that had to be perfect to get his man. . . . He fielded for an average of 1.000. Than perfection, there can be nothing better . . . And with such a brilliant batting record, there can be no doubt that Koenig has lost the horns that sprouted as he earned the title of goat, and in their place is the laurel wreath as the hero of 1927.''

Koenig has particular reason to remember the year, then. But it stands apart as something more than a great year for him, just as it was more than the year Ruth hit sixty home runs, the year Gehrig batted in 175 and Hoyt won twenty-two games, more than the doubleheader massacre of the Senators, the turning back of the As and the Tigers, the winning streaks, the historic sweep of the Series, all the records. It is the coming together of all these things at a time when life itself seemed as exuberant as the moment of the sixtieth homer, so that Koenig might speak for all of them, the living and the dead, as decades later, the steady gaze fixed on the far, bright California hills, he says that when he thinks of baseball, he thinks of 1927. There were other clubs for him but, he says, ''I think of myself as a Yankee.''

Madrid,
mayo de 1983

Roberto Gonzalez Echevarria
47 Mather St.
Hamden, CT 06517